Stuck Together

Books by Mary Connealy

From Bethany House Publishers

THE KINCAID BRIDES

Out of Control
In Too Deep
Over the Edge

TROUBLE IN TEXAS

Swept Away
Fired Up
Stuck Together

A Match Made in Texas: A Novella Collection

Stuck Together

MARY CONNEALY

BETHANYHOUSE
a division of Baker Publishing Group
Minneapolis, Minnesota

Published by Bethany House Publishers
11400 Hampshire Avenue South
Bloomington, Minnesota 55438
www.bethanyhouse.com

Bethany House Publishers is a division of
Baker Publishing Group, Grand Rapids, Michigan

Printed in the United States of America

Library of Congress Cataloging-in-Publication Data
Connealy, Mary.
    Stuck together / Mary Connealy.
        p.   cm. — (Trouble in Texas ; book 3)
    Summary: "They may be the last two single people in Broken Wheel, but
Vince Yates and Tina Cahill are determined not to end up stuck together"—
Provided by publisher.
    ISBN 978-0-7642-0916-1 (pbk.)
    1. Man-woman relationships—Fiction. I. Title.
PS3603.O544S88 2014
813'.6—dc23   2014003383

Scripture quotations are from the King James Version of the Bible.

Cover design by Dan Pitts
Cover photography by Mike Habermann Photography, LLC

Author is represented by Natasha Kern Literary Agency

14   15   16   17   18   19   20   7   6   5   4   3   2   1

Stuck Together is dedicated to my oldest daughter, Josie. Josie may be the first person to read what I was writing and say, "She's pretty good." And say it like she really meant it.

My husband likes to tell about the time he was complaining about the time I spent writing—long before I was published—and Josie said to him, "You know, Dad, she's pretty good. She's as good as some of the books I'm reading that are published." And because my husband respected Josie's opinion, he decided to stick with me, go along for the ride, slow and meandering though it was, and see where we'd end up.

Josie was the first one to answer the phone when I called after I got my first contract, too. I'd called my husband but got no answer, and then Josie was next and she was there. She was just so genuinely thrilled for me. It was wonderful.

So thank you, Josie. There were a lot of times early on when it might have been easy for me to give up. Having you say "She's pretty good" really helped.

CHAPTER 1

Tina Cahill finished hammering a hefty board across the front of Duffy's Tavern. Carefully printed on the board were the words *Abandon Hope All Ye Who Enter Here*.

It sent a message at the same time it nailed Duffy's door shut.

Tina's plan was to get his notice.

"That tears it!" Duffy roared from inside the saloon.

He'd noticed.

She stepped well out of the way, expecting only one reaction from the galoot, and she got it.

With one hard shove he swung the batwing doors open and knocked down her sign, which clattered across the wooden sidewalk. Tina was encouraged when it stayed in one piece. Her construction skills were definitely improving, and that was good because she meant to be at her mission for a long time and she'd need that sign again later.

Duffy Schuster glared at her.

Wagging her finger under his nose, she said, "Close this den of iniquity, Duffy Schuster."

To make her point more fully, she looked behind her for her placard, which she had in addition to the sign so she could nail shut the tavern door with one and march back and forth carrying the other. Her placard read, *Whiskey, The Poison Scourge* on one side, and *LIQUOR, A Thief in Your Mouth that Steals Your Brain* on the other.

She spied the placard on its long, sturdy pole leaning against the saloon and picked it up, intending to wave it in Duffy's face.

"I am sick of you—" Duffy's hot breath blasted her neck.

Startled to feel him so close, she whirled around. It was a complete accident that her placard slammed Duffy right in the head.

Duffy staggered backward through the swinging doors of the saloon, howling in pain. An unfortunately located spittoon tripped him and he fell, pinwheeling his arms.

He backhanded his brother, Griss.

Griss, the worse for drink, bellowed a word that made Tina want to cover her ears. Her hands were busy with the sign, though, so she had to listen to every bit of the foul diatribe.

Tina peeked over the top of the slapping doors. "I'm sorry, gentlemen."

She wasn't really. Well, she was. She hadn't intentionally clubbed Duffy in the head. And it was just the worst sort of luck—for Duffy—that her placard was on a very stout stick. And it wasn't her fault about the stick, either. Why, just last week, Griss had snapped the handle of her sign right in half. So of course she'd chosen a thicker length of wood this time.

But if ever a man needed a few feet of lumber taken to

his head, it was Duffy Schuster, and his brother right along with him. So in that sense she wasn't all that sorry.

Griss threw a punch at Duffy, who tumbled out of the saloon and landed with a thud on his back, saloon doors flapping. Tina jumped away or he'd've landed right on her stylish black half boots.

"Get back, Tina!" Jonas, her brother—who was turning out to be a scold—shouted from behind her. "I told you to stay away from that saloon, today of all days!"

Duffy regained his feet and met his angry brother with a wild roundhouse. Griss ducked and charged, head first, ramming Duffy in his sizable belly.

The two grappled, shouting absolutely improper words that made Tina want to whack Duffy again, and Griss too, while covering her ears.

A woman in this situation definitely needed extra hands.

The two men staggered right toward her.

"Tina! Look out!" Jonas's feet pounded faster on the board-walk. He grabbed her around the waist and whirled her away from the mayhem. Her sign swung, too. She felt it smack someone and hoped it wasn't Jonas.

Tina twisted in Jonas's arms to see her placard had re-directed Griss's next punch intended for Duffy, so it hammered Jonas in the back of the head.

Jonas, the peacemaker, the town parson, her loving brother, shoved her to safety and turned back. "Now, you two settle—"

Jonas took the next fist right in the face.

Tina tried to catch him and went down under him in a whirl of her pink calico skirts. The trusty placard went flying off the board-walk and onto the street. Probably

9

best to get it out of the scrap anyway lest it be broken. She'd hand-lettered it and it took quite a while to get right.

"You keep your stinking hands off the parson." The smithy, Sledge Murphy, came out of the saloon. None too steady on his feet, but apparently drink didn't stop him from respecting a man of the cloth.

Then Sledge cursed the air so blue that Tina dramatically reduced her opinion of his piety. In fact, it appeared the man just wanted an excuse to jump into the fight. He was a massive man, his arms huge from his heavy work swinging a hammer against an anvil, besides wrestling the horses he had to shoe. When he tackled Griss, it was inevitable that Griss give way and fall backward into Duffy, who flew off the board-walk to land with a thud on the packed earth of Broken Wheel's Main Street.

Duffy's feet swung wide and whipped behind Jonas's knees. Jonas, who probably should have known better than to stand up, tumbled right after Duffy. Griss and Sledge jumped after him.

Jonas went down in a pile of howling drunkard.

Vince Yates—the big oaf—came running out of his law office, charging straight toward the trouble, yelling threats that no one paid attention to. He found time to give Tina one very dire look from his blazing brown eyes, blaming her without saying a word.

Tug Andrews, an old curmudgeon who owned the general store, slammed the swinging doors open and stood for a second looking at the mayhem before him. He had a ragged leather coat on and a battered fur cap. The man looked like he'd just come down from a decade spent in the mountains, and Tina judged him to be old enough and wise enough to stay out of the fray. Through his thick gray beard he hollered, "Fight!" Then went feet-first into the brawl.

Two more ruffians boiled out of the saloon as if called there by Tug's shout. They jumped into the chaos with a howl that would do justice to a pack of wild dogs. Jonas rolled out of the midst and crawled two feet before Sledge dove on him. Rude, considering Sledge had gotten into this to save a parson.

Vince reached the group, jerked one of the newcomers by the collar, spun him around and pounded a fist into his belly. The man doubled over. Vince caught him by both shoulders, straightened him up, and with two wicked blows sent him reeling to the ground unconscious. Vince turned back to the fight and hauled someone else out. He looked set to end the whole battle single-handedly, dealing with one man at a time.

How organized!

Then Duffy got knocked out of the pile, rolled hard against Vince's legs and he went down. The man he'd prepared to knock into a sound sleep was free to start whaling on Vince, and he did it with zest.

Tina decided to adopt Vince's systematic approach. Retrieving her sturdy placard, she jumped off the board-walk and clubbed the blacksmith over the head. He fell over, cold as a carp. One down, four to go.

She changed that to five when another man rushed out of the saloon. This one shouted "Yee haw!" as he threw himself into the fight with flailing fists, as if fighting were fun.

Men were so strange.

The man Vince had dealt with came around and threw

himself back into the tumult. Six to go. The blacksmith stirred, too. Seven.

Two more men came out of the saloon, and Tina quit counting.

Tina hauled back to whack Griss just as Glynna Riker came rushing out of her diner. Her eyes met Tina's, which caused Tina to hesitate, embarrassed. She had to fight the urge to hide her sign behind her back. Glynna had already seen it, and the placard was taller than Tina, so it would have been pointless anyway.

Her hesitation came at just the wrong time.

Griss reeled back from some blow or other and shoved her into a full horse trough.

With a loud splash she went all the way under the water, frigid in the cold December weather. She surfaced from the distinctly brackish-tasting water and clawed at the sides of the wooden trough to get back on her feet and back to saving her brother. She'd save his friend Vince while she was at it, no matter what a waste of breath that man was.

She lost her grip on the slippery trough edges and went under again.

"Dare, get out here!" Glynna's voice cut through the chaos only because it wasn't a dull masculine roar. Glynna's shout didn't cut through enough to stop the brawl, just enough to be heard by Tina, even with her head submerged.

Trying again, Tina heaved her heavy sodden skirts out of the water, and the whole side of the trough snapped off. She flowed out and splatted face-first onto the muddy mess she'd made of Broken Wheel's Main Street.

Shoving herself to her feet, she slipped and sat down hard, the fall broken mercifully by what was now a mudhole. She saw the trough's water wash over the fighting men, and the slippery footing was too much for a few of them, who went down. They churned up a growing swamp as she crawled out of the mire. When finally she got her feet under her, she saw the men now slogging through muck to land a blow. A good dousing hadn't cooled them off one speck.

She saw someone tackle Jonas; enough of his bright red hair still showed through the mud for her to identify him. She waded through the mud to her placard, grabbed it, and charged back into the fray. One good whack on Duffy's shoulders got his attention. He turned, swinging as he pivoted. He realized it was her, and a horrified expression came over his face to see who he'd be punching. Texas men didn't punch women, after all.

But Duffy had already thrown his weight into the swing. Tina jerked the sign up to shield her face, and Duffy slugged it, then shouted in pain. Tina nearly got popped in the nose by the sign, and she fell back into the mud. With her sign knocked away, she saw Duffy clutching his hand, howling, the big baby. He staggered, his feet skidding out from under him. Griss tripped over Duffy and fell. Both Schuster brothers came up coated in mud with drawn-back fists. They recognized each other, smiled—which Tina could not understand at all—then pivoted to dive back into the madness.

Their joint assault knocked men over like ninepins, and now the fight turned into more of a mud-wrestling contest than fisticuffs.

Resolutely regaining her feet, Tina fetched her sign. It was proving to be a fair weapon and decent shelter. She felt as if the good Lord himself was providing armor from such ruffians, so she refused to fear for her own safety.

With right on her side she went back at the crowd of rioting sots, except for Jonas. And Vince. Rioting, but not sots. Looking into the fracas, she added Dr. Riker. Even coated in mud, she recognized the doctor in the middle of the battle.

She took a solid grip on her sign and got a good back-swing. A blast knocked her onto her backside in the cold mud. Every man froze in his tracks and pivoted to see Glynna with a shotgun, aimed up in the air.

"One more man throws a punch and I'm gonna fire Tina from the diner and go back to cookin' myself," Glynna said. Her voice rang out, but you couldn't call it shouting. It was too musical with her sweet Arkansas twang.

A gasp tore through the crowd. Nothing could have cooled them down more effectively.

They all loved Glynna.

They all hated Tina.

Tina accepted that—the righteous were always perse-cuted.

Not that Glynna wasn't righteous.

But no one wanted Glynna cooking again. Several of the men gave Tina a grudging look of appreciation as they picked themselves up out of the muck.

She knew her biscuits alone had earned her the respect of every man there. True, she was no Lana Bullard, the former cook at Glynna's diner. Tina couldn't touch that woman's fried potatoes. But since Lana was locked up for trying to murder Dr. Riker, the men in town had to settle for what they could get. And no doubt they had all found religion just from praying that sweet, beautiful Glynna Riker would never go back to her daily burnt offerings.

Even the Schuster brothers ate Tina's food with enthusiasm. Decent of them, considering her only goal in life was shutting down their loathsome saloon.

The men abandoned the fight and stood with only a bit of grumbling. So covered in mud they were barely recognizable, they filed back into the saloon. Tug Andrews, distinct because of his long hair and bushy beard—though it was less bushy due to the mud—slung a friendly arm around Griss's neck.

The two exchanged a smile, then Griss hollered, "The house is buyin' a round."

A cheer went up as the swinging doors flapped shut behind the last of them.

That was so annoying, Tina looked around from where she sat in the mud and found her placard within reach, thinking to make her point by cracking a few more heads.

Jonas crawled onto his hands and knees, then shoved himself to his feet with a grim look aimed straight at Tina.

Vince rose from the muck, his sodden, formerly black vest had an armhole ripped open, and it hung from one shoulder. Vince gave Dare a hand up.

She could see that, under the mud, Dare's eye was swollen.

Jonas had a fat lip, his right arm hugged up against his body, and when he finally moved, it was with a limp. He limped straight for her, a scowl on his mud-caked face.

"Can't you get her under control, Jonas?" Vince used his forearm to clean his face, which made things even worse. His brown eyes burned with irritation, but at least he didn't have that usual stupid smile.

Tina felt some satisfaction in knowing she'd had a hand in wiping it off.

"Me and what army?" Jonas ran his good hand over the mud dripping into his eyes.

"It's a good cause and you all know it. Why won't you help me?" With a generous smile that none of them deserved, Tina added, "I'd be glad to make you placards of your very own."

"Why do you persist in picketing the saloon, Tina?" Jonas reached down for her, flinched with pain, checked the motion and pulled his arm back to his side. "It doesn't change a thing except to stir folks up."

Vince came to Jonas's side, took one look at Tina sitting in the mud and flashed her that bright smile of his. The man must be bankrupting himself with tooth polish.

Tina looked down and remembered she'd been on her face and on her back, so she was coated with mud all around. It was as well her pink gown was an old one.

Shaking his head, Vince said to Jonas, "Let me get her."

Somehow that sounded like a threat.

"I don't need anyone to get me." Tina tilted her nose in the air. "My aunt Iphigenia always told me a woman needs to know how to take care of herself, and I can certainly get myself out of this mud."

She shoved herself up, her feet slipped out from under her, and she landed on her backside again. She was very grateful that the mud most likely covered her blush.

Dare came up. He squeezed liquid out of his mustache for a second while he glared down at Tina. He then studied Jonas, shook his head. "Let's take a look at that arm. Come on over to my office."

Jonas gave Tina such a beady-eyed look, she almost faltered in her determination to stop the scourge of demon rum that flowed from the unholy saloon. The Schusters actually only sold cheap whiskey, but demon rum still described the problem nicely in Tina's opinion.

Jonas quit glaring and limped off. Once he was around the corner and no longer looking at her, she renewed her resolve to serve the tiny mission field right in front of Duffy's Tavern.

Glynna asked, "Do you need help, Tina? Maybe a bath?"

Both of Glynna's children, mostly grown Paul and little sweetheart Janny, stood close at Glynna's side, staring. Tina considered telling them it was rude to stare, but then Vince grabbed her under her arms and dragged her to her feet.

She stood, slipped in the mud, and fell against him, adding mud to the front of his ruined vest. He closed his eyes as if he were exhausted, then scooped her right off her feet, swung her into his arms, and sloshed through the mud as he marched down to the diner.

Glynna shooed her children inside with Vince right behind, Tina being toted along like a parcel. A muddy parcel.

Glynna held the door. Once inside, Vince set Tina down on one of the benches that lined Glynna's tables. The man showed little if any care for Tina's rather tender backside — she'd sat down too hard, too many times. Of course she hadn't mentioned her tender backside and she never would. Still, she gave him a disgruntled look, wasted on him because he was already walking away.

He left the diner, closing the door firmly behind him. Tina went ahead and admitted that he just plain slammed it. He went along the board-walk past Glynna's large front window until Tina couldn't see him anymore. Standing quickly to catch him in the act if he went into that vile saloon, she watched him walk straight for her placard, pick it up, and swing it into a post holding up the porch roof. The stick held, but her painstakingly hand-painted placard smashed into four pieces.

Tina didn't bother to scold the brute. She would nail those pieces back together and be right back on her picket line tomorrow.

Vince picked the pieces up and threw them in the mud, then stomped on them until they were toothpick-sized.

"Fine, I'll make a new sign." She spoke aloud, but of course Vince couldn't hear her.

Then Vince took two steps and found the sign that had started this whole thing.

Abandon Hope All Ye Who Enter Here.

Tina hoped he appreciated her literary leanings. Not everyone could apply Dante to her daily life.

Vince turned to look at the diner and saw her watching him. Glowering, he took the sign along with her stick and stalked off. Tina lost sight of him as he rounded the short row of Main Street buildings. Tina hated to lose her stick. She'd be hard pressed, in this little Texas town, to find another one half as nice. She was still trying to figure out how to get it away from him when she heard the crack of an ax.

With a sigh of disgust, she didn't even run to stop Vince from turning her placard stick into kindling.

"If he knew me well, he'd know I don't discourage easily."

"We all know you very well, Tina. Why do you think Vince is being thorough in his destruction?" Glynna came out of the kitchen. Her words were withering, but she

18

didn't seem to be overly upset at Tina. No decent woman wanted that saloon in town.

"Let's go over to the parsonage. You need a bath. I'll pour the rinse water for your hair."

The hacking stopped, and Tina followed Glynna out the back door of the diner just in time to see the door to Dare's doctor's office shut hard with a loud *click*. But why not call it as it was? Vince slammed a door again.

CHAPTER 2

Vince walked into Dare's office and slammed the door hard. He'd brought firewood.

He took some pleasure in stoking Dare's stove with Tina's picket stick and what was left of her sign marking Duffy's Tavern as the gateway to hell.

Vince wasn't a drinker, but honestly, Duffy wasn't so bad.

"She'll just find another stick." Jonas sounded exhausted. Being a big brother was too much for him and that was a fact. Vince couldn't see a single strand of hair that showed red on Jonas's soaked head. His face was so muddy none of his freckles showed through. And as Jonas sat there, getting Dare's examination table filthy, a big clump of mud fell off his shoe.

Jonas didn't notice. Right now it was the least of his troubles.

Dare was busy bending Jonas's arm one way and another. At a glance, Vince diagnosed his friend from across the room. Jonas wasn't bad hurt, no real swelling; he'd just taken a good whack. He'd be fine.

Even though Dare's eye was covered in mud, Vince could see it was going to be black.

"You know, Duffy doesn't really serve a lot of liquor out of that saloon." Vince figured it was worth mentioning.

"He does all right." Dare almost sounded envious. He'd washed his face and hands, probably some law against doctoring with dirty hands. But his hair was starting to stand up in mud-hardened spikes, and his clothes were filthy.

Vince thought that if Dare were doctoring him, he'd insist on the doctor taking a bath first even if he had a bone sticking out of his skin.

It was no secret Dare didn't make much money with doctoring. He'd had a growing practice for a while, back when Glynna was cooking at the diner. She had no gift for it, and Dare kept busy treating stomach ailments of men who'd eat at the diner in order to see Glynna's pretty face. But Glynna had hired a cook and Dare had gone back to making a bare-bones living. "He built a house with real boards."

"You've got real boards too, Dare." Vince swept a pointing finger around the room.

"Yep, but only because someone abandoned this house, and I just moved in. Although"—Dare raised his head, perked up—"Duffy was here before us. Maybe someone abandoned his house, too."

"Can you think of anything that will get her to stop walking that picket line, Jonas?"

Jonas gave Vince a disgusted look. "I've known her for the same length of time you have. You're as likely to figure out a way to handle her as I am."

Vince had one very vivid, very shocking image of himself "handling" Tina Cahill. He'd toted her into the diner. She was slick with mud. An armful of shivering-cold sass. Her shining blue eyes like to stabbed holes in his hide. Like somehow he was to blame for her condition. Her pretty blond curls were dripping brown and plastered to her face. Her dress, earlier in the day, had been pink, and he had a particular fondness for the way Tina fit in her dresses. But now it was so coated with mire, the color was impossible to confirm. She was soaking wet—that dress clinging to her everywhere.

Vince veered his thoughts away as fast as they occurred and hoped nothing showed on his face.

Jonas wasn't overly fond of any man paying attention to his baby sister. Which wasn't much of a problem here in Broken Wheel, Texas, Tina being Tina.

"You knew her when she was a child."

"I barely saw her." Jonas flinched, so Dare must've found a tender spot. Jonas didn't comment on Dare's doctoring skills, or the lack thereof. "I was grown and gone from the time she was a toddler."

Jonas's father had died, and his mother remarried a brute who took his temper out on Jonas and his ma. Jonas had run off several times before he'd left home for good when he was a half-grown boy. His one regret was abandoning his defenseless baby sister to the ugliness in his home.

Because he'd ended up riding the outlaw trail for years, he'd only found out his stepfather had killed his ma and been hung for it after it was all over. When he'd gone home to see to his sister, he'd found her living with Jonas's starchy aunt Iphigenia—Jonas's father's sister, who resented being asked to raise a child who shared no blood with her.

Iphigenia had refused to let Jonas stay with her; neither would she agree to let Jonas take Tina. And Jonas had to admit he was no fit caretaker for a little girl. He'd stopped by to see Tina, only being home a few times through her childhood. Tina had adored him and barraged him with letters in Andersonville. Those letters had helped keep Jonas and all the Regulators sane in Andersonville Prison.

"Well, you got all those letters from her during the war." Tina Cahill had been a letter-writin' fool, no doubt about it.

"I let you read them when we were locked up together. You learned everything I ever learned about her."

Vince, Dare, and Jonas had all spent time in Andersonville, a prison notorious for starvation, deprivation of every kind, and the relentless, ugly deaths of its inmates. Dare had learned doctoring there, which mostly amounted to throwing a blanket over a man's head when he died. It wasn't the finest medical training ground known to man. Still, Dare did okay.

"You need a sling." Dare went to get a rag out of his stack.

Vince was relieved Dare didn't resort to his main skill: amputation. That and blanket throwing were about all he had real experience with.

Vince said to Dare's back, "You should put a cold cloth on your eye before it swells all the way shut." There, Vince was now a doctor, too. He was a doctor *and* a lawyer. Neither job paid much, and that made Vince glad he hadn't bothered with law school. No sense making an investment like that for a job that earned a man so few dollars.

Of course, he might've made a better living elsewhere. Broken Wheel was a north Texas town set smack-dab in the middle of Indian Territory. Only idiots lived here, and idiots rarely needed a lawyer. Vince figured it was only fair to count himself and all of his friends among the idiots.

Vince could have gone home, of course. His father had written about building a new mansion on South Prairie Avenue, no doubt the fanciest address in Chicago. For that was how Julius Yates did things.

Vince had stopped home for a time after the war to regain his health, and he'd only done that because he was too weak to direct his own affairs. The Army had simply shipped him home. He'd been half starved and weighed barely one hundred pounds when he'd gotten there. Father had seemed unable to even look at him. Mother had gone one better. She'd forgotten she had a son. Vince had left as soon as he was able. Except for that visit, he'd been away from home for most of his adult life. He wondered if a new house, with no old memories, would be easier to handle.

Not likely.

Any home shared with his father would be a bigger wasteland than this Palo Duro Canyon.

Now Luke was married to a woman he'd rescued from a flood, then brought along to a land war. Not the usual courtship.

Dare was married to a woman whose husband he'd killed. Even though Flint Greer had needed killing bad, that wasn't the normal way to round up a wife.

And Jonas had been hunted down by his baby sister, Tina the Picketer, who had moved in and promptly turned the whole town on its ear.

Well, not the *whole* town, just the saloon. But there were really only five businesses in Broken Wheel: Sledge Murphy's smithy; Tug Andrews's general store; Glynna's diner; Asa Munson's boardinghouse; and of course Duffy's Tavern. Vince didn't count his own law office, nor Dare's medical practice, as both were mighty quiet establishments.

So Tina threatened one-fifth of the Broken Wheel economy, and that attracted notice.

Most of the townsfolk had gotten used to her walking back and forth, her little twenty-step-long picket line. Her cute little boots clicking out a persnickety rhythm on the boards of Broken Wheel's short sidewalk.

She was there five days a week, from one to three in the afternoon, weather permitting. And this was Texas desert country, so the weather usually permitted. She picketed right after she'd gotten the diner cleaned up after the noon rush.

The men tipped their hats, admired her pretty face and fussy dresses, complimented her biscuits, ignored her scolding and went about their drinking.

But it was the end of December, payday at a few of the area ranches and New Year's Eve besides. The cowpokes had a bit more cash money than usual and they were in high spirits. That had drawn a slightly bigger crowd to the saloon than normal. And that crowd had more to drink than was probably wise.

"I warned her things would be different at Duffy's today," Jonas said, wincing at Dare's medical treatment. "I told her it was payday, besides being a holiday, so Luke and the other ranchers around these parts weren't expecting a long workday from their men."

"You shoulda warned her a little harder," Dare said, rigging the sling.

"And louder," Vince added. "Maybe you should've applied your hand to her backside."

26

Jonas rolled his eyes. "I might not survive giving Tina a hiding. I'd rather take a beating in a brawl at Duffy's than even attempt it."

Vince had to admit he agreed with that.

Even though Tina's presence had become routine, today—probably because the liquor was flowing more freely—just as Jonas had feared, Tina had stirred up a hornet's nest. Vince thought of that *Abandon Hope* sign. He was surprised by a momentary urge to smile over the sign the little minx had come up with. She was a bright little thing. It wasn't everyone who could apply Dante to her daily life.

Part of Vince thought it was just as well to ignore the whole thing. They could just make a note on a calendar and worry about Tina once a month—on payday.

The other part of him lingered over the thought of turning her over his knee and spanking some sense into her.

Vince didn't figure he dared do that. And he knew better than to volunteer. Not just because Jonas would object. Dare once in a while made some comment that reminded Vince that Tina was the only single woman in this town—if he didn't count crazy Lana Bullard, and he didn't. And Vince was single himself, which was just how he liked it.

If the men in town were to vote on it, they'd probably elect to throw Tina into the jail along with Lana. They'd probably amend the vote to allow both women—who were both mighty fine cooks—out to make breakfast and dinner at Glynna's diner.

Vince wondered, not for the first time, how that diner qualified as belonging to Glynna. She had just moved into an abandoned diner, then hired a cook.

The fact that Glynna claimed to own it and then kept all the money she didn't spend on supplies and wages was a deeply questionable legal issue that a lawyer might be expected to have trouble with. But no one seemed to care, and so Vince didn't, either.

A knock on the front door of Dare's house sent Vince, the only one not busy, to answer it. Paul, Glynna's son, stood at the door, holding a letter. "Mr. Andrews had a letter for you at the general store. He said you hadn't been in to check and I oughta bring it over."

"I never get mail." Vince looked at the handwriting and felt a chill rush up his spine, because he did in fact on rare occasion get mail. His father's letters were never easy.

Paul shrugged.

"Are you done at the diner, Paul?" Dare called to his stepson. The two of them had a rocky start, but they were getting along well now. Paul was a more cheerful youngster than he'd been when his ma was married to Flint Greer. Who wouldn't be upset about his ma being married to a hardfisted sidewinder like Greer?

"We're done for the day. Ma's busy helping get Tina cleaned up from the mud-wrestling fight." With that, Paul turned and left.

Vince's eyes were frozen on the unmistakable handwriting on the envelope in his hand. He walked over to a chair at the side of the room, away from his friends.

As he sat, his stomach twisted, which made Vince mad. He'd have sworn nothing about home could touch him anymore.

He'd repeated that vow when he'd left after recuperating from Andersonville, but he'd made that decision a long time ago—long before he was old enough to strike out on his own. The day his father had taught him to always be on his guard.

❦

"Vincent, darlin'." Mother fluttered her pretty fan as she stepped into his playroom.

She came. Today was his seventh birthday, and he'd hoped she would come. He'd dressed in a little black suit and had a neat neckcloth on and his black boots shined. He felt very grown up.

"Yes, Mother?" Vincent said.

"Your grandmama sent you a present for your birthday." She smiled her beautiful smile and spoke with her musical Southern accent.

His only living grandparent was his mother's mother, who lived in Georgia. She was kind and lavished wonderful gifts on him, and he and Mother spent at least a month with Grandmama every winter at the plantation.

"Can I see it?" Vincent threw himself at Mother and hugged her.

"Vincent, land sakes!" Mother's voice broke.

Vincent stepped back so fast he stumbled and fell on his backside. Sitting, braced on his arms, he looked up knowing what he'd see and dreading it.

Mother dabbed at her eyes. Tears. Always he upset her, and he hated doing it.

"Children are such undisciplined creatures." Mother cried delicately into her lace handkerchief while she brushed at her skirts, as if they were now ruined. "I despair of your manners, Vincent."

He tried to remember not to touch her, but he loved her so. Struggling to his feet, he said, "I'm sorry, Mother." He clasped his hands neatly behind his back and looked up at her. Terrified of her tears.

"I declare, you will never grow up to be a gentleman if you can't remember simple decorum."

Mother stood before him like a magical creature. So fine and beautiful, how dare he touch her? What if she gave up on him becoming a gentleman and never came to see him again? What if she banished him? His best friend had already been sent away to boarding school, and Vincent knew that his time would come, but not yet. He couldn't bear to be away from Mother.

Her tears eased and finally, with trembling hands, she tucked her kerchief away. Slowly, as if she feared what he'd do next, she reached out her delicate white fingers and took his hand. That was more gift than he'd expected.

"If you can mind your manners, then come along."

Vincent quivered with excitement, yet he was quiet and didn't squeeze Mother's hand or touch her skirts. But there was a gift that required them leaving the room? He was rarely allowed outside of this suite: his bedroom, the play-room where he also took his meals, the schoolroom, and the room where his nanny slept were his world.

He went downstairs sometimes, summoned to his father's study, only when he was in trouble. And of course he was allowed down to walk to the park on fine days. But it was improper for children to have the run of the house. A young gentleman remained in his rooms unless he was summoned elsewhere.

They moved sedately down the wide, curved staircase

and went straight to the front door. Mother nodded at a liveried footman, who swung the door open for them.

Vincent saw a beautiful sight. Gerald, the Yateses' head groom, stood holding the reins of a brown-and-white-spotted Shetland pony, its thick mane shimmering like silk. The pony shook its head, and the harness bells jingled a pretty tune.

"A pony? And a cart, too? Mother, are you saying this is all mine?"

Mother said, "Calm yourself, Vincent. Yes, it's all yours. You'll be allowed to drive it to the park when the weather is fair. You'll have a groom riding beside you so you'll be safe, of course."

Vincent's heart pounded to think of the freedom being offered him. He'd had very little of it up to that point. His studies were taken seriously. His playtime away from the house was carefully planned with his nanny, and at least one footman was always there to watch over him. Vincent had been reminded many times of all the dangers in the world, especially when a boy was the heir to a great fortune. His father scolded him about any recklessness.

"And it's all right with Father?" Vincent regretted that question when he saw Mother's smile fade a bit.

"He hasn't seen the pony yet. It arrived with a letter from Grandmama just today. But your father will abide by my mother's wishes."

Grandmama was wealthy, a fact Vincent was never allowed to forget. Much of the wealth they had was a result of Mother's family. Though Father was prosperous in his own right, too.

Father worried overly about Vincent's safety. He liked

to pinch Vincent's shoulder when he came in with torn trousers and scraped elbows. There were also scoldings and even whippings when Vincent didn't attend to his studies.

Mother bent down and straightened Vincent's neckcloth. "I must get on now, honey child. My maid is waiting to dress me and do my hair. But Gerald will ride with you to the park for your first lesson."

Vincent looked at the man who ran his father's stable. There was no way to hold back a smile. "Thank you, Mother." Vincent squeezed her hand, too happy now to risk wrinkling her more.

"Happy birthday, Vincent." She smiled and went back inside.

Running down the broad stairs to the sidewalk, Vincent reached the pony. His exuberance caused the animal to dance a bit. A hoof lashed out, and Vincent jumped back and tumbled to the sidewalk. A second later and he was right back on his feet. The kick hadn't come close.

"Have a care, Master Yates." Gerald had a firm hold on the reins, and the cart didn't move even an inch.

Then Gerald's eyes moved past Vincent and widened just as a hard hand came down on Vincent's shoulder. Only one person in the world had a grip like that.

Father.

A shudder of fear coursed through Vincent's body. He spun Vincent around, and the scowl on his father's face was dreadful to see.

"Have this dangerous animal destroyed." Father never looked away from Vincent. His hand became a vise as he dragged Vincent by the arm into the house. Just as the door slammed, Vincent heard the soft *clip-clop* of shod feet and the joyful jingle of bells as the pony was led away.

"I have warned you about being reckless, Vincent. A reminder you won't soon forget is in order."

The whipping Vincent received left marks on his backside and legs that were a long time fading. Even at such a young age, Vincent knew his father did more damage with his whip than the pony would have done with a kick. But the pony had died because Vincent was reckless.

If he'd known Father was standing nearby, he'd never have upset the pony and then he might have saved its life. Father's seventh birthday gift to Vincent was one he never forgot.

He learned to always be on guard.

⌒∞⌒

Vince remembered his father's icy rage. For so young a boy, Vince had managed to return that rage full force. It was the first time Vince had ever seen shades of his father in himself.

That day marked the end of Vince trying to win Father's approval. Instead he learned to sneak. He learned defiance. He learned to bear, in unrepentant silence, the scoldings and whippings if he got caught.

Shaking off the ugly memories, he tore open the envelope, prepared to be hostile to whatever Father said.

He read one sentence, then his eyes fell shut on a surprising wave of tears.

Shocked by such a show of weakness, he fought them and blinked his eyes open to stare at the letter—which was several pages long. But his vision was too blurred to keep reading after the first few lines. Mother had the same madness her father had, but at a much younger age. Vince had seen plenty of evidence. He'd gone home after the war so sick from the time in Andersonville, he had no choice but to find a place to recuperate.

Mother hadn't recognized him.

Vince knew it ran in the family. When would his turn come?

Father said that without Vince's help, Mother couldn't stay at home anymore. Father had written to order Vince back to Chicago if he didn't want his mother locked away in a madhouse.

Locking Mother away would be a public admission of failure. And Julius Yates didn't fail at anything. It was probably just more of Father's usual threats aimed at getting Vince to come home and take over the family business—as if Father would give up an ounce of his authority.

But it was the ugliest threat yet, and as much as Vince doubted Father would ever do such a thing, Vince remembered that beautiful pony. He never underestimated Father's cruelty.

Vince tucked the rest of the letter, still unread, into his stiff, mud-caked shirt pocket. Tina wasn't the only one who'd been in a mud-wrestling fight. Remembering that gave Vince the excuse he needed. "I've got to get cleaned up," he said.

He stalked out then, not even looking at Dare and Jonas. He wasn't absolutely sure a tear or two hadn't escaped his eyes, but he didn't want to risk the others noticing if they had.

CHAPTER 3

The hot water was shocking and set her teeth to chattering. "I d-didn't know how c-cold I was."

Tina and Glynna had come back to Jonas's parsonage and only now, as she sank into the tin tub of steaming water, did Tina realize her whole body was numb from taking an icy mud bath.

"Let me know if you need help washing your hair." Glynna stood in the next room to give Tina privacy for her bath. She could have gone back to the diner. Tina knew Glynna had been trying hard to see that her children spent time with book learning every day, and this was definitely a disruption. But Tina appreciated that she stayed.

Tina was a while ferreting out all the mud, but finally she felt clean again—except for her hair, which she'd pinned on top of her head. Glynna had stoked the fire in Jonas's kitchen to a blaze while Tina had gotten the tub ready, so the kitchen was well heated. Tina finally lifted herself, dripping, out of the tub, dried quickly and pulled on a clean dress. Tina had dressed in the most modest and respectable style when she'd lived with Aunt Iphigenia, but since she'd come to Broken Wheel, she was learning to leave off the extra petticoats and corset. Her life was much easier without them.

"I'm ready."

"Tina, no offense, but . . ." Glynna was talking as she stepped in the room, but she hesitated and shuddered just a bit as she looked at Tina's hair. "Go ahead and bend over the tub. I'll pour water over it. We don't dare use the muddy water from your bath."

Glynna hefted a steaming kettle off the stove and touched it to make sure it wasn't burning hot. Glynna was a delicate woman, her hair gold, her skin bronze, her eyes hazel, until she seemed to be the same tawny color all over. Though she worked hard, she managed to look so pretty all the time. Tina had to fight not to be envious of her. And of course the envy was about more than how Glynna looked; it was also about her happy marriage.

Glynna had found love and that added a glow to her sun-warmed coloring. "I'll get your hair wet and scrub the mud out."

Tina pulled the pins out of her hair, and it stayed in the knot she'd formed. Dried solid.

"This is going to take a while." Glynna came up beside her.

Tina leaned over the tub of brown water. They didn't speak as Glynna poured a bucket of water over Tina's head, then scrubbed and rinsed.

Water ran brown into the big tin bathtub.

"I have to give it one more scrubbing." Glynna went back to work.

While Glynna lathered up a second batch of foam, Tina decided they could talk. "Earlier, you said something about 'no offense'?" Tina braced herself to be deeply offended. That was usually the way when someone said "no offense."

There was a long hesitation, which Tina appreciated. It wasn't as if Glynna was *eager* to be offensive.

Glynna was always quiet and sweet, but now she was more hesitant than usual. "I am not sure you're doing the Lord's work with your picket line."

Tina wasn't surprised that this was the topic. It stood to reason and she was fully prepared to defend herself. "I can't imagine the Lord isn't fully supportive of my cause."

"Yes, well, that's true, I'm sure. The Lord most likely has no use for a saloon. Although Jesus did turn water into wine at that wedding in Cana, so clearly some drinking is acceptable."

"This is no wedding, and the only thing miraculous in Duffy's Tavern is how easily a fool hands over his hard-earned money."

"I'm ready to rinse."

Tina braced her hands on the edge of the tub and relished the feel of warm water washing away the soap and the last of the chill from her body. This time the water ran with clean white suds that gave way to clear water. Her friend wrapped Tina's dripping hair in a towel.

"I'm wondering if maybe . . . well, the men now mostly just ignore your picketing." Glynna and Tina each took a handle on the metal tub of muddy water and carried it together out of the kitchen.

As they lugged the heavy tub out of the parsonage, around back and poured the water onto the cold ground, Tina said, "Not all of the men ignore me."

Vince was the first face that popped into her head. Then

Jonas and Dare. Really, with those exceptions, most of the other men walked right past her as if she were invisible. Although Sledge Murphy was inclined to speak to her favorably about biscuits, and Tug Andrews had a tendency to growl. That was how he acted with everyone, though, so she hadn't taken it personally.

"Most of them. The thing is, it's possible your picketing has lost any effectiveness it ever had."

Tina noticed that Glynna was too kind to say it never had one speck of effectiveness.

"Maybe we should think of something else. Some new approach. I saw Duffy's face when he almost punched you."

"Duffy didn't punch me. And I know he didn't set out to."

"Which means you recognize at least some decency in him." Glynna poured water from the kettle on the kitchen stove, then began shaving soap into the steaming tub.

Tina sniffed and didn't respond to the comment about that low-down, whiskey-selling Duffy Schuster.

Glynna plunged Tina's muddy clothes into the sudsy water.

"I'll wash those, Glynna. You don't have to."

Glynna, kneeling beside the tub, smiled. "It's one of my few housewife skills. Let me do it while you dry your hair."

"Thank you. I appreciate the help."

Nodding, Glynna went back to her worrying. "The thing is, if Duffy—or any of that crowd—had punched you, I think that would be deeply shaming to a man."

Tina thought of Glynna's husband, the one before Dare, who'd put his hands on her in violence. Glynna had come to Broken Wheel as a mail-order bride for Flint Greer, the man who'd killed Luke Stone's father. She'd thought she was rescuing her children from an ugly life when her traitorous first husband, after years of stealing from the Confederate Army, had been hung. But her life with Greer had turned to one of heavy fists and constant fear. Jonas, Vince, and Dare had fought at Luke's side to free Glynna and get the ranch back. Through all that, Glynna had ended up married to Dare Riker, the doctor in Broken Wheel.

"Are you saying I should just give up?" Tina didn't want to, not one bit. "My aunt Iphigenia taught me to persevere. She always said, 'Do what is right, come what may.'"

"Yes, well, of course you need to do what is right, but I'm wondering if perhaps a fresh approach might be needed to achieve your ends. It can't be God's will that you were involved in a fistfight on the street in the mud, can it? I know things are a bit different here in the West, but it isn't at all proper."

Put that way, Tina had some doubts of her own.

"I think if Duffy had struck you, if you had in any way been hurt in that ruckus, it might . . ." Glynna's eyes met Tina's.

Glynna was a true friend, one of the few Tina had ever had. Aunt Iphigenia's home hadn't been the type of place a young girl brought her friends. So Tina didn't want to upset Glynna. "It might what?"

"I don't know how a man's mind works." Glynna was silent a moment, focused on her washing. "But any man has to hit a woman for the first time." She stopped and looked up, and the gentle sound of sloshing water ended. "Do you think the second time might be . . . be easier maybe? Do you think a woman being in the middle of a brawl such as that one today could harden a man? Maybe turn him into a man who hits women? You wouldn't want to have any part in bringing a man to that, now, would you?"

"A woman can't be blamed for a man hitting her. It's not your fault your husband struck you." Tina combed her tangled, wet hair in front of the stove with its crackling fire. The kettle was steaming again, the stove's water wells heating. It made her furious to think of Glynna somehow blaming herself for what Greer had done.

And yet it was an intriguing and upsetting question. What if Tina had been punched? How would that have made a man—one who knew better than to hit a woman—feel?

"I have to admit that in the midst of all this, I haven't spent much time considering Duffy's feelings."

Glynna smiled. "He doesn't seem like the sensitive type, for the most part."

"So do you have any idea what else I might try?" Tina stopped her combing and looked at Glynna. The woman was older, and she'd certainly lived through more troubles than Tina, though Tina's own life couldn't be considered an easy one. Still, Tina was willing to take advice.

"Not really. Can you think of anything?" Glynna went back to her washing, while Tina had the snarls in her hair to consider.

Finally, a bit nervous to mention it, Tina said, "There is one more cause in this town that concerns me."

Glynna lifted Tina's dress out of the water and wrung it out. "What's that?" Looking cheered by Tina's mention of a different cause, Glynna worked as she waited.

But that cheerful expression wasn't going to last. "I've been up-upset . . ."

"About what?"

Glynna might not like this.

"Well, about the way they've got Lana Bullard locked up."

Glynna froze, the dripping dress in hand. "Um . . . they locked her up because she tried to kill Dare. And me. And Vince. And Paul."

"Vince and Paul were only attacked in the fight afterwards."

"Which wouldn't have made them any less dead." Glynna's friendly expression had turned wary.

"And you were a hostage, not her true victim."

"It felt very true while that knife was at my throat." Glynna ran a hand over the barely visible nick on her throat, where Lana had held a knife while she made accusations against Dare, who had already been stabbed. "Lana is a dangerous woman." She set the dress aside and pulled a chemise from the rinse water next. She spoke very precisely, as if carefully weighing each word. "What exactly do you think should change about her current imprisonment?"

"I've heard that if a person commits a crime while they're insane, they aren't really responsible for the crime and they need some kind of treatment, not prison."

The two women scrubbed and combed in silence for a while. At last Glynna said, "I suppose there's no denying she's furiously mad. But how do you treat such a thing? She can't be let out of jail. She's too dangerous to be on her own."

Tina nearly had the tangles out of her hair before she came up with an answer. "I think we need to see if we can cure her of her madness."

"How in heaven's name do we do that?" Glynna shook

out the dress and took it to a clothesline strung along one wall of the kitchen. She pegged it by the shoulders and reached for the next piece of clothing.

"I thought maybe, since he's a doctor, Dare might know."

"But Dare's who she wants to kill." Glynna was clearly more interested in her husband not being subjected to another attack than she was in justice. "How could he possibly help her?"

"Who else?"

"Why would Dare want to help a woman who stabbed him and almost killed me?" Glynna was asking a really good question.

Tina set her comb aside and gave Glynna a sheepish shrug of her shoulders. "Do what's right, come what may. I'm hoping he thinks it's the right thing to do."

CHAPTER 4

"I'm never going to help with something so wrong." Dare skidded to a halt in his pacing.

His attitude disappointed Tina mightily. She'd convinced him to come to the jail and had carefully and thoughtfully laid out her arguments. Dare seemed unable to get over Lana's string of murder attempts. There had been three—on Dare. Tina wasn't counting Glynna and Vince and Paul, though Glynna, Vince, and Paul sure counted them.

So six murder attempts. But Lana had never succeeded, for heaven's sake!

"You think we should just throw open the cell door and let her loose?" Vince, of course, never failed to disappoint her. Tina didn't even consider appealing to Vince to show some mercy to poor Lana.

But she'd hoped for better from Dare.

His momentary stillness didn't last. He went back to his customary pacing back and forth from one side of the small jailhouse to the other, a bit faster than before, shaking his head emphatically.

"No, it's a ridiculous notion. She can't be allowed to run around free."

Lana lay on her side on the thin mattress in her cell. She drummed her fingers on the mattress, her head propped up on her fist, watching them with sharp eyes. She seemed to have gotten used to being in there. Now she watched silently as Dare, Tina, Vince, and Mitch Porter, the former sheriff of Broken Wheel, talked about her fate.

Somehow in the midst of Lana's madness she'd also found time to strike up a more-than-friendly acquaintance with the ex-sheriff. Porter had been bought and paid for by Flint Greer, and Porter had twisted the law around to suit Greer's best interests. Now Vince was the sheriff, sworn in by Big John Conroy, but it was an unpaid job without Greer to supply the money as he had for Porter.

Porter meanwhile had moved into one of the vacant houses in Broken Wheel and lived on money he must have saved up from Greer's salary.

Tina knew that besides fetching food for Lana, the job of sheriff didn't take much time, so Vince had been a good sport about being stuck with the job.

Tina sat ramrod straight. Aunt Iphigenia had always insisted on correct posture, and never more so than when a woman needed to make a case for something. "I know she's dangerous."

"You figured that out all by yourself, huh?" Vince stood behind his desk with his back leaning against the wall. The jail had two cells that took up half the back of the building. A small hallway led between the cells and a tiny storeroom. There was a rack for rifles at Vince's back that had no rifles in it. If Vince wanted a gun for sheriffing, he needed to bring his own.

Vince had his arms folded and his ankles crossed, looking calm as ever. But his eyes were alert and they were staring at Tina so hard they seemed to punch holes in her very compassionate idea.

"She can't stay here any longer and you know it." Tina tapped her foot.

The question was, if not here, where? Big John, who made his home in Broken Wheel, even though he traveled most of the time, would make that decision next time he was in town.

Until then, Vince, the town lawyer, sworn deputy and unpaid public servant, was in charge of the prisoner.

"She needs to be released," Mitch Porter shouted. He was sweet on Lana, which might be why he thought letting her loose was a good idea.

"Women are locked up in the same prison with men in Texas," Tina said. "We can't let that happen to her."

"Yep, we can." Vince's eyes shot fire at Tina.

"It's too horrible." Tina surged from her chair, tempted to start pacing right along with Dare. "It's unspeakable! She'd be at the mercy of evil men."

Vince didn't even quit his easy leaning. "I hope the poor men survive her company."

Tina seriously considered whether Vince was going to survive her company. "I can't believe you don't see we have to help her."

"What I *see*," Vince said as he straightened from the wall and uncrossed his arms, so Tina knew he was serious, "is the knife sticking out of Dare's back. I see Glynna and

Dare bleeding when that avalanche came down on their heads."

"We don't know Lana was responsible for that." Tina needed her placard. She could've brandished it to underscore her seriousness.

"I see my friend's house burning down around his ears. I see him getting ready to jump from a third-floor window to escape. Lana stays locked up. For good. She's a menace, and none of us are safe if she's set free."

Lana said from where she lay, "I done some bad things, but I was plumb out of my mind. I'm fine now. You got my word I won't burn no one up, nor stab them in the back, never again."

As a defense against her crimes, that wasn't going to be much help. "There have to be ways besides turning her in with a prison full of men."

Tina stood and moved very deliberately into Dare's path.

He stopped pacing rather than run her down. He said, "Vince is right. She's a killer, Tina. Crazy doesn't excuse that."

"By law it does."

"She'll hurt someone if we turn her loose." Dare was trying hard to be kindhearted about refusing Tina's request.

"I just said I wouldn't," Lana snarled.

"That's what jails are for," Dare said, giving Lana a nervous glance, "to protect innocent people from dangerous ones."

"She had a bad night," Tina said.

"The avalanche, the fire, and the stabbing. Three separate attacks, all premeditated, and they happened weeks apart. That's not a bad night."

Tina shrugged one shoulder. "Now, Dare—"

Porter shouted, "She's been sane and peaceful as can be ever since."

Of course she'd been locked up tight.

"She doesn't seem real dangerous right now, I'll grant you that." Vince gave Lana a glum look.

She arched a brow at him. "I said I was sorry. And I probably need a lawyer for when I go to trial. You're the only lawyer in town, Yates. So I'm hiring you."

"You can't hire me. I'm probably going to be prosecuting you, not to mention being the one who arrested you, and you can add in I think you're guilty as charged. Find another lawyer."

"I can't. You're the only one in town."

"Then you're out of luck, Lana."

"I need a lawyer so I can get out of here. I want to go back to cooking at the diner."

Dare made a purely rude sound. "You expect my wife to give you a job after you stabbed me and held a knife to her throat?"

"I wasn't thinking clear. I'm better now." Lana rolled onto her back and wove her fingers together and rested them on her chest, staring at the jail ceiling. As if saying she was sorry was enough. She did seem mighty sane lying there in her cell.

"I can see myself being driven mad if Big John doesn't get to town soon and haul Lana away." Vince sounded irritable, but he leaned back against the wall again.

"You're all a bunch of lying cowards. Blaming her for something she never done."

"Porter," Vince said, not bothering to even look at the

man, "I'm going to see you hung just to shut you up. Now, get out of here."

Tina wondered just how the law worked in Texas.

Porter glared at Vince for a few seconds as if daring him. But Vince had eyes that could make a man back down, and finally Porter dropped his gaze and stormed out in a huff, slamming the door behind him.

"I know she's dangerous, Dare." Tina went back to her wheedling. "The thing is, maybe we could make her come to her senses."

"I *have* come to my senses," Lana said. "Stop bad-mouthing me."

Lana glared at Tina, who realized she was more than a bit afraid of upsetting Lana. "I mean . . . we can make it safe to turn her loose."

"How?" Dare asked.

This was the tricky part. "I thought that since you're the doctor, you might know."

"I know enough to believe it's not possible. Once a mind is broken, it doesn't come back."

"I'll say," Vince muttered.

"Mine did." Lana twiddled her thumbs and seemed to be memorizing the number of flyspecks on the ceiling. There were plenty of them.

Tina looked over at Vince, but he didn't notice. And Vince was a noticing kind of man. "What do you mean, 'I'll say'?"

Vince glared at her and didn't answer.

"So she's going to prison?" Tina wanted to start screaming at the very thought. To put a woman in a prison full of men was—

"Maybe not." Vince cut into her panic. "There are asylums. I don't know where, but Texas is getting plumb settled these days. We could find out where the closest one is and take her there."

"Do they need a cook in an asylum?" Lana asked. "Cooking in the diner was the best job I ever had."

But then Lana was known to have worked her whole life abovestairs in one seedy saloon after another, so it didn't take much to improve on that.

Dare ignored the question. "I heard of one called Bedlam that became famous in London. I know they had them in Chicago."

"We can look into an asylum." Vince gave Tina a kind look that seemed sincere. It was as if he understood her fears, which seemed strange when he was the most vocal about locking Lana away.

"I can't imagine anyone being able to bear caring for a building full of furiously mad patients." Tina felt sick at the very thought.

"Like feeding a pack of cowboys, I reckon," Lana said.

"I can't either." Vince strode to the door and wrenched it open. He paused. "I'm going to ride out until I find someone who knows about asylums, and while I'm at it, I'll ask about treatment for madness."

"There are books about that kind of thing." Dare frowned. "But we might need a medical school to find them. You can't ride there. The closest colleges are in . . ." Dare pondered that for a minute. "There's one in New Orleans. St. Louis has one. Memphis too, I think. It would take weeks to ride to one and get back."

"It's not like I'm real busy here."

"You're guarding the prisoner!" Tina jammed her fists on her waist.

Vince looked at Dare for a moment, then at Tina. "Can you be sheriff while I'm gone?"

"No! A woman can't be sheriff."

"I guess I could ask Griss to do it." Vince peered through the open door toward Duffy's Tavern.

"You would give my sworn enemy the job of upholding the law?"

With a shrug Vince said, "Just because he sells cheap whiskey doesn't make him a bad man."

"As a matter of fact, it does. He can't be sheriff and neither can I."

"Well, why not?"

"Because women aren't sheriffs."

"This is the West. Women can do anything they want . . . so long as the men let them. And what man in this town is gonna stop you from doing *anything* so long as you keep making them food and don't let Glynna go back to cooking?" Vince flinched and glanced at Dare. "Sorry."

"I'm sorry, too," Dare said.

Vince turned back to Tina. "Dare can be sheriff except when he's doctoring. Luke's probably too busy. I'd ask Jonas, but it don't seem proper that a parson be sheriff. What if he had to shoot somebody? It'd be hard to preach his way around that come Sunday morning."

"I don't think—"

"Good, because your thinkin' has caused nothing but trouble. Consider yourself sworn in." Vince plucked the star off his vest and tossed it to her. She caught it by reflex.

"Dare, try to remember any specific books you've heard of while I pack a bedroll. If you remember in time, I can ride to Dahl's Pass and send a wire ordering them. Then we can ask the supply wagon driver to bring it along with him on his next trip. Otherwise I'll have to ride farther afield." Vince charged out and slammed the door.

"I'm the one who got a knife in my back," Dare said, sounding exasperated. "What's he so all-fired upset about?"

"I'd like to know the answer to that, too." Tina held up the tin star and scowled at it. Sheriff? For heaven's sake, how had that happened?

She thought of the strange way Vince had acted. It was important to him to track down this information, and Tina had a strong feeling it had absolutely nothing to do with the care and treatment of Lana Bullard.

Tina felt her shoulders square as her spirits rose to meet this challenge. "I see no reason I can't be sheriff. My aunt Iphigenia always said a woman needs to know how to take care of herself. I think being sheriff means I can take care of this whole town."

"You're not going to start picketing again, are you?" Dare asked, rubbing one hand over his face.

"Of course I am. Right after the noon meal, unless my sheriffing work keeps me busy." Tina pinned on her shiny badge.

"You can start your job by getting me some more food." Lana sounded pathetic. "Dinner was mighty skimpy today."

Tina wondered if being hungry might make the woman go crazy again. "I'll get you something right away."

Dare shook his head and walked out of the jailhouse. Tina went after him.

Lana called from the cell, "I wouldn't mind a sip of whiskey with my meal."

Tina shut the door, wishing Vince hadn't gone and destroyed her placard. She'd like to wave it at Lana while she served up a whiskey-less meal.

CHAPTER 5

Tina had been sheriff for a mighty long time when Vince finally came back.

It was a wearying job. She'd slept fitfully in the sheriff's chair for the first three nights. Then Dare found out she was doing that and said she could leave Lana by herself overnight.

Even after she got her own bed back, she waited on the prisoner hand and foot. Lana was always hungry, and Tina would do about anything to shut her up. And Mitch Porter was always around clamoring for Tina to let Lana go, as if Tina had the authority to drop the charges. It was ridiculous, but she had no way to avoid listening to Porter's endless complaints. Honestly, he was such a pest that Tina wanted to arrest him. She might have too if she thought she could wrestle him into a jail cell. But if she did manage it, then she'd have to start hauling two caterwauling prisoners their meals. She wondered how many meals Porter would demand a day.

It was doubly annoying because Vince hadn't trusted her with the key. He'd given it to Dare, who'd refused to let her have it back. He'd called her a bleeding heart and said if she needed to open the cell door, he wanted to be right there with her in case she decided to let Lana make a run for it rather than see her locked up in a prison full of men. Tina had to admit, it was an idea she found tempting.

Fortunately, Lana's food could be shoved into her cell through a space near the floor.

Besides being a sheriff without any authority, she'd been cooking breakfast and dinner at Glynna's diner. She was worn clean out and about ready to join Lana in Bedlam.

Now here she sat, right during her normal picketing time, while Lana snored through her afternoon nap. Tina did find the long hours of boredom gave her time to paint a new placard. It was tricky because mostly she wanted to paint Bible verses, but her board wasn't long enough for most of them. The sign was nearly done, though, so she was ready with her mission just as soon as she had a few moments of free time.

The sound of clopping hooves drew her attention to the window, and she saw Vince ride in, his black duster flapping in the sharp January breeze. Vince, tall and slender, with neat dark hair, was the best-looking man Tina had ever seen. Which didn't make him any less exasperating. He was also a tidy man as a rule, though right now he was filthy.

Tina grabbed her coat off the hook in the jailhouse and rushed outside. Then she realized what she was doing. Why had her spirits lifted at the sight of Vince Yates? Why had the sight of Vince made her run out to greet him? And why had she looked at how dirty and tired he was and wanted to take him in and feed him and care for him?

Since she was already outside, she reasoned that she was

54

just eager to quit being sheriff. Whatever her excuse, there was no denying that she was glad Vince was home.

Vince spotted her and rode straight to the jail. Even though he had lines of exhaustion on his dirty face, he managed to flash a smile at her that she couldn't help but return. Despite his habitual torment of her, the man seemed almost as happy to see her as she was to see him.

"Did you find that book for Dare?"

Vince patted the bulging saddlebag. "I got a book and a stack of journals, besides some medical publications with articles in them. I ended up riding all the way to New Orleans."

With a gasp, Tina said, "That far?"

Nodding as if the effort were almost beyond him, Vince said, "The Medical College of Louisiana is there and it has a good library. I also found a humane asylum."

"Humane asylum, is that different than an insane asylum?"

"It's a special home for the furiously mad with rules promising kindness. I asked about Texas, but no one could tell me if there was one here. Maybe a private one somewhere."

"Well, at least you found the books." Tina knew she sounded doubtful, but the whole idea of an asylum—a building packed with lunatics—made her queasy in her stomach.

Nodding, Vince went on, "On the advice of the folks at the college library, I ordered more writings. Did you know there's an actual magazine called *The American Journal of Insanity*?"

Tina shook her head. "Strange to think there's that big a need for information."

"They'll be shipped here as soon as possible. And the Louisiana Insane Asylum was begun due to pressure from a lady named Dorothea Dix, who's made a crusade out of getting decent treatment for the insane. I wrote to her with more questions. I'm hoping she'll write back."

Tina thought of her quiet little work toward the cause of closing the tavern and caring for one madwoman, and now there was a woman who'd changed the whole state of Louisiana with her efforts. It made Tina feel like a failure.

The kind of girl whose parents vanished out of her life.

And whose brother could rarely be bothered to visit.

And whose aunt, after a lifetime of preaching on how a woman needed to take care of herself, had married a poor excuse for a man, then chosen that man over Tina.

A woman who'd been abandoned as many times as Tina could only conclude that her whole life was a failure. Shaking off the demoralizing thought, she went back to thinking about what Vince had just done for one poor woman. Why, he'd done more for Lana Bullard than Tina had.

"New Orleans is a long trip." Tina knew Vince had gone on the trip due to pressure from her to keep Lana out of prison.

"It is for a fact." Vince swung himself off his horse. His boots hit the packed dirt of the street, and dust puffed off him in a cloud. He tied his black gelding to a hitching post.

"It was nice of you to go." In fact, it was so nice that Tina suddenly couldn't quite believe he'd done it, not for Lana, who'd tried to kill Vince's friend, and Tina seriously doubted he'd done it for her.

"How's my prisoner?" he asked.

Tina forgot wondering about his generosity and the

56

long, hard ride he'd gone on, and remembered Vince the Coyote who'd stuck her with this job. She remembered with a shudder of relief to have something to be annoyed with Vince about. She was far more comfortable with that than with being charmed by the effort he'd just gone to or how nice it was to have him back.

"She's getting fat. I've taken to feeding her six times a day just to shut her up."

"Six times?" His disgusted expression hurt more than it should have.

It shouldn't bother her, because the man was as tired as she was. With a tiny shrug of one shoulder, she said, "She was hungry."

"Look, I shouldn't have expected you to know what you were doing."

"Because I fed her too much?" Tina arched a brow.

"I didn't mean you—"

"You left me with a madwoman and now you're criticizing how I did the job I never wanted in the first place?"

Vince raised both hands as if in surrender. "I should have known a woman—"

"You're the one who gave the job to a woman. You've got a lot of nerve riding off without a by-your-leave"—or had she pushed him into going?—"and then coming back here to find fault."

"Stop putting words in my mouth." Vince ran both hands deep into his hair.

"Take over, Mr. Lawman." She was happier now that she was sparring with Vince. Those soft feelings just plumb scared her to death. She jerked the badge off her shirtwaist and threw it at him, just like he'd thrown it at her.

Vince let the badge bounce off his chest and fall to the hard ground, too busy scowling at her to even try to catch it.

"The truth is, you're no more skilled at being a sheriff than I am. How many weeks ago did your friend baptize you into the job?"

"Deputize, not 'baptize' for heaven's sake." He pulled his hands free from his hair and kicked up a little dust doing it, then took a step toward her.

"You know what I mean." She took a step toward him just to make sure he could hear every word she said.

"Stop fussing at me, woman."

It would be her pleasure to never speak to him again. That ought to end any fussing. "If you're done with your unkind assessment of my efforts, I'll just go." Thinking to sweep around him and walk away in grand style, she took one step and got too close.

He grabbed her arm and pulled her to face him. "I was only saying I shouldn't have lassoed you into a job you're not suited for."

"Because I'm a woman and not up to it?"

"Yes!"

"Why, you—"

"No!" Vince grabbed her other arm. "I mean no. You're up to it. You did fine."

Because she was very close, Tina saw the lines of exhaustion on his face. A spark of compassion made her want to hold him and soothe him and tuck him into bed with a nice kiss.

She immediately went back to picking a fight—much safer. "Let me go, Vincent Yates. Get your hands off me or so help me you're gonna draw back a stub."

He laughed.

Which was about the worst thing he could've done.

She jerked her arms to no avail. With motions too smooth and fast for her to overcome, he dragged her inside the jailhouse.

A quick glance told her Lana was still fast asleep, the lazy lout. "Take your hands—"

"Hush!" Vince gave Lana a quick, hard look. He whispered, "I'm sorry."

"No you're not."

"I'm exhausted." His eyes flickered to her lips, then right back to meet her gaze. "Tina, I never meant to . . ."

He looked down again.

"Meant to what?"

Only silence met her question.

Tina, barely able to form a coherent thought, asked, "What should we do?"

His warm brown eyes sparked. Absently he said, "Oh, woman, I have got me some ideas what we should do."

"I meant . . ." Her voice faded as she looked into those dark eyes and lost her train of thought. She might have looked at him all day. She might've done more than look. She'd never felt this kind of longing before. She'd never had a man hold her. Well, Jonas, but that was entirely different.

Vince's grip on her upper arms loosened, and his hands shifted into a much gentler touch. He lowered his head, and she thought she was going to get the first kiss of her life. Instead he rested his forehead against hers. "What am I doing?"

Tina knew what he *wasn't* doing. And she was mighty

ashamed of herself for being disappointed. She just stood there, her breath unsteady, her pulse pounding.

Vince ran his hands up and down her arms, the caress as warm as firelight. Their eyes met. Tina knew the heart wasn't meant to beat this hard, and it wasn't supposed to ache like this. Heaven only knew what damage being in Vince Yates's arms was doing to her insides. Her brain was certainly working strangely too, because it felt so good to be held she couldn't put a stop to it.

Then, with halting movements, Vince pushed her away and turned his back.

Her knees wobbled, and she had to fight to keep standing.

"I shouldn't have put my hands on you." He refused to look at her. "I'm sorry."

He was sorry. It was the sweetest moment of Tina's life and he was sorry. She wanted to demand he take that apology back, but suddenly all Tina could think of was the little girl whose parents had died. She couldn't even remember them, and she'd never been told what happened.

The little girl with the stern, critical aunt who had never given hugs.

The little girl desperately in love with her heroic big brother, who hadn't even bothered to come and see her when he'd been released from his prisoner-of-war camp. Instead he'd gone west on a quest to serve God. Tina had meant nothing to him.

Just as she meant nothing to Vince.

He could hold her close, then brush her away with an apology.

"Would you mind getting those books out of my saddle-bag and taking them to Dare?"

It wasn't enough for Vince to apologize; now he wanted her to get away from him. Clenching her jaw to keep from crying, she decided getting away was an idea with merit. She went out as silent and unwanted as a ghost who haunted the lives of others.

As she removed the books and papers from Vince's saddlebag, she shook off her thoughts of loneliness.

Jonas wanted her. She'd had to foist herself on him, but once she was here, he'd welcomed her nicely. Of course, Jonas made almost no money and she did quite well at the diner.

On her way to Dare's house with her armload of books and papers, she realized how precarious her position was. If Vince put his mind to it, he could probably persuade Jonas to send her away. Squaring her shoulders, she resolved to work hard and give Jonas every penny she made in hopes he'd let her live with him forever.

She thought of Duffy's selling of demon rum and Lana Bullard's madness, and decided, since Jonas seemed inclined to tolerate her mission in those areas, she'd focus on them. She'd work hard enough to never be cast out and guard her lonely heart.

It wasn't that hard a decision to make. It was how she'd been living since her earliest memory.

CHAPTER 6

The hurt in Tina's eyes made Vince wish his legs were long enough he could kick his own backside.

He was tempted to try it, until Lana snorted and grumbled in her sleep. Vince decided to just kick himself mentally to keep his prisoner's sleep from being disturbed.

He knew why it'd happened. He'd come riding in and seen the prettiest woman he'd ever known, and all he'd wanted to do was go to her. Be near her. He'd been unable to think of anything else. When she'd picked a fight with him—for no reason he could figure out—he was glad because he'd been thinking all the wrong thoughts from the minute he'd laid eyes on her.

They seemed to be forever fighting. Normally the little spat would have kept them apart well enough, but Vince was all in from his long ride. He was badly in need of a meal, a bath, and a good night's sleep. All those things played havoc with his self-control, and confound it, when she'd smiled at him, all he could think about was how much he'd missed her.

He'd even missed watching her picket every afternoon. He was inclined to help her make another placard.

He didn't think anyone knew it, but he'd made a habit of setting a chair by the small front window in his lawyer's office and watching Tina march back and forth. He hadn't missed an afternoon since she'd begun with her cause. That was one of the reasons he'd jumped into the middle of that fight so fast, because he saw the whole thing start.

The fight didn't bother him overly. A fistfight was fun once in a while, so he couldn't get too upset that she'd started one. He knew now that he'd hurried back to Broken Wheel partly because he wanted to see what trouble Tina had gotten herself into.

It seemed that a man could be entertained by a woman's strange ways.

She'd snipped at him, and he'd answered back, glad for a reason to put distance between them. He never should have touched her. That was when things had gone wrong. Her sassy mouth and his firm grip on her supple, slender arms had struck a spark.

Moving restlessly, he admitted that spark was there before; she'd just fanned it into a flame. And that fire was still alive in him, deep in his gut. He'd tamped it down the best he could, but it was still there, smoldering, glowing hot.

He thought of how she'd looked when he'd apologized. Vince knew a thing or two about women. He'd hurt her. Shaking his head in self-disgust, he gave some thought to how he'd held her and then insulted her. He should've pulled over on the trail and slept, scrounged a meal somewhere, and come into town less on edge.

Except who could predict a thing like this would happen—just because a man was hungry and tired? He'd been hungry and tired plenty of times and nothing like this had ever happened before. And it wasn't going to happen again, and for one very good reason.

Mother.

Something was very wrong with her. Worse yet, it ran in her family, which meant it ran in him.

And if he didn't get Mother's madness, Father was even worse.

Vince had known since he went home after the war that he never dared pass on any blood from his veins. He'd either be a tyrant or a burden. He imagined Tina being saddled with a man like either of his parents and felt only pity for her.

It was a mighty good reason for a man to never marry.

When he'd stopped in to see his parents in Chicago right after the war, he'd been sick in both body and soul. He needed care and time to heal. Vince had hoped he'd be welcomed home. Surely his parents had been informed he was a prisoner of war. Surely they'd worried. He'd hoped he and his father could mend fences and get to know each other as adult men.

Father was only interested in Vince if he came into the family banking firm. Vince wasn't even that much opposed to banking. He just knew he couldn't live his life under his father's thumb, and his father would never treat him as anything resembling a partner. Father didn't know how to share power with anyone.

The visit had been unpleasant between father and son, and worse because something had happened to Mother.

She hadn't known who Vince was. She'd acted afraid and then cried out when he tried to hug her. At first he tried to excuse it because he knew how awful he looked. Though being looked at with fear by his mother was devastating, he knew she was a sweet but shallow woman and he forgave her, hoping she'd get used to the idea of his being home. He hadn't really understood until he'd been there a month that she wasn't upset by Vince going off to war and coming home sick and half starved, a burden to his family. She honestly didn't know who he was. In fact, she didn't seem to remember having a son at all.

On the day he'd realized that, he'd had to admit finally that something was really wrong in Mother's head. She'd lost her wits in strange little ways. The one that was most glaring to Vince was that she couldn't remember his name.

As soon as Vince was strong enough to get around, he'd asked Father what was wrong. Father wouldn't talk about it except to say she was an embarrassment, just as her father had been. He had hired a companion for her, and Mother still dressed beautifully and went out to tea with her society friends. She seemed to manage fine.

But she'd forgotten her only son. Worse yet, she couldn't even treat him as a friendly stranger. She feared him when he would enter the same room with her.

Vince had understood she wasn't thinking right. But it had hurt so badly to have his mother as good as run away from him sobbing that Vince couldn't stay. Between Mother's fear and Father's tyranny, Vince had moved along as soon as his health allowed.

Eventually he let his family know where he came to live, but he'd never gone home again.

Because of the recent letter from Father, demanding that Vince return to Chicago and take up the reins of the bank, they'd exchanged a wire or two when Vince was in New

Orleans, just to make sure the man knew he wasn't coming, ever. And he'd hunted through that medical library as if he were searching for the keys to escape from eternal fire.

It had nothing to do with Lana, and it wasn't just to cure Mother. It was to save himself when his turn came.

He needed to apologize to Tina again. Only this time he needed to do it in a way that didn't hurt her feelings but also kept her away from him.

And he needed to do it in a way that wouldn't make Jonas load his rarely used pistol.

Vince wracked his brain. He'd always had a charming streak that worked well with women, not that he'd practiced it in a while, having kept to manly places since the war. But there had to be a right way to handle this. The right words . . . words that wouldn't get him shot.

Rubbing both hands through his hair, he mulled it over, stumped, distracted by how nice it was to hold her in his arms.

Before even an inkling of an idea began forming, he heard the rattle of wheels and looked out the window to see a beautiful coach rolling into town. Black-lacquered paint with scrolled golden decorations. The elegant coach was pulled by a team of four shining black geldings and driven by a man in a black uniform.

Vince had never seen such a conveyance in Broken Wheel before, and he couldn't imagine why anyone wealthy enough to own such a thing would bother to come to Broken Wheel. It flickered through Vince's mind that it was as richly appointed as the carriage his father owned back in Chicago.

The coach was going too fast and it skidded as the driver pulled it to a halt. Dust enveloped the rig.

Then the dust settled. The coach door swung open. There was a long moment that for some reason riveted Vince's attention on that open door. Of course any newcomer to this quiet town was interesting.

And then Father stepped out.

Dread kicked Vince in the belly. He had the wild notion that his father had appeared just because Vince was thinking about him.

He blinked to clear his vision in the hopes Father would go away.

But sure enough, there stood Julius Yates, wearing a tall silk hat and a black travel-stained woolen frock coat. He carried a black cane with a silver wolf's head on its top. The same cane Father had carried for years with no real need for it, except that Father liked carrying something so costly.

Today Father was leaning hard on that cane.

Watching through the jailhouse window, Vince was frozen.

Pure stunned surprise accounted for part of it. What had Father been thinking to come out here? He must've headed out with all possible speed the moment he got Vince's wire saying there would be no homecoming. Father had never in his life come to Vince; it had always been the other way around. Father would demand Vince's presence, and Vince would appear at the appointed time. That defined his childhood, those audiences with Father. And Father had always had the knack of keeping Vince off-balance, appearing at unexpected times, turning his moods from cool tyranny to white-hot anger. Dealing with Father was where Vince had learned to get himself out of dangerous scrapes, which had served him well in the war and earned him the nickname Invincible Vince.

The other thing that struck Vince hard was realizing his father had gotten old. It'd been three years since Vince had seen Father, but the man had aged a decade. Or maybe Vince had been too sick to really see that the years were catching up to Father. Maybe this was why he'd increased the pressure on Vince to come into the business. Father's hair was now heavily streaked with gray. He was bent over, moving slow, his hand trembling on the head of that wolf. He depended on his cane for balance as if the trip had almost done him in.

He'd been older than most fathers when Vince was born, near fifty, which made Father in his seventies now. Mother had been much younger than her husband, in her mid-twenties when Vince came along. Of course they were both getting older now.

But they'd always seemed ageless to him. His mother's fragile blond beauty never changed. His father's rigid spine never bent.

Father owned the biggest bank in Chicago and had his fingers in many other pies.

Beautiful Virginia Belle was the privileged daughter of a Southern plantation owner. Father had married her, and when Mother's parents died, Father had gotten out of all investments in the South. He'd always been savvy about money, and he'd made a fortune to add to the one he already had.

Mother's parents had also left a nice inheritance directly to Vince, though he'd still been young. His crafty grandmama had set it up so that Father couldn't get control of it. It left Vince with more money than he could spend in a lifetime.

Another person stepped out of the coach and pulled his attention away from Father.

A tall, dark-haired young woman Vince had never seen before. She was a perfect female version of Julius Yates. Even from across the dusty street, Vince saw that her eyes were the same dark brown as Father's and his own. She wore a dark woolen coat and a tidy black bonnet, none of it made with the fine quality material and expert tailoring of Father's clothes.

But his father wasn't the biggest surprise in that carriage, nor was the young woman who might be proof of his father's lack of honor.

A slender, trembling, white-gloved hand stretched out from the dark core of that coach. Father ignored it, but the young woman quickly reached to offer assistance.

With agonizing slowness, one last person appeared. First, Vince saw the elegant glove. Next came a velvet reticule dangling from a wrist, followed by blue silk, ruffled cuffs. Past the blue cuffs emerged a beautiful mink coat. Finally, Vince saw the blond hair and light blue eyes. . . .

He tried to deny it just because he wanted to so badly, but the truth was inescapable.

Mother was here.

Mother, who belonged in Bedlam right alongside Lana Bullard.

CHAPTER 7

Even as Vince shoved the jailhouse door open, he was struck by how filthy he was. He should have snuck out the back of the jail, rushed home, bathed and changed into clean clothes.

Father was going to judge him harshly.

Nothing new there.

"Father? Mother?" Vince strode across the street. Words jammed up in his throat. He wanted to start demanding answers. What were they doing here? What were they thinking?

Vince saw the driver begin to unload a huge stack of luggage roped onto the roof.

"Be very gentle with the basket inside the coach," the young woman instructed the driver.

All this luggage, including apparently fragile things, for these three people in Broken Wheel, Texas, where most people were lucky to have one change of clothes?

It could mean only one thing.

They were planning to stay awhile.

And there was nothing Vince could do about it.

There'd never been much to do about Father. Which was why Vince had left.

He realized Mother's face was deeply lined. The years had been kind to Mother, but she was in her fifties now and there was no hiding her age. Mother turned her eyes on Vince, and joy lit up her face.

Vince braced himself. Mother had a knack for saying upsetting things.

"Julius," Mother said. Her smile bloomed as she greeted Vince by the wrong name. "It's so wonderful of you to meet our train." And with the smile, as it always was with Mother, tears filled her eyes.

Happy tears. Sad tears. Frightened tears. Bored tears. Every dealing with his mother came served up with tears, and they made Vince feel like a brute.

Eyes brimming, Mother came toward Vince, with the young lady at her side steadying her.

A tiny place in Vince's heart died as his mother rushed for him, thinking he was Father. It had been better when Mother had thought he was a stranger and been scared of him, because Father was exactly who Vince never wanted to be.

Shoving aside the hurt, Vince hurried forward and swept her into his arms with the gentle skill of a man used to being a foot taller than his favorite woman in the world. She'd loved him in a negligent kind of way . . . before she'd forgotten his name.

He pulled her close and looked past her to his father, whose eyes were razor sharp. Those eyes could cut Vince to ribbons and had done so regularly. The lines in Father's face showed his age as much as the white hair. And yet that hard, ruthless intelligence was still there.

Nothing on his father's face said, It's good to see you, son.

"If we can't get you home, then we'll have to come here to see you. Even if it does nearly kill Virginia Belle. The time has come for you to help with her care, Vincent. I'll not allow you to shirk any longer."

"What? You mean you're here to stay?"

Mother's tears spilled over and she began crying softly. Through her sobs, she said, "I've missed you so." Mother's accent was thicker, far more Southern than when Vince had gone home after the war, even though she'd lived in the North for thirty years. "My dahlin' Julius, why did you leave me?"

Julius. His father's name.

A movement drew Vince's gaze to the young woman who'd accompanied his parents.

"Vincent," Father said in a voice so cold it made Vince want to hunt up a thicker coat, "I'd like to introduce your sister, Melissa Yates."

Vince didn't bother to look at his father. There was no point. Melissa Yates, his sister. His father had found companionship outside his marriage, and Melissa was the result. Vince wondered if there were other "results" around. And now Mother, already so fragile, was forced to live with the proof of Father's infidelity.

"Hello, Melissa."

At the sound of Vince's voice, Mother pulled back so suddenly she'd have fallen if Vince hadn't caught her arms. "Missy, you're here, finally!"

The surprise sister came up to slide an arm around Mother's waist. With a glance at Vince that revealed an embarrassed flush on her cheeks, Melissa said, "I'll see to her."

Mother leaned on Melissa's arm with a bright, if vacant,

smile. Vince knew Mother wasn't well. He knew it wasn't personal. She couldn't help that she didn't love him enough to remember him.

"We need a place to rest, don't we, Virginia Belle?" Melissa murmured.

"Bless your heart, Missy." The tears forgotten, Mother produced a lacy fan from her reticule and, disregarding the chilly Texas breeze, fluttered it flirtatiously. She spoke with the genteel drawl of a Southern belle. "I would dearly love to rest, honey child."

Melissa turned to Vince. "Perhaps you have room?"

A direct question was about all Vince was capable of answering. "There is only one bedroom where I live." He jabbed a thumb at the small building where he practiced law, then made a grand gesture to the south end of town. "You'll have to get a room in Asa's boardinghouse." It was easily the nicest house in town. Asa called it a boarding-house, but there was no food available. Asa thought calling it a hotel was too high and mighty, and he saw himself as a humble man. So he called it a boardinghouse without quite realizing it made him sound not so much humble as stupid. "We'll get rooms for you all. Follow me."

Father made a sound of disgust. As if he'd expected Vince to have a twenty-room mansion available, with servants to quickly see to unexpected guests.

Vince wanted to tell his father uninvited guests had no right to expect a welcome, but he didn't. That would come later, when Mother was resting.

As they walked down the street toward Asa's, the diner door swung open and Glynna stuck her head out. She was rapt with curiosity, and she didn't even bother to hide it. "Vince, who are your . . . your friends?" She looked confused, glancing from Father to Vince to Melissa, their resemblance clearly marking them as family.

"Glynna Riker, I'd like to introduce you to my family." Gesturing to each in turn, he said, "This is my father, Julius Yates, my mother, Virginia Belle, and my . . . sister, Melissa." Vince was proud of himself for only stumbling for a second over the sister part of his introductions.

Melissa gave him a sharp look, almost as if she expected him to denounce her. But he didn't bother. She was the least of his troubles.

"Would you all like to come in?" Glynna asked. "Vince is a good friend, and I'd love to get to know his family. I'm sure you're exhausted and hungry. I've got apple pie."

Which reminded Vince of Tina, the one who'd made that pie. The woman he'd almost kissed only minutes ago.

He was about to say no. He saw his father open his mouth, and Vince saw the determination in Father's eyes to say no, too.

"Apple pie sounds lovely." Mother, however, spoke first. "My old mammy used to bake an apple pie fit to make the angels weep." Mother leaned on Melissa and asked in a childlike voice, "Where is mammy? Why didn't she come on the train with us?"

Melissa whispered something Vince couldn't hear. Mother started for the diner, while Father said in a resigned voice, "Very well. We can stop in for a moment."

"Do come in and sit down. Were you heading for the boardinghouse?" Glynna smiled, and as a rule, her smile made the sun shine brighter in the sky. It had no effect on Father, though, and Vince was beyond smiling.

"Yep." Vince sort of wished Glynna would leave off her smiling. It clashed with the general mood. "They're staying at Asa's."

"I'll have my son, Paul, get your trunks toted down there, and tell Asa to expect company." Glynna's smile brightened even more. "We'll insist he give you clean sheets."

Father glowered.

Melissa winced, but quickly covered it.

Vince wondered if the young woman got punished for having an opinion. Vince had grown up knowing to keep his mouth shut, and there was no sign that Father had mellowed with age.

"Two rooms?" Glynna asked.

"How many rooms are there?" Father studied the two-story house.

"Four," Vince said.

"Get all four. I'd as soon not share the house. And tell the proprietor we'll want them indefinitely."

Indefinitely? Vince shook his head to clear out his ears. He must be hearing things.

Glynna's blond brows arched, but then she swung the door wide and stepped back.

Paul was there and had heard them talking. The boy was shooting up taller every day. He had his mother's blond hair, and shining blue eyes that must've come from his father. His voice broke and jumped from low to high and back again as he said, "What does 'indefinitely' mean? And 'proprietor'?"

Glynna whispered definitions to him. She'd started overseeing the children's studies since she'd married. Dare helped too. He seemed determined that his children would learn, even though there was no school in Broken Wheel.

Vince didn't mention to his father that Asa lived in the boardinghouse, so they wouldn't exactly have the house to themselves. Of course, Asa wasn't one to intrude . . . unless he felt the need to shoot someone.

"That large basket needs careful handling," Melissa said to Paul. "I think I should—"

Mother's knees buckled suddenly, but Melissa caught her. She seemed to have forgotten what orders she was giving Paul. Vince helped to steady Mother from behind.

"I'll tell Doc Riker to come over, then get the bags moved and talk to Asa." Paul ran toward the back of the diner.

"Hurry, so Mother can lie down," Vince yelled after him.

Paul called over his shoulder to Melissa, "I'll take extra care with your basket."

Vince and Melissa got Mother up the two steps to the board-walk, inside the diner, and settled at a nearby table.

Eight-year-old Janny came in with four pie plates in her little hands. The girl was getting to be the best cook and waitress in the family. She was the spitting image of Glynna with her golden-hazel eyes. Janny being the best cook honestly wasn't saying much, considering Glynna blackened everything she cooked. Paul was pretty good in the kitchen too, so it wasn't like Janny didn't have some competition.

Janny arranged the plates on the table before they'd all had a chance to sit down on the long benches. She then headed back to the kitchen to fetch coffee.

"Apple pie!" Mother clasped her hands together with childlike glee. "Mercy me, this looks delicious."

Vince did his best to conceal it, but it hurt that she recognized apple pie when she didn't recognize her own son. What had he done to make himself so forgettable?

In truth, Vince had been a handful all his life. Something he took some pride in, however misguided that might be. He'd've bet neither of his parents could forget him, no matter how hard they tried.

The back door opened and closed as Dare came in. Somehow, just knowing Dare was here made the worst of the tension ease out of Vince's spine. Yet even with his friend there, this situation was still looking like a world of trouble.

Another racket from the back and Jonas came in, followed by Tina. Paul was a regular town crier.

Vince found himself distracted from the disaster that had climbed out of that regal carriage by the disaster that was Tina Cahill. His family showing up was so bad that he was grateful he'd almost kissed the troublemaking little reformer, just because the stupidity of that was enough to distract him from how badly his life had just been blown apart.

Dare slid onto the bench beside Mother on the far end of the table and spoke quietly to her, then took her pulse. Mother simpered under the attention.

Several minutes passed with Dare checking Mother over, and then, looking at Vince, Dare said, "I think your ma is just worn out from the trip. A bite to eat and a good long rest will set her to rights."

Glynna bustled in with empty tin cups hanging from one hand, a finger through each handle, and a heavy coffeepot in the other. "Sit on down. We've got plenty for everyone."

As if pie and coffee were going to fix anything.

Tina sat at the far end of the table from Vince without once looking at him. He knew because he hadn't been able to take his eyes off her. Tina was straight across from Mother.

Jonas sat on the end of the bench past Vince, as if he knew Vince needed a friend nearby. Or maybe Tina had told Jonas what had gone on in the jail, and Jonas wanted to keep an eye on Vince in case Vince needed a thrashing.

Dare took a cup of coffee from Glynna and began pacing. Vince felt his muscles tighten, and he itched to go stand by the door. Keep watch. Someone was always bringing trouble. Except all the trouble in the world was sitting right here at this table with him.

His friends all thought he'd gotten in the habit of posting himself as a sentinel during the war, but Vince had learned to be on guard by Father. Vince could never make Father happy, so he learned to hide when he could, sneak when he had to, and delight in driving Father mad when there was no escape.

A quick glance at Mother—eating her pie with enthusiasm while not knowing who Vince was—made him regret thinking of madness in any context.

The coach driver came in at that moment, hat in hand. The man was covered in trail dust and dressed all wrong for Texas. How had Father managed to get themselves a driver in such formal clothing? Had he ridden all the way from Chicago with Father, to have handy for when they had to leave the train and ride in a carriage?

"Is there any food left for me?" the driver asked. He looked right at Glynna, then at Tina and Melissa. The man looked stunned to be surrounded by so many pretty ladies in a little town like Broken Wheel. He dragged his hat off and couldn't know that his hair stood straight up on top of his head. Clutching the hat brim, he looked around at the women, seemingly in no hurry to eat. The man even took a long look at Mother. Flattering, considering she was thirty years his senior.

Vince noticed Paul go by the diner window dragging something. It had to be one of the trunks, which must weigh so much the boy couldn't entirely lift it. Had they moved their entire household to Broken Wheel?

Janny quickly got the coach driver a meal, and he took a seat at an adjoining table, as if content to sit there and wolf down his food while leering at the women.

Glynna hurried to get more cups before her daughter could take over and run the whole diner herself. A scraping sound from outside drew Vince's attention, and he saw Paul pass by the window going back toward the carriage. The boy had gotten himself saddled with a big job.

"So, Vince, introduce us," Jonas said, always the one doing the thinking.

"Father, these are friends of mine from the war," Vince replied.

There was no attempt to conceal Father's sound of disgruntlement. He'd had the money and influence to keep Vince out of the war, yet Vince had shoved the offer back in his father's face.

"I was in Andersonville Prison with Jonas and Dare. Jonas Cahill is the parson here in Broken Wheel, and Darius Riker is the doctor."

Father gave Jonas a dismissive glance. A man of God didn't warrant much notice from Julius Yates. No money

80

in that profession. Then he turned to watch Dare pace. A doctor could be successful, if he was shrewd.

Dare was shrewd enough to note the dismissal of Jonas, the best and most decent of them. Jonas had a streak of shrewd in him too, because he noticed the lack of respect and tensed beside Vince.

"This diner is owned and operated by Dare's wife, Glynna. Her son, Paul, is lugging your trunks, and her daughter, Janet, is serving your coffee."

That earned a grunt from Father. Instead of appreciating the help, he'd just lowered his opinion of Dare's whole family because serving others marked them as low class.

"Sitting beside you is Tina Cahill." A woman I would like to drag outside and kiss the living daylights out of. There was an introduction that would get a strong reaction from everyone. "She's Jonas's sister."

Vince sincerely hoped Jonas couldn't read minds, because he was an overprotective big brother. If Jonas caught him kissing Tina, he'd probably shoot Vince dead, even though that was completely against Jonas's religion. Anyway, Vince knew it would never happen, because getting shot would be a relief about now and Vince just wasn't that lucky.

Vince was discovering all his childhood training in manners was easy to use if he had a mind to. "These are my best friends in the world." He glanced around the table, and even Tina looked at him for a second. "I'd like you all to meet my father, Julius, my mother, Virginia Belle, and my sister, Melissa."

"Julius." Dare reached out a hand to Father.

Who nodded and shook it. "Dr. Riker."

In that moment of tension, with Father looking down his nose at everyone, the women bustling in and out with coffee and pie, Janny asking questions quietly in the background, Vince only distantly noticed the diner's front door open and close quietly.

Several minutes had passed before Melissa cut through the chatter. "Where's Virginia Belle?"

Vince jumped to his feet. Father scowled and looked around the room.

"She must've gone out the front." Glynna stood in the kitchen door, the only back way out of the place. She looked confused. As if wondering why someone stepping outside would be a problem.

Unless that someone wasn't thinking right.

Vince whirled and nearly fell over the bench seat. He caught himself and raced for the door. He barely noticed Melissa only steps behind him.

He rushed out of the diner, looking all around. "Where did she go?"

"We have to find her before she gets out into the countryside. Where did my basket go?" Melissa demanded it like it was life or death.

"Paul probably took it to the boardinghouse. What difference does a stupid basket make?" Vince hurried toward the boardinghouse. On all sides of this tiny town lay trackless miles of rugged wilderness. If Mother got lost out there, she might die before they could find her.

He looked back to see the rest of his friends pour out of the building and took command like he had so many times in the war. "Fan out. She can't have gotten far. She's not . . . not thinking right."

"We'll split up." Dare let Vince know he'd caught the meaning behind those few words.

Vince saw a flash of white on the ground right in the middle of the street. He raced for it and picked up a delicate lace handkerchief. It had to be Mother's. Common sense dictated that he check the buildings, and he did take a quick look inside the coach, thinking Mother might be drawn to the familiar. But this was Mother, so once the coach proved to be empty, he ignored common sense and ran toward the wilderness to the west of Broken Wheel. If she'd stayed in town, they'd find her fast, as there weren't that many buildings to search. It was only if she'd wandered out of town that she'd be in trouble.

A motion to his right caught his attention, and he saw Melissa running for Asa's. A good place to search, but Vince thought they should get to the edge of town and fast. Just then a crash sounded from inside the boardinghouse, followed by a shout of fear. A boyish shout, not Mother's voice. The noise brought Vince to a stop. The boarding-house door slammed open. Paul came tearing out, yelling for all he was worth.

Behind him, a blur of brown-and-white fur howled, snapping its teeth. Vince reached for his gun.

"Livvy, heel!" Melissa shouted. When Melissa shouted, Vince recognized it was a dog chasing Paul.

There were no dogs in Broken Wheel.

It stopped nipping at Paul and whirled to charge Melissa, baying with every long pace.

Vince pivoted to save Melissa, knowing the dog was going for her throat. Vince was too far away to protect her.

She was standing between him and the dog, so his drawn gun was useless.

He'd taken two running steps when the dog skidded to a halt, turned to stand at her heel, and plunked its backside down, panting. It looked at Melissa with devotion, its long pink tongue lolling out of its mouth.

It was a foxhound. Vince had seen one often enough. They used them to hunt runaway prisoners in the South. Runaway slaves too, it was said.

Maybe the midsize, short-haired dogs even hunted the occasional fox.

Melissa dropped to her knees in front of the white dog with its big brown spots just as Vince came up beside them. He wanted to yell at her for playing with a dog when Mother was missing, but he didn't have time.

"Livvy, find Virginia Belle," Melissa commanded. She ran a hand gently over the dog's head. The dog yipped once, then stood, wheeled in a full circle as if planning to start chasing its tail, and froze, facing the west. With a deep-throated howl the dog raced away. Melissa ran after it.

That dog was hunting his mother. It took Vince a moment to overcome the horrible image. Then he took off in pursuit of Melissa, who was in pursuit of the dog, which was in pursuit of Virginia Belle Yates.

CHAPTER 8

Tina had no idea what was going on. Vince's mother had gone outside? Why in the world did that cause such a fuss? Why were they all running around hunting for her?

But they were, and Tina didn't get a chance to ask questions.

Vince had yelled at Dare, "She's not thinking right."

Then Melissa had raced out of town after a dog. Where had the dog come from?

Vince was hard on Melissa's heels. A ladylike woman such as Melissa sprinting somehow scared Tina more deeply than seeing Vince run.

Why would Vince and Melissa assume Mrs. Yates would head out of town? The woman had most likely gone looking for a privy or walked over to the boardinghouse to see about her luggage. It made no sense to race out of town, but their worry was undeniable.

"She's not thinking right." Those were Vince's words.

"Mother!" Vince's deep voice sounded from behind the jailhouse.

Back there was nothing but red stone, scrub juniper, cottonwood and mesquite trees, and cold, cold wind. A woman might want to go for a brisk walk, stretch her legs after a long carriage ride, but she would mention it, tell them where she was headed. No one in her right mind would leave the warm diner to go for a stroll in the cold, and certainly not without saying she was going.

"She's not thinking right."

Tina's gut twisted. There'd been no chance to exchange a word with Mrs. Yates. The woman had quietly eaten her pie and sipped at her coffee. Beyond noticing the woman was very pretty and dressed in lovely clothes, she'd barely drawn Tina's notice.

Deciding to eliminate the obvious before chasing out into the countryside, Tina hurried across the street toward the jail. She was in and out quickly and quietly. A snoring prisoner, but no sign of Virginia Belle Yates.

Glynna stepped out of the general store at the same time Jonas emerged from Duffy's Tavern.

He had Duffy and Griss with him, all three of them talking fast in the blustery wind. The Schuster brothers headed for the livery stable. Helping. Tina was almost sorry she'd spent the last few months tormenting the lousy gin-peddling coyotes. Almost . . . but not quite.

Dare came around from behind the saloon. His house, which was also his doctor's office, was back there. Tina and Jonas lived in a house back there beside the church, and most of the other houses in town were on that side, as well.

Glynna emerged from the boardinghouse.

Even the driver, carrying his plate in hand and chewing as if he were starving, was walking around town, poking his nose in each building. Between bites he called out for Mrs. Yates.

"Virginia Belle?" The high, falsely perky tone of Melissa Yates's voice could be heard in the wooded area to the west of town. Vince's voice, on the other hand, was a deep echo.

Why would they think Mrs. Yates would leave town on foot?

"She's not thinking right."

Tina rushed toward Dare, Glynna, and Jonas. All four of them met in the middle of the street.

Taking a look around, Dare said, "We've got someone searching every business, home, barn, shed, and privy in town, including the abandoned ones. I told them to check the storerooms, attics, cellars, and crawl spaces."

"What's going on?" Tina looked between the others.

Dare shook his head. "No idea. But Vince said to search so we're searching."

Glynna asked, "Did I hear a dog?"

"Yes, I suppose there was a dog on the coach with the Yates family. I didn't notice it when they arrived, but Melissa called it by name. Vince and Melissa ran after it. I can't figure out why they're chasing a dog when they should be hunting for Vince's ma. And I can't figure out why we're even hunting for Mrs. Yates. Surely she wouldn't leave town in this cold."

Tina scanned the area. She saw people still scurrying around, everyone hunting. Tug stomped out of his general store toward his house, the man tugged on his beard, a constant habit that had earned him the nickname. As he walked home, he muttered words Tina was glad she couldn't hear.

Duffy poked his nose out of the haymow window of the livery. Sledge headed toward his ramshackle cabin behind the parsonage.

And that was when she noticed the door to the diner ajar. Julius Yates was eating a bite of his pie.

"If we're all searching, why isn't Vince's father? We must be overreacting just because Vince did."

"Melissa did, too," Glynna pointed out. "Vince hasn't seen his mother in years it sounds like, so he might be overreacting. But Melissa should know if there's reason to worry."

"Virginia Belle?" The voice was unmistakably Melissa's. "Virginia Belle, come on back." The tone of her voice was strange, coaxing, almost like she was playing hide-and-seek, but also touched with fear. "Virginia Belle, where are you?"

The foxhound bayed in the distance.

"So why not Mr. Yates?" Tina thought for only seconds. She trusted Vince's and Melissa's reaction, and yet . . . "My aunt Iphigenia always said 'A body should remedy suspicion by procuring to know more.'" It was an old saw that Aunt Iphigenia usually used as an excuse to gossip. But in this instance it made sense. "I think I'll go *procure* some knowledge from our very unconcerned Mr. Yates."

She strode toward the diner. If they needed to search, she'd search, but first she'd get some answers.

Inside, she couldn't fathom Mr. Yates's relaxed demeanor. He was refilling his coffee cup. The pot had been left sitting on the table by Janny when she'd run out to help locate Virginia Belle.

"You don't seem that worried about your wife, Mr. Yates."

He took a long sip of his coffee, grimaced over it like it didn't meet his exacting standards, and said, "She'll turn up. She always does."

Vince and Melissa could still be heard in the distance, calling.

Vince infuriated her. Always interfering with her mission to close the saloon. Unkind toward poor Lana Bullard. And the big lout shouldn't have pulled her into his arms the way he had. And she certainly shouldn't have enjoyed it so much. Even so, he was out there now, frantically searching, fearful for his missing mother.

Yet here sat the man who'd taken vows before God and witnesses to love and protect his wife, calmly sipping coffee.

Tina had a few more questions for the strangely indifferent man.

Oh yes, she had a few more questions indeed.

⚭

The dog dashed at a clump of scrub juniper, yelped, and spun away.

Vince heard an all-too-familiar rattle. "Stay back!" He rushed forward, grabbed Melissa around the waist, and whirled her away. "Rattlesnake."

Melissa gave him a frightened look over her shoulder. The rattle sounded again as Vince hauled her to safety, giving the snake a wide berth.

Livvy vanished around a man-high slab of red rock, then reappeared, charging straight for Vince. The dog ran in circles around Vince's legs, sniffing his boots and Melissa's legs.

Melissa stopped and waited for the dog to pick a direction. Vince stood at her side, half crazed with the need to move, to hunt, to do *something*.

Looking at the hound, Melissa said, "What's the matter? She always runs right for her?"

"Always." Stomach twisting at the word, Vince kept a firm grip on his little sister. It helped to have someone to hang on to. "She's confused by all the new smells, I reckon. Let's give her a few minutes to settle down."

Forcing himself to stay still so as not to distract the dog, Vince said to Melissa, "You said 'always'—does this happen often?"

Melissa looked up at him, true sadness and worry on her face. "That's why we got the dog. We take a lot of precautions. I lock the doors day and night. The windows are now impossible for her to open. Virginia Belle never goes out alone. With all that, still, sometimes she slips away. Not very often anymore. A few times she's gotten out through the kitchen door when it was left unlocked just for a moment. Twice she vanished while we were walking in the park. Livvy found her every time."

"In Chicago?" Vince swallowed hard. "With all those busy streets and crowds of folks? How does the dog find her there?" And how had Mother kept from being run over or assaulted?

Melissa shrugged. He felt her slender, strong arm move, saw her square shoulders that looked used to bearing weight. "That's why this surprises me. Livvy has followed her scent in really difficult situations."

"My mother seems fond of you. She . . . she knows your name." He didn't add that Mother hadn't known his, but he suspected she got the point.

"She doesn't really. She calls me Missy, while no one else does. It's not really my name but the name she gave me. Your . . . uh, our father said she has a cousin who was a close childhood friend named Missy. I think your mother has me confused with her. But she does remember it, almost always." With a sad smile she added, "She never forgets the dog's name. She really seems to like her."

The foxhound snuffled at a clump of blue-stemmed grass, and Melissa snapped, "Livvy! Find Virginia Belle."

The dog looked up at Melissa and whined, then came up and sniffed Vince's hand.

Looking down, Vince realized he still clutched the handkerchief Mother had dropped on the street.

"That's what's stopped her. He smells Virginia Belle on that kerchief." Melissa yanked it out of Vince's hand and crouched in front of the dog so it could sniff the cloth. "Find Virginia Belle, Livvy. Go on."

The dog spun and began moving again, but slowly, sniffing left and right.

Vince itched to set off on his own. He'd give the dog a few more minutes, then he'd resume his own hunt.

"So you're my little sister? I reckon there's a story there." Vince did his best not to sound like he blamed Melissa for that. It sure enough wasn't her fault.

"Our father was with my mother for years. I didn't know they weren't married until I was around twelve years old. There were two other children, a set of twins younger than me, a boy and a girl."

"God have mercy," Vince muttered. "He had three children with your ma?"

Nodding, Melissa said, "Elizabeth and Richard. They favored Father in appearance just like we both do. There was a scarlet fever outbreak when I was around fifteen, and it killed Ma and both of the younger ones. Father had sent me away to school, so I didn't catch it."

"I went to boarding school too, but I had a tendency to run off," Vince said. "Father finally gave up on me."

"I liked school. By then I knew my parents weren't married and I was ashamed and glad to get away. Two years ago I finished school and he took me to live with him and gave me the job of caring for Virginia Belle."

"That was shortly after I was home for the last time."

"I had no idea he had another son until I went to work for him and I saw your picture hanging in his house. It's true he's my father, but he treats me like a servant, not a daughter. I sleep in a room beside your mother, so I'm not in the servants' quarters, but that's just so I can be on hand to care for her."

"But he introduced you as my sister."

"When he said that, it was the first I've heard him admit it to anyone, and my picture certainly isn't hanging up anywhere. But the resemblance is so strong I'm sure most people who see me guess the truth. During my growing-up years he had little to do with me or my sister and brother. We were banished to another part of the house with our nursemaid when he came over and we only rarely saw him. I didn't understand what his relationship was with my ma until I figured out they weren't married."

Ma seemed like an affectionate name for a mother. Vince had felt affection for his mother, but it was a distant, almost worshipful feeling. More longing than actual love. Father was busy with work, and apparently with his mistress. Mother had her high-society friends, her lavish teas and dress fittings. She'd been kind when she stopped in the nursery, and he desperately looked for some sign of affection from her. And he'd hated it when Mother cried, feeling like he needed to fix whatever had hurt her. His father had been nearly as lacking from Vince's life as he'd been from Melissa's.

Vince had done wild things and earned a certain amount of Father's attention that way. Angry, punishing attention, yet Vince had preferred it over being ignored. But even misbehavior like running away from school hadn't interested his mother. When he thought back on her absent-minded kindness, it somehow made sense that she'd forgotten his name.

The dog suddenly lifted its pointed nose, wheeled to the west and took off running, its distinctive baying echoing in the canyon that surrounded them.

"Maybe she's picked up Mother's scent." Vince ran after the dog, still hanging on to Melissa's arm. The ground was scattered with red stones, stunted trees, ragged grass, and weeds.

Vince caught a glimpse of the dog. He ran, dragging his sister along, only vaguely aware it felt better to have someone to hang on to.

The dog appeared from behind a boulder, then vanished into a clump of mesquite trees, streaked into the open again and rounded a tall mount of grass and began baying. The dog didn't reappear.

"Livvy's found her!" Melissa moved faster, now ahead of Vince.

"Or she found another snake." Vince hurried to keep up. They rounded the grass blocking their view, and there was Mother, lying on her side, her forehead bleeding.

Livvy was sniffing at her still form, whining as if worried sick.

With a cry of alarm, Melissa dropped to her knees beside Mother. Vince knelt across from Melissa and did a quick examination for injuries beyond the small wound on her head, which looked to have been caused by a jagged rock smeared with blood.

"She probably just fell and knocked herself insensible," Vince said. "C'mon. Let's get her to Dare." He slid his arms under Mother and stood, moving as smoothly as he could so as not to jar her further. He ached for his confused mother. She would wake up from this blow and wonder why she hurt so and maybe be terrified to find herself in Vince's arms.

He looked at Melissa, realizing he had no idea how to deal with Mother. Oh, he'd get her to Dare's doctor's office as fast as possible; he needed no one to tell him that. But in so many ways, Mother made him feel as helpless now as she had when he was a child. Melissa knew how to manage far better than he did. He was a man who took command, a trait inherited from his father, but right now he'd give anything for someone to tell him how to understand his own mother.

Striding back to town, with Melissa rushing along beside him and Livvy whimpering at his heels, he saw Dare coming out of the back door of Vince's law office.

After reaching Dare, Vince said, "I found her unconscious. She must've fallen and hit her head."

"Let's get her to my place." Dare looked at Melissa. "Check in the diner. Glynna is my right hand when I'm doctoring. If she's there, tell her I need her. If she's not there, find her."

The three of them rounded the row of buildings to Main Street—such highfalutin words for the cold dirt between Broken Wheel's two short rows of businesses.

Dare, always a restless, fast-moving man, led the way across the street and around the other row of buildings.

Melissa said, "Livvy, come!" as she veered off toward the diner.

Vince was hard on Dare's heels, holding his mother as gentle as he could while they made their way to the doctor's office.

"Your pa never even left the diner, Vince. I know there's trouble between you and your pa, so I hope you don't take offense. But what kind of a low-down coyote sits around drinking coffee while his wife's gone missing?"

Vince wanted to stop Dare from asking such an ugly question. It was probably a good thing he was still carrying Mother, because listening to Dare's questions made him want to swing a fist. But if Vince went to shutting someone up with a punch in the nose, it'd probably be Father who deserved the beating.

Because Vince had shared the worst a man can share with his friend during their imprisonment in Andersonville, there was little that could earn Dare a punch. That desire was all coming straight out of Vince's upset, and Dare didn't deserve a bit of it.

"Let's just take care of her. No sense fretting about my father. He won't ever change."

"Tell me why she ran off. Did something upset her? Or scare her?"

Dare pounded up the two steps to swing open his door.

Vince followed right behind, turning sideways to get through with the small burden he bore.

He rested Mother on Dare's examining bed. As he laid her down, she moaned and turned her head from side to side. Lifting one of her hands to touch the cut on her head, Vince caught her wrist. "No, Mother. Let the doctor have a look."

Mother resisted, tugging against Vince's grip. Dare pressed a cloth on the bleeding wound, and Vince's restraint, along with the pain of Dare staunching the trickle of blood, pulled Mother's eyes open. She looked straight at Vince.

"My son." Mother blinked, and her eyes filled with tears. "Vincent, my sweet boy, I've missed you so. I'm glad you've come home."

Vince thought his heart would rip open from the sweet pain of Mother saying his name. Her eyes fluttered closed again. Vince reached to shake her shoulder, gently but insistently.

"No, Vince." Dare stopped him. "I need her to be still. She may need stitches and she'll at least need a bandage. That's easier to do if she's fainted."

Looking at the closed eyes, Vince said, "She knows me. Right now she knows who I am. You asked me why she ran off; it's because something's wrong with her. Something in her mind. One of the reasons I wanted to try and find a way to help Lana Bullard is because I thought then maybe we could help Mother."

"She's that bad?" Dare looked up sharply. "As bad as Lana?"

Lana, who'd tried to kill Dare.

"I don't think she's dangerous." Then again, Vince

hadn't been around his mother for a long, long time. "Not to anyone but herself. But she's . . . addled. Like she's living in a world only she understands. When I went home after the war, she didn't know who I was. I was sick and starved down to bones."

"I remember," Dare said somberly. Dare had been the same—they all had.

"I suppose I looked so awful she couldn't see her son in me. She acted scared of me and ordered me out of the house every time she saw me. I learned to stay out of her way. And she gets upset if we don't go along with whatever nonsense she's talking about. Hearing her say my name is . . ." Vince swallowed the lump in his throat.

Dare went back to working on Mother, probably because he was afraid Vince was going to shame himself with tears.

Vince would do no such thing. He went on, "You didn't hear her when she got out of the carriage and hugged me. She called me Julius. Father's name. If she passes out or falls asleep, who knows if she'll ever—"

Glynna hurried in and rushed to Dare's side. "What can I do to help?"

Only then did Vince realize no one had closed the door. Had Glynna heard any of this? How loud had Vince been talking? He knew it didn't matter, but it was so shameful to have a mother who wasn't in her right mind. And it tore at the very fabric of his soul to be so worthless that his mother couldn't remember his name. And he couldn't help but wonder if whatever madness plagued her might one day come over him.

He heard another step and saw Tina pulling the door

shut. His eyes met hers. Knowledge of what Vince had said was there. She'd heard everything.

"It doesn't matter that you overheard," Vince said quietly. "You'll all have to know in order to protect Mother."

Vince prided himself on hiding his feelings and keeping his life private. He didn't even like his Regulator friends to know what he was thinking. Now he'd have to live with the whole world knowing how mixed up his family was.

"We need to talk about what care she needs." Dare seemed to understand how Vince was feeling. He lifted the cloth from Mother's forehead and studied the wound, talking the whole time. "We'll all need to know, because if she's not thinking right, then she'll need constant attention. If we're all alert, we can prevent another incident like what happened today."

Dare focused on his patient. He'd always been good at this, ignoring distractions and focusing on whoever was sick. It was what made him a good doctor. "Glynna, I need warm water and bandages."

Glynna was turning into a first-rate nurse, too. She had the basin of water within Dare's reach almost before he'd asked for it. Tina moved for the bandages. She was here to help, not watch. Glynna brought carbolic acid without being asked. Dare thought the liquid was a powerful help in preventing infections, and he put it on nearly every wound.

Dare wrung out a clean cloth in the hot water and cleaned the cut. After a few long minutes and a closer inspection, he said, "It won't need stitches. It's not that deep."

Vince heaved a sigh of relief just as the door behind him swung open.

Father. Finally.

Melissa was right behind him. Livvy trotted at her heel.

The dog laid her muzzle on the bed and gave a little whine. Livvy seemed more upset about Mother getting hurt than anyone else. A sad commentary.

In fact, it was so sad that Vince had a momentary burn in his eyes that in a weakling might've meant tears. But men didn't cry, so Vince dug deep and found anger instead. At last he was ready to say out loud all that had been pressing to get out.

A volcano didn't have this kind of pressure.

"Well, how is she?" Father asked impatiently.

Turning to face Father, Vince saw no reason anymore to pretend like he'd ever find a way to get along with his arrogant, cheating, ruthless tyrant of a father.

CHAPTER 9

Mrs. Yates jumped at the sound of her husband's voice. She twisted on the bed and jumped again, this time at the sight of Dare leaning over her. "Why, I declare, whatever is going on here? Who are you, young man?"

Tina was glad for the interruption, because she saw the storm clouds churning in Vince's brown eyes.

"I'm a doctor, and you bumped your head." Dare's soothing tone darkened and grew louder as he looked up. "I need quiet in here."

Mrs. Yates didn't jump this time. Instead her eyes went wide and she leaned a bit toward Dare.

"My patient needs to stay calm. Make yourself useful, Vince." Dare's voice returned to being calm as he drew Vince back from glaring daggers at his father.

Tina saw so much pass between Dare and Vince. It then struck her hard that she'd never had a real friend. Her growing-up years had been lonely beyond belief. Now, here with Jonas, despite her picketing, she'd been drawn into her brother's circle of friends and she loved it. And they let her be part of their circle, even if she did have to give them an occasional scolding to get them to do as she asked. She'd noticed well enough that none of them hesitated to scold her right back—Vince most especially. But they never withdrew their friendship when they did so.

Now here was Dare, seeing a fight brewing, trying to head it off so they could focus on what was most important: his patient's health. Although heading off a fight between a father and a son was a good cause all of itself. Such a good cause in fact that Tina, despite her annoyance with Mr. Yates, should probably paint up a sign and march around with it, advising against fathers and sons fighting.

"Mr. Yates, your presence here is disturbing your wife." Dare spoke with all the authority of a doctor. "Maybe you could occupy yourself settling into the boardinghouse."

Tina saw Mr. Yates stiffen, not happy to be dismissed. He looked at his ailing wife, pulled his pocket watch from his vest pocket, snapped it open and studied it for a moment. Looking up he said, "You're right, Doctor. I think it's high time for me to go." With a humph he snapped his watch shut, tucked it away, turned, and with a steady thump of his cane, left the building.

A bit more gently, Dare said, "Help me hold your ma's hands, Vincent."

Using his full name brought Vince's eyes to his ma. Dare had done it deliberately, probably hoping Mrs. Yates would recognize it in her muddled state. A taut muscle worked in Vince's jaw, but he got a grip on his temper and turned back to his ailing ma.

As Vince sat on the bed beside her, his ma smiled up at him. "Son, it's so nice to see you. When did you get home?"

Vince drew in a breath so deep his whole body rose. He

leaned close. "I just got here, Mother. The doctor needs to help you. You have a cut on your head." Vince's voice dropped to an inaudible murmur, and his mother seemed enthralled with him.

Then she turned to Dare. "I'll be still, Doctor. Thank you ever so much for your assistance." She lay utterly still, but her eyes slid to Vince. "You've gotten so handsome, Vincent. I declare you are the very image of your father."

She continued to speak to Dare and Vince in turn in her pretty Southern drawl.

Ruthy Stone stepped out of the barn, her milk pail brimming over. She ran smack into Quince Wilcox, a recently hired cowhand.

He stumbled and fell against her. Milk slopped out of the pail. Ruthy was quick to steady it before more spilt as she backed away into the barn. Quince lurched backward and hit the wide open door, then stumbled to a halt. "Sorry about that, Mrs. Stone."

He was tall and skinny, with a scruffy beard and dirty blond hair that hung in his light-blue eyes. He was older than Ruthy, and most of the cowpokes, except for Dodger and their cook, were young. Riding herd was a job for youngsters.

Quince leaned toward her and Ruthy, who'd never considered for a moment not feeling safe around their hired men, fought the urge to take a step back. Quince blocked the door so she couldn't get out without pushing him aside. But it didn't suit her to retreat.

He grabbed the barn door as if to steady himself, then

stepped just a bit closer and caught her arm. "There now, sorry about the spill, ma'am."

Ruthy didn't back up, not wanting to allow the man to step in and shut the door on them. That was when she smelled liquor on his breath.

He held on longer than was appropriate in Ruthy's opinion but made no further move. She didn't like his touch, though she sensed no real threat. He held on to keep himself upright.

Controlling her expression to show no fear, she said crisply, "Please step aside, Mr. Wilcox. I'm late for preparing the evening meal. Your supper will be ready in the bunkhouse by now I'm sure."

Quince narrowed his eyes. Ruthy suspected he was seeing two of her. He shook his head, dropped her arm, and turned aside.

"Supper in the bunkhouse." He nodded as if trying to understand what that meant. Then he staggered away without another word.

Ruthy was shaken by the unpleasant encounter. She closed the barn door, watched Quince walk on tottering legs for a bit, then hurried inside.

By the time Luke came in, she was calm again and wondering why she'd let something so small upset her. It reminded her too much of Virgil—the son of the family who'd raised her when she'd been orphaned as a child. He wasn't a drinker, but he'd liked putting his hands on her. She might be overly disturbed by Quince because of Virgil, and that wasn't fair to the man. She set fried chicken on the table while Luke washed up. She decided not to talk about Quince grabbing her. But she could mention the whiskey breath and unsteadiness because that made him a problem around the ranch.

Once settled to her meal, she said, "One of your hired men was the worse for drink when I saw him outside a bit ago."

Luke had just torn a bite off a chicken leg, and he watched her closely as he chewed. After swallowing, he asked, "Who was it?"

Ruthy didn't like the tone of Luke's voice, and she hated to get one of the men fired. "The newest one, Quince Wilcox."

Taking another bite of chicken, Luke mulled that over. "I know some of the men like to go into the saloon on payday. I don't like it, but I've never felt right about saying they can't, not as long as they don't get into trouble in town. I always figured what a man does with his money and his time off is between him and God, so long as he don't hurt anyone. But they usually keep that kind of ruckus in town and settle down after they've taken a chunk out of their month's pay. I've never caught one back here drunk. Payday was two weeks ago. You say he was drinking now? Here on the ranch?"

Ruthy rested one hand on her rounded stomach and felt their child move. She hadn't liked Quince touching her. But she didn't like turning a man out of a job. Neither was she about to lie. "I didn't see him drink, but I smelled liquor on his breath."

"You smelled it?" Luke's eyes sharpened until he was utterly focused on Ruthy—and he'd been paying real close attention already. "Just how close did Wilcox get to you?"

Luke had grown up here in Indian Territory in Texas. He'd fought in the Civil War, and when his pa had been murdered and his ranch stolen he'd gotten it back by facing the man who'd killed his pa and battling it out. Luke was as sweet and gentle as a man could be, but there was no denying her husband was a tough man. It was one of the things she liked most about him.

But she felt guilty to say the words that would get a man fired. And she knew she *could* say those words. Luke was so protective he'd never keep a man around who bothered her in any way. All she'd have to say was that his actions had backed her into the barn and she'd been afraid to be shut up in the barn with him. "Well . . . uh, he staggered. I . . . I swung the barn door open right as he was passing. He stumbled into it. That was mostly my fault." Except he was walking so close, while normally a person gave doors a wide berth just because they could swing open. She wondered if Wilcox had been leaning on the barn to keep himself steady. "It was when he stumbled that he got close enough I could smell his breath."

Luke's jaw formed a tight line, and he put his chicken back on the plate. A bad sign because not much came between Luke and her fried chicken.

"This just happened now? Tonight?" Luke's tone gave Ruthy a little chill down her spine. She was glad she'd told him right away, because she knew he'd've been unhappy if she'd kept it from him, then he'd found out later somehow. He wouldn't even like it if she waited until tomorrow to tell him.

"Yes, just after I milked the cow tonight."

"So Wilcox was drinking during the workday?" Luke went back to eating his chicken.

106

No answer to that question was required, so Ruthy went on with her meal, too.

Luke finished in half the normal time. As he rose from the table, a knock sounded at the back door. He went to it, and Dodger, the S Bar S Ranch foreman, stood in the light cast from the kitchen lanterns.

"Are you all right?" Luke asked Dodger. Ruthy came up beside him.

"Yep, just getting back." Dodger stepped inside. He was a mess. His right eye was swollen shut. His hat was missing. One sleeve of his coat was badly ripped, and he limped with every step. "I found a cow that'd dropped her calf and it had stumbled into a spring. The calf was soaking wet, shivering so bad I figured it wouldn't survive without help. I had a time convincing the mama I oughta bring the baby in where it's warm."

"Get in here." Luke stepped back.

Ruthy knew Dodger had been around since Luke was a boy. The foreman had white hair and a thick gray mustache. He wasn't a fast-moving man, but there was no job on the ranch he'd ask anyone to do that he couldn't do better himself. Ruthy had trusted him ever since he'd helped Luke get the S Bar S back from Flint Greer.

"Yep, that cow didn't think I needed to touch her baby. But the calf's in the barn now and the mama alongside it. They'll be fine."

"Sit down and share our meal." Luke glanced at Ruthy.

She smiled and waved Dodger to the table. "There's plenty. Get off your feet for a spell."

"That chicken looks mighty good, Mrs. Stone. I'm sure the food in the bunkhouse has gone stone cold by now. I'm

107

obliged for the offer." Dodger sank down at the kitchen table with a muffled groan. One arm went to his ribs, yet he didn't complain. Ruthy resisted the urge to offer medical help. Dodger wouldn't appreciate his weakness being pointed out. He was banged up, but if he was really hurt, he'd probably say so.

Ruthy bustled about, getting a plate and filling it with chicken and mashed potatoes and gravy. She laid a slice of freshly baked bread on the plate, pushed the butter and jelly closer to Dodger, poured everyone a fresh cup of coffee, and sat down to join them.

A few minutes of silence passed, the only sound that of their clinking silverware. Ruthy saw the determined expression on Luke's face. But he bided his time, letting Dodger eat in peace.

Finally, Dodger swallowed the last bite and lifted his coffee cup, turning to Luke. "What's going on, boss? I've seen that look before. It means there's a problem."

"There is a problem, for a fact. Wilcox was drunk today at work."

Dodger set his cup down with a click of tin on wood. "He was?"

"He bumped into Ruthy. She smelled liquor on his breath."

Dodger turned and locked his eyes on Ruthy until she wanted to squirm. "Is that all he did, ma'am? You've got a mighty kind heart. Are you saying less than the full truth because you're worried about him losing his job?"

Luke turned to study Ruthy closely while waiting for an answer.

Dragging in a calming breath, Ruthy said, "I am worried

about him losing his job. We can't have a drunkard around the place, but just because he had a drink today doesn't mean it's a habit."

She hadn't answered Dodger, not completely. She sincerely hoped no one noticed.

"More often than not, drinking during the day, especially a workday, does mean it's a habit." Dodger took a drink of his coffee.

Luke worked his jaw until she saw muscles tense in his face. She thought he was reading her mind, seeing the few moments when she'd been just a bit frightened.

Without goading her to say more, Luke turned to Dodger. "I've never had a hard-and-fast rule about drinking on the job because I've never needed one. No man tries to work cattle while nipping at a bottle."

Dodger shrugged a shoulder. "No man who wants to live to an old age anyway. A cowpoke needs his wits about him when he's out dodging hooves and horns."

Though Dodge sat there exhausted and battered, Ruthy knew he'd be fine. What if he'd been as unsteady as Wilcox? Ruthy knew there was no sense letting an already dangerous job get worse.

"Let's go talk to the varmint." Dodger pushed back his chair.

"Reckon he's asleep by now." Luke waved at the cup in front of his foreman. "Finish your coffee. We'll talk with him first thing in the morning, if his head'll stay on his shoulders."

"Why wouldn't his head stay on his shoulders?" Ruthy gasped.

Luke gave her a tight smile. "A drinking man tends to

wake up with a sore head. And the best cure for it, to a drunkard's way of thinking, is to take another drink. A man can have a heap of trouble getting out of that cycle."

Turning back to Dodger, Luke went on, "A man unsteady because of drink can put himself, the other cowpokes, and his horse in danger."

"You sure we shouldn't go see the coyote now?" Dodger took one long, last swallow of his coffee.

"Let's wait. If he's worse for drink, we'll only be wasting our time. In the morning we'll have it out with him when he's sobered up. Maybe it's time to talk to all the men. Make some rules. Just so no one can say they're surprised that I frown on drinking hard liquor."

"I suppose morning would be better. But we'll make it early, before he starts guzzling again." Dodger rose from the table, stiffer for having stopped and rested, but he kept moving and that was about all any man could do.

He swung the door open just as a gun fired and a bullet ricocheted off the doorframe just inches from his face.

Dodger dove backward.

Luke launched himself toward Ruthy and dragged her to the floor.

"She's going to be fine," Dare whispered as he stepped away from the now-sleeping Virginia Belle. He'd been all afternoon tending her, most of it spent just being kind and letting her rest.

Vince had spent that time talking with Mother, and she'd known he was her son. She'd been moved to tears a few times, but Vince had stuck it out when he wanted to run. Afraid she'd forget him while he was hiding from salt water.

Now the lantern lights were turned high, and the sun had dipped behind the mesa west of town. Dare rubbed his back as he straightened from his patient.

Vince knew Mother *wasn't* going to be fine . . . ever. But he would hold this day in his heart. His mother had remembered him.

He'd felt plenty of guilt for leaving home once he'd regained his strength after the war. Mother had needed someone to care for her. But she wasn't about to let that someone be Vince, not back then. And for him it had been a kind of torture to see Mother tremble at the sight of him.

Father had never been proud of Vince, and Vince had learned to handle that. But Mother could be kind if Vince was very mindful of her feelings. Having her forget who he was crushed him until he could barely breathe in that fancy house in Chicago.

So he'd left, wandered, spent a winter reading law books, and finally ended up here to help Luke Stone get back his ranch. And he'd kept his father aware of where he was if he ever quit drifting long enough to have an address. Then Father would write to him, demanding he return home and assume his responsibilities, and Vince would write back and refuse.

Vince had no confidence that Mother would still remember him when she awoke. He braced himself to accept that.

He turned and saw his little sister had leaned forward where she sat and fallen asleep face-first on the table. "Melissa."

She jerked upright at the sound of her name.

"You're exhausted." Vince was surprised at his reflexive interest in protecting her. The thought that Tina was someone's little sister skittered through Vince's head, and he banished it the moment he thought it.

Melissa shook her head as if to clear it. Vince realized she still had on the dusty clothing she'd been wearing when she'd stepped out of the coach hours ago.

Vince hadn't cleaned up all day, either.

Melissa knew how hard Father must have pushed to get across the country as fast as he had. Mother clearly was all done in. Vince felt much the same.

Father had probably washed up, demanded someone make him a meal, and then gone to sleep. Vince hadn't seen him since he'd left after visiting Mother hours ago.

"You need to rest, Missy. But first, do you have the energy to tell us more about Mother's condition?"

Melissa rubbed her eyes. She spoke quietly of Mother's inability to remember dates and names. Melissa's voice started out rusty from sleep, but she gained energy as she talked. She told them how Mother sometimes got lost in the house where she'd lived for years. And then Father had built a new house. A mansion so huge it was beyond Melissa's ability to describe.

"Since we've moved, Virginia Belle is always restless. I think it's because she just can't remember where she is. I suspect she's searching for anything familiar, and when she's slipped out of the house, I think she's trying to go home.

"Until recently she often had tea with old friends, but ever since the move, she's far more apt to forget names, and she's always wandering off. Our father finds that embar-

rassing and has more or less confined her to the house."
Melissa's eyes shifted to Vince. "She asks for you quite
often. Father wanted you to come home, and when you
wouldn't, he made a snap decision to hunt you down. We
set out very suddenly and pushed as hard as possible, racing to make train connections, hiring fast-moving coaches
when no train went the direction we wanted."

"Father doesn't make snap decisions," Vince said. "He
plots. He decides every move in advance." For some reason, when Vince said that, he got a chill up his spine. He
wasn't sure why, and he didn't have time to think more
about it now.

"I think he must have been planning to come and see you
for a while. Has he known you were living here for long?"

"Long enough." Vince frowned as he imagined Father
getting things in order, then picking his moment to leave.

"All the horses were ready at every stop. Things went
too smoothly to be arranged at the last moment, even with
money smoothing the way. But I think he was still hoping
to get you home. He must have either given up or decided
he had a better chance of ordering you home if you met
face-to-face."

"I exchanged telegraphs with him on my trip to New Orleans. I made it clear I wasn't coming home. That must've
been the final straw that set Father's plans into motion."

"We need to let your mother sleep awhile." Dare began
cleaning up his supplies from the bedside table. "Then you
can get her to the boardinghouse, Vince. Your father's
probably all settled in by now. I need to run over to the
livery. Sledge cut his arm last week and it's time for me to
take out the stitches. I was on my way there when your

folks climbed off that carriage. I forgot all about it until now."

"Go ahead." Vince waved Dare off. "I'll be here."

Melissa said, "There should be two of us. I've learned the hard way that just because she's sleeping isn't reason enough to stop our caretaking. One person can't watch the front and back door all the time. One person has to take occasional breaks, and trouble can happen in an instant. We had two people with her at home at all times."

Vince looked at the dark circles under Melissa's eyes. "You're all in from the trip, Melissa. I'll be all right with her for a while, if Dare hurries back."

Melissa said uncertainly, "You look tired yourself."

Vince remembered the shape he'd been in when he rode into town. He was just as bad now, just as dirty and exhausted and hungry. Only more so because the day had passed and the sun was now setting.

At that moment the door to Dare's doctor's office swung open, and Tina came in carrying a tray that smelled wonderful. A red-and-white-checked cloth covered what looked like heaped plates. His stomach growled, and he had his hands full not grabbing the tray away from her.

Dare smiled at her. "Just what we needed. Can you stay with Vince for a little while? Melissa needs rest, and I need to run and check on Sledge's stitches."

Tina's smile faltered, and she gave Vince a quick glance that reminded him of what had happened the last time they were alone together. But Tina couldn't very well explain that she didn't want to be alone with Vince for fear he'd kiss her.

"Of course I'll stay. I left Jonas eating and have nothing to hurry back for. Melissa, I brought a plate of food for you."

"I'll take it to the boardinghouse with me. I'm afraid the moment my stomach isn't poking at me to remind me to eat, I'll fall asleep where I sit. Best to be near a bed then."

"Your room's at the top of the boardinghouse steps, the room farthest to the left. Livvy's already asleep in there. Paul got her some food. Mr. Yates has the corner room, and he's gone to bed for the night. I knocked on his door to offer him a meal, though he did stop by the diner earlier and ate. He didn't answer. I'm sure he was exhausted, too." Tina added the last part doubtfully. No one could fail to notice how completely unconcerned Father was about his injured wife. Now he was sleeping and no doubt clean and well fed while everyone else hovered at Mother's bedside.

"Thanks, Tina." Dare rolled his sleeves down. "I'll walk you over to the boardinghouse, Melissa."

Melissa shrugged into her woolen coat and took the plate with a smile of gratitude.

Dare grabbed the doorknob, then paused. "I won't be long. If your ma keeps sleeping, Glynna and I can watch over her through the night. I haven't seen Glynna for hours. Heaven only knows where she's gotten to."

"She spent the afternoon and early evening with the children, working on their lessons in the room above the diner, and now she's feeding the prisoner." Tina set the rest of the food on the table, where Melissa had been napping.

Dare froze, his eyes wide.

"I cooked," Tina added quickly.

Vince blew out a sigh of relief. He wasn't sure exactly where cruel and unusual punishment kicked in, but

Glynna's cooking might come real close. He'd hate for Lana to get out of jail on a technicality.

"I cooked food for you all and the prisoners and Jonas." For a moment Tina looked disgruntled, and why not? She was feeding the whole town and she wasn't even making wages at the diner, not since it closed at noon.

"We still don't know what to do about Lana." Tina had a fussy expression, the one that tended to make her grab a picket sign.

"I don't think we can talk about it now without disturbing Vince's ma." Dare frowned at his patient. "Then I'll be back with Glynna and the youngsters to take over."

Vince wanted to add, We're going to have to spell each other forever. Because Mother's problem wasn't going to go away and somehow they were going to have to find two people available at all times to watch over her.

Dare held the door, and Melissa left, carrying her dinner plate.

Once the door closed, Vince turned to Tina and they stared at each other.

All Vince could think of was that unfortunate moment they'd shared earlier at the jailhouse. After all that had gone on today, that was a plumb stupid thing to be remembering.

And yet . . .

Vince wanted to run. He even took a step back. Tina could handle this for a while.

He'd go clean up, change his clothes, read a book.

Maybe he could guard the front door by standing outside. True, it was cold, but cold might be just the thing.

If Tina was to guard the back door, she could go stand in the kitchen.

116

With him outside and her in the kitchen, they wouldn't even have to see each other.

Mother stirred.

Vince thought of the windows she could climb out.

He wasn't going anywhere.

For now, he and Tina were stuck together.

CHAPTER 10

Luke threw his body between Ruthy and flying lead. Someone unloaded what sounded like a Winchester rifle into the south side of his cabin. His thinking got very fast, and the world seemed to move at a fraction of its usual speed.

He dragged Ruthy to the floor, twisted so he didn't land all his weight on his little wife, or crush his child, and laid out his body to block a bullet.

With nearly the same motion he kicked the door shut. Three more bullets slammed into it.

"Get in the closet, Ruthy. Now!" He felt her leave. But they'd talked about what to do in a time of danger. He knew his Ruthy. She was a savvy woman and didn't waste one second asking to stay. He knew she preferred to face a fight. But he also knew she understood that if Luke knew she was safe, he could concentrate on the danger. And she wasn't just going to cower in that space beneath the closet floor. She had a gun tucked in there, so she could fight if she had to.

That same shelter was where Glynna Greer had hid from her husband to make him think she'd run off. It had sent Greer riding after his wife and given Ruthy a chance to

119

sneak Glynna out while Luke was busy fighting Greer and his henchmen. The shelter had been built by Luke's pa, and Glynna had only found out about it because Luke had passed her a note through Dodger telling her to hide, hoping Greer didn't know about the secret trapdoor.

Now Ruthy was gone, down those steps to safety, going through the trapdoor that locked solid from inside. But Ruthy was tough. She'd have a gun in her hand, make sure it was loaded, then be back up those steps. Ready for trouble, ready to duck underground if need be. And smart enough not to be in the way while Luke had a fight on his hands.

He thanked God for this woman as he crawled along on his elbows to his Colt. Two more shots slammed into the thick log door. Pa had built this house to withstand just this sort of trouble.

Luke drew the pistol from where he hung his gun belt every night, right inside the back door.

Then silence.

He looked over to see Dodger crouched low, his gun leveled.

There was another blast of gunfire, but it was aimed in a different direction and came from a different sort of gun. He recognized an old Sharps fifty caliber and knew it belonged to Marty, a young cowpoke who was a steady hand. Marty carried his pa's old gun and wouldn't part with it. It was the only Sharps on the ranch.

Marty's gun quit firing. Luke crawled to the lantern hanging by the cookstove and snuffed it. The kitchen now cloaked in darkness, he went to the door and stood to the side of it. Dodger jumped up, went to the other side and flattened his back to the wall. They looked at each other, both with their guns drawn and pointing straight up.

"Ready?" Luke said to Dodger as he reached for the door handle.

Dodger nodded.

Luke eased the door open and waited.

Dodger stepped around it and let it swing all the way to the wall.

"Whoever it was is gone now, boss," Marty called.

Luke trusted the young man, but even trustworthy men could be wrong. "Stay back, Marty. Dodger and I are coming out, and I don't want you in the line of fire."

"Five of us came out of the bunkhouse. We heard the shots, and I just heard someone running off on foot. We're ready for you, boss. Come on out."

Luke swung out the door and dropped behind a watering trough next to his hitching post.

No one took a shot. Dodger's running feet were the only sound as the old-timer went in the opposite direction of Luke, to spread the gunfire. Luke could hear Dodger round the side of the house and stop.

Then there was nothing but a gusting wind and the hoot of an owl stirred up by the ruckus.

Slowly Luke straightened.

Gun in hand, he listened, let his eyes adjust to moonlight and waited until he was certain whoever had done the shooting had for sure gone.

"All right, he's taken off." Luke made certain his men knew exactly where he was before he came out from cover and strode for those who'd come out of the bunkhouse and took positions with their firearms.

"Did anyone see him?" Luke took a quick count. Everyone was here. Including Quince Wilcox, the man Ruthy had seen drunk earlier. He looked pretty steady now, though Luke couldn't tell for sure in the moonlight.

Luke felt a twist of indecision. He'd intended to fire the man first thing in the morning. He didn't like a drunkard working for him, and he was sure Ruthy had been upset by the encounter and was making light of it to keep the man from losing his job.

But now with the shooting, he wasn't so sure. He didn't keep a lot of hired men around after the spring roundup, and he was already shorthanded. And it looked like he needed to start posting a stronger night watch.

"Did anyone see anything? Get a look at who was shooting?"

"I did, boss," Wilcox said.

Luke felt his tension rise. He didn't like the idea of accepting the word of a man who'd been drinking. It'd been several hours ago, though, assuming the polecat had quit drinking when Ruthy had seen him and hadn't been pulling a cork the whole night.

"You got a look at the man who shot at the house?"

"Yep, one man, alone and on foot, unless he had his horse tied up away from the ranch. I didn't get a good enough look to pick out the man, but I did see one important detail."

"What did you see?"

Wilcox gave Luke a long look that had a mean edge to it. "You ain't gonna like it."

Luke didn't respond. Wilcox looked to savor the moment, enjoyed that he was the center of attention. The silence stretched, and Luke fought back the urge to shake the answer out of Wilcox.

Finally, sounding smug, Wilcox said, "I saw him well enough to know he was an Indian. One of those Kiowa you're so fond of. Might've even been the one you let come around here from time to time, Red Wolf. And the way he was swinging that rifle, then running, unsteady-like, I'd say he was drunk."

⌒◇⌒

"You eat now, Vince." Tina hurried to Mrs. Yates's bedside. The woman had shifted and moaned. Her eyes flickered open. Blue eyes, but so light blue in this light they were almost gray, nothing like the warm brown of Vince's.

The lack of resemblance seemed wrong. Why had Vince and Melissa taken after their father so completely?

Tina looked nothing like Jonas, her brother. How did God work it all out? How was it arranged who to hand down the hair color and eye color, the height and even the personality traits to?

Vince ate silently while Tina pondered these things. She kept her gaze fixed on Mrs. Yates to stop herself from looking at Vince.

Finally he finished his meal and came over to his ma's bedside across from Tina.

"That was mighty good, Tina. I appreciate you taking care of us."

Tina couldn't be so rude as to not look at him when he complimented her, so she gave him a quick glance and a smile. "You're welcome. I was glad to do it."

Mrs. Yates's eyes had closed as Tina watched over her,

and she settled into a sound sleep, which was a shame, considering Tina was stuck in here alone with Vince. Mrs. Yates needing attention would be a nice distraction.

Tina had to come up with a way to spend time with Vince and yet stay far away from him. Then she thought of a few questions she'd been harboring that he wouldn't want to answer. In fact, they'd annoy him something fierce. All the better to keep him on his side of his mother.

Besides, she was dying to know what was going on. Watching him closely as he stood staring at his mother's still form, she said, "I couldn't figure out why you rode off like that, to New Orleans, over Lana Bullard."

Vince's eyes lifted until they locked on Tina's. His dark eyes shifted from concern while he'd watched his mother to blazing lightning now. Oh yes, she'd annoyed him, all right. That gave her the courage to go on, despite his forbidding expression.

"It wasn't Lana you were worried about, was it? When I asked Dare if there was some kind of treatment for people who are . . . are . . ."

"Mad?" Vince suggested with sleet in his voice. "Insane? Lunatics?"

"Impaired," Tina said. She'd jumped at that word when it came to her. "You thought if there was a treatment for Lana, it might work for your mother."

Silence stretched between them. Tina wondered if he'd toss her outside and take over watching his mother himself.

"What makes you so stubborn about protecting Lana?" Vince's voice was quiet, smooth, but carried a harsh warning. "I have to wonder if there isn't someone in your life who reminds you of her."

124

"No, there's no one like that in my family, but I was taught by my aunt Iphigenia that a woman needs to know how to—"

"Take care of herself. Yes, I know. You say it about twice a day."

"So it seems like there should be a way for a woman to overcome whatever's wrong with Lana. But you're changing the subject. You're looking for a cure for your mother's . . . confusion, aren't you? Has she always been like this?"

"My life before Broken Wheel is none of your concern." Vince turned from the bed and went to the front door. She half expected him to walk out. Instead he turned, leaned his back against the door, and crossed his arms. Sentry position. Vince did dearly love to stand guard.

Tina decided she'd ask him about that next. "It's clear you love your mother, just as it's clear your father isn't a kind man. I heard she mistook you for your father at first. That must hurt."

"I've been around my mother and father enough not to let them get my feelings ruffled." Vince settled in. His voice smoothed out, and he was fully in control of himself. Which was exactly what Tina didn't want.

"Then if it doesn't hurt your feelings, why not talk about it?" This had started because Tina very deliberately wanted to be a pest. But with her question and his reaction, she realized she really could hurt him. It had been a mistake to bring up his trouble with his parents.

"Listen, Miss One Woman Picket Line, my mother was confused when I went home to heal up after the war."

"Heal up? You mean you were wounded?"

"I was never wounded. All my troubles were as a result of

the terrible conditions at Andersonville. I was half starved. No, truth be told, it was more like three-fourths starved. I was down to skin and bones. I was ailing from every disease in that place except the ones that killed quick. I just plain needed a place to lie down, eat right, get a doctor's care for a while and regain my strength. I stayed at home as long as I could stand it."

"Did your mother mistake you for your father back then?"

Shaking his head, Vince said, "She thought I was a stranger. She'd get upset every time she saw me in the house. I ended up hiding from her as much as I could because she acted like I was there to harm her. I stayed mostly to my rooms. The servants brought food. The doctor stopped in. I learned Mother's routine and could avoid her, but every so often she'd run into me and there'd be trouble."

"Trouble?"

Tina saw his jaw working as he gritted his teeth and looked into the middle distance, as if he were seeing the past. "As soon as I could get around, I took to leaving the house all day. I should've just found someplace else to live, but I needed to rest. I needed steady meals. I needed home." Vince shook his head. "Those are excuses. I was weak and I let myself depend on my father. He got it in his head I was back to stay, even though I told him I didn't want any part of the banking business."

Tina decided Vince was more comfortable complaining about his father than talking about his mother. She wasn't going to let him get away with changing the subject. "So your mother was showing signs of confusion back then? Or has she always been like this?"

"This was new. She'd always been . . ." Vince's voice broke. He lapsed into silence and looked at his mother.

Tina also looked at Virginia Belle, an aging Sleeping Beauty. A lovely, fragile Southern belle who'd probably always given her care over to others. But she'd never needed it as much as now.

Then Vince gave his head a hard shake and glared at Tina. She could see that he preferred anger to sadness, and all these memories were enough to make a grown man cry. And for all her resolve to stay away from him, Tina found her feet carrying her to stand facing him.

"It's not unheard of for an older person to get a bit absent-minded, Vince."

"Absent-minded?" A harsh laugh replaced the sadness. "That's what you call it when you forget your own son?"

Tina decided anger was better than tears, at least from a man's point of view. "Call it anything you want, but yes, sometimes older people begin to get a little dotty."

"She's not that old, and . . . and her father was like this, too. Both of them were much too young to be entering their dotage."

"And this is why you were so interested in Lana's troubles?" It made sense now. "You wanted to see if those papers might also help your mother."

Vince's shoulders sagged just a bit, and his eyes lowered to the floor. Tina thought she was wearing him down, but then she noticed the dark circles under his eyes, his dusty clothing. He'd lost weight since he left Broken Wheel. She could smell him: horse and sweat and dirt and fresh air and strength. Those last two weren't a smell, yet somehow they were part of him. She wasn't sure how far it was to New

Orleans, but she was sure it was a long, hard ride and he'd pushed himself to the limit to get there and back in such short order.

The man was at the breaking point, and she didn't want to say the word that would make him snap. She opened her mouth to change the subject. She decided she'd bring up a lengthy discussion about the weather while they waited for someone to come and take over for them. But before she did, she had to tell him one last thing.

She rested one hand on his shoulder. He'd deny it, of course, but she thought he could use the support. "I see no sign that your mother is dangerous in any way, except maybe to herself. I don't think your mother's problems are of a similar nature with Lana's."

At her touch, Vince looked her square in the eye. "Father writes from time to time and I knew she'd gotten worse. His last letter he talked about locking her up if I refused to come home and help with her care. I'm sure Father meant Mother would go to some asylum, though he didn't say it directly. He looks at sending Mother away as a failure, which is why he's kept her at home with caretakers. But in his last letter he told me he'd built a new house, a bigger house than the one I grew up in. He said she's worse since they moved."

"A woman who's a bit confused in familiar surroundings," Tina said, clenching her hands without really noticing until Vince removed her fingernails out of his shoulder, "is bound to get worse in a place that's unknown to her."

"If you can figure that out here after knowing Mother for less than a day, how come my father couldn't figure it out? Why didn't he see that a new home was a bad idea?"

Temper simmered in his eyes. Behind the anger, whenever he looked at his mother, was worry mixed with love. "And now they're here. I didn't find answers that were a comfort in New Orleans. Mother isn't going to like wherever he sends her, and how unhappy will she be in a place surrounded by strangers?"

That worry and love made him so vulnerable. When he was at his usual tormenting best, Tina had no trouble staying firmly at odds with him. But here he stood, worried about his mother, hurt and angered by his father, exhausted because of the long ride he'd taken based on things Tina had said. He'd held on to her hand when he'd tugged her nails out of his hide, and now he raised their hands, his eyes locked on hers, and touched his lips to her fingertips.

"What am I going to do about you, Tina Cahill?"

The suggestions that popped into her head were firmly out of the question. Aunt Iphigenia would be scandalized.

Even knowing that, it was all too easy to rest her other hand on his shoulder, then slide it over to his shirt collar, then his neck. Their entwined hands were between them, but Vince lowered hers from his lips and leaned down—and butted her in the head.

For a moment Tina thought he'd attacked, and she balled up a fist to hit back. Then Melissa called out, "What's blocking the door?"

Tina rushed to Mrs. Yates's side and stood with her back to the door, rubbing her bruised nose. Vince stepped aside.

"Be careful." He glared at his sister.

Melissa swung the door open. "Why are you standing by the door?"

Tina knew the answer to that question. Vince had gotten as far away from her as he could. And then she'd gone after him like some kind of hoyden chasing after a man. It's a wonder she didn't try and lasso him.

Why hadn't she stayed away from him? Why? Why? Why?

Banging her head on the nearest hard surface was an idea with merit, and only the spectacle she'd make of herself stopped her. That was when she noticed Mrs. Yates staring at her, her eyes wide open and a tiny smile on her lips.

Had Mrs. Yates seen Tina and Vince almost . . . almost . . . Tina quickly veered her thoughts away from *almost*.

"Virginia Belle, you're awake." Melissa rounded the bed so she stood straight across from Tina, though she only looked at Mrs. Yates.

"Missy." Mrs. Yates smiled as she reached up to take Melissa's hand.

"How are you feeling?" Melissa's voice was so kind, so patient. Mrs. Yates responded well to it. Tina vowed to learn that exact tone. She realized then that she'd never fully relaxed her fist. Wiggling her fingers, she ignored Vince when he came up beside her, closer to Mrs. Yates's head.

"Julius, what are you doing home from work?" She'd forgotten her son again, mistaken him for her husband.

Tina couldn't stop herself from looking at Vince. Only a glance, but that was long enough to see the hurt in his expression. "I'm glad to see you awake, Moth . . . uh, Virginia Belle."

"I thought you were going to rest." Vince looked across the bed at Melissa, who'd washed up and changed clothes but still had dark circles under her eyes from exhaustion.

She gave him a helpless shrug. "I was, but . . . well, something's come up. I need to talk to you." Melissa's eyes went to Mrs. Yates, so this was not about witnessing Vince and Tina standing too close.

"I'll stay right here." Tina was glad for anything that got Vince away from her. "You two can have yourselves a talk."

"It won't take long." Missy headed for the door.

Tina sat down on the side of the bed. "Tell me about yourself, Mrs. Yates."

"Well, bless your sweet heart. I would like nothing better than a chat."

"Where did you grow up?"

"Daddy owned a cotton plantation, and Mama was the finest hostess in the South. When I was a little girl . . ." Mrs. Yates began talking about her childhood.

Melissa and Vince stepped close to the door. Tina couldn't hear Melissa's words, just an urgent murmur.

"What?" Vince shouted.

Mrs. Yates frowned and tried to look past Tina, who took her hand. "Go on, you said you were an only child?"

The furrow eased from Mrs. Yates's forehead. "I was, and oh, mercy, I was a spoiled little thing. Why, I had a pony with its own tiny carriage by the time I was—"

"How long ago?" Vince's voice had fallen, but it was still impossible to miss.

Melissa responded too quietly for Tina to hear, then Vince stalked out of the house.

Melissa came up to sit across from Tina. She had a sheen of tears in her eyes. Tina opened her mouth to ask what had happened.

Melissa met Tina's eyes and shook her head to stave off any inquiry. She then took Mrs. Yates's other hand and without comment listened to Mrs. Yates tell of her early life of privilege and ease in a gracious, gentle world built on the backs of an enslaved people. A world that was gone with the wind.

CHAPTER 11

Vince had never gotten along with his father. The man was a tyrant with never a kind word to say to Vince or his mother. There was no denying Julius Yates had a knack for making money, but he had no knack for inspiring love. Nor did he consider that a failing. There was no failing allowed in Father's world.

Which was why Vince had delighted in it. He'd gone to private schools and delighted in getting expelled. Father would rage at Vince, then get him into another exclusive school, and Vince would get himself tossed out of the new one. And so it was that a boy with all the financial advantages in the world grew up with almost no schooling. Later, when his mother's mother died and left him a fortune all his own that meant Vince never had to work a day in his life, it was even easier to defy Father.

But even with the antagonism between himself and his father, honestly the whole world and his father, Vince had never imagined this.

Father was gone.

He wasn't just gone from the diner or the boardinghouse. He was gone from Broken Wheel, and all his things had gone with him. The carriage he came in was gone too, along with the driver. He'd come halfway across the country just so he could dump his unwanted problems—namely his mad wife and his illegitimate daughter—on his trouble-maker son.

There was more.

Asa was moving out of the boardinghouse, and he was the one who gave Vince the news that Father had bought it and paid a ridiculous price for it. Asa showed Vince the bag of gold double eagle coins that made Asa one of the richest men in the territory. Although that wasn't saying that much, Asa was mighty pleased all the same.

"He said I had to move out, but that suits me. I'm sad-dling up my horse and going to Californy. My brother owns a farm out there, and he invited me once to come and stay with him. I never could see my way clear to show-ing up, hat in hand, with nothing to show for a lifetime of work."

Vince thought that was strange, since he'd never seen Asa do any real work.

Asa opened the heavy-looking cloth bag and held it out so Vince could see the gold coins. More money than Asa's boardinghouse was worth, ten times over. If the old codger was smart—and Vince had no reason to believe he was—Asa could live out a comfortable life with the contents of that cloth bag.

"Now I can go to my brother with some pride, and I aim to." Asa shook the bag and gave Vince a gap-toothed smile at the sound of the gold jingling.

Vince was too furious with his father to comment on the fact that Asa's "lifetime of work" was pretty much spent lazing around in a house he owned through squatter's rights. Even furious, he felt he had to warn the old man.

"Don't wave that gold around, Asa, or you'll never live to spend it." Vince knew plenty about what money could do to people. It'd had a real undesirable effect on his father. Vince sincerely hoped Asa survived to enjoy his newfound wealth. The fact that the man was braying about the gold and waving that bag around didn't make Vince optimistic.

"Your pa left money for you too, Vince. He told me to tell you it was your turn." Asa scratched his head thoughtfully. "I wonder what that means? Your turn for what?"

Vince knew very well what that meant. His turn to care for his mother and sister. Father had found both women embarrassing, and he'd moved the shame a long way into the wilderness.

He thought of his mother and how addled she was and how unkind Father was, and mixed in with the fury was a hint of relief that his mother was away from the old tyrant.

Vince turned to look at his humble room above his humble lawyer's office. Then he turned and could see Dare's house, with Mother in there. They'd already lost track of her once. And Melissa said two people had to watch Mother at all times.

Vince trudged toward the doctor's office, his mind a wrangle as he tried to imagine what he had ahead of him. It was a mighty good thing that being a lawyer never took a moment of his time.

He reached Dare's front steps just as Melissa came out. Vince stood facing his sister. She was part of that heap of wrangled-up thoughts. She was a living, breathing reminder of his father's unfaithfulness and the burden of being a big brother. But honestly he didn't even have time to ponder all that. Mother was taking up too much of his thinking time.

Melissa frowned. "He abandoned us. Left his wife and daughter and son without a backward glance."

"Oh, I reckon he looked backward," Vince said, picturing it in his mind, "just in case someone spotted him running off."

"All his problems solved in one easy jaunt."

Shaking his head, Vince said, "A one-thousand-mile, exhausting and expensive jaunt."

"When he told me we were going to see you, I never even suspected he had such a thing in mind, but he planned it from the first."

"How are we supposed to take care of someone who needs so much?" Vince really hoped she could tell him.

Melissa stomped down the steps fronting Dare's place. "In Chicago we had a staff of twelve people, each working a four-hour shift, so two people would be with her at all times. We tried six people doing eight-hour shifts, but it was hard to stay attentive for that long. I have no idea how we can duplicate that situation out here. Of course, there aren't busy streets with rushing horses and wagons. There aren't big buildings and thousands of bustling strangers."

Then Melissa looked at the wilderness that surrounded the town. "But there's that." She waved her arm at the rugged terrain. "Miles and miles of places to get lost, with rattlesnakes and cactuses all around . . ."

"Don't forget outlaws, cougars and buffalo, pits you can fall in, and avalanches that can rain huge stones down on your head." Vince shook his head. "I found a scorpion in my office just the other day."

"What's a scorpion?" Melissa had her hands twisted together as Vince listed some of the ways a person could die in the Texas desert.

"A big old poisonous bug-lizard thing. Likes to sting." Vince saw her flinch and was sorry he'd mentioned it.

"Well," Melissa said, "we need to—"

"Who's with her now?" Vince interrupted.

"Glynna and Dare are both in there with their children." Melissa squared her shoulders. "I'm not sure how much time you're willing to give to this, Vince, but I'll plan on staying with her as much as possible. I imagine there's nowhere else to go, anyway. We'll have to move her to Asa's boardinghouse."

"It's the Yateses' house now. Asa told me I own it." Vince glanced at the big two-story house built as if to block the south end of Main Street.

Melissa rolled her eyes. "Of course you do. Your father—"

"Our father," Vince reminded her.

Nodding, Melissa said, "Our father would see that as providing for everyone. He could just buy that house—no doubt he left a stack of gold coins behind—and then he could ride away without a twinge of remorse."

Melissa scowled at Vince for a long moment, and Vince let her because he was curious as to what she planned to say next.

"Just how much like your father are you?" she asked.

And there was a question that stung like a scorpion.

Jonas picked that moment to round the corner of Dare's house, coming from the parsonage. His canny dark eyes flicked between Vince and Melissa exactly once before he asked, "What happened?"

Vince liked to think he was pretty hard to read, but either he was so upset he couldn't keep that fact off his face, or Jonas was unusually sensitive. Which would be a good trait in a parson, yet it annoyed Vince to no end. On the other hand, there was no sense pretending what had happened hadn't. Maybe talking it out with Jonas was a good idea.

"My father left town," Vince began.

"For how long?"

Shaking his head at Jonas's innocence, Vince said, "I don't mean he left town for a while, like on a trip or for an errand. He left town *for good*. He's gone. He only came here to leave Mother and Melissa with me. He finds them both an embarrassment—me too, for that matter."

"You find your mother and Melissa an embarrassment?" Jonas sounded personally offended.

"No, Father throws me in with the two of them. The three of us are an embarrassment. I suspect he'll go on back to Chicago and tell all his business cronies I invited both of them to stay with me."

"He won't include me. I doubt anyone outside the house has ever heard of me." Melissa didn't seem to care overly.

"Probably not. I'd bet Mother is a forbidden topic, too. No one will even know she's gone. The big crisis will be if Father has gotten behind at work, but he'll soon catch up."

Jonas's eyes widened. "He left them both here?" They'd been talking quietly up until now. But now Jonas lost control of his voice. "Just up and abandoned his wife and daughter?"

"Shh!" Melissa looked over her shoulder at the closed door. "Yes," she said quietly. "No sense upsetting Virginia Belle with the news. If we're lucky, she may not even notice he's gone. And since she just recently moved out of the home she'd lived in most of her adult life—and that move confused her terribly—this change may not increase her addled state."

Vince looked again at the boardinghouse. "You said the new house was so big she couldn't begin to find her way around. Maybe a smaller house will help. She'll still have to learn it, but there isn't much to learn, honestly. Four rooms upstairs, four down. Twelve people, though. How in tarnation are we going to find twelve people to help us?"

"What do you need twelve people for?" Jonas really was behind.

"Mother can't be left alone. She wanders off."

"Tina and I will take a shift." Jonas was a good friend and quick to step in and help. But Vince wondered if maybe Jonas oughta ask his feisty little sister first.

"You mean Tina will help if she can find time between working at the diner and the saloon."

Melissa gasped and took a quick look at the white parson's collar Jonas wore. "Your sister works at the saloon?" She rested her hand on Jonas's wrist. "Is she a dance-hall girl? She seems a bit edgy. I can help you get her out of that life. If you want, I can—"

"I'm *not* a dance-hall girl, Melissa." Dare's front door closed with a solid thud.

Melissa flinched and turned around.

Tina had come out of Dare's house without anyone noticing. "And I am certainly not edgy." Tina plunked her little fists on her hips and glared at Vince's sister in the edgiest way imaginable. "And I don't expect to ever hear anyone say different."

Melissa took a quick step back and bumped into Jonas, who steadied her with a hand on her waist. Vince couldn't help noticing Jonas didn't move that hand. And then he still didn't move that hand.

"Of course you're not," Melissa said to Tina, sounding pretty scared. "That's just my . . . my upset at Vince's father running off affecting my thinking."

"Vince's father ran off?" Tina screeched. Again, a bit edgy.

Vince found he liked the distraction. "Yep."

Dare stepped outside. "Quiet down. Virginia Belle is sleeping."

Jonas still hadn't moved his hand.

It made Vince think about how he'd almost kissed Tina, and how much Jonas would have to say about that. Well, Jonas could just get his hand off Vince's sister.

Glynna was right behind Dare. "Vince's father ran off?"

Vince rubbed his eyes, hoping his vision had failed him and he'd look up and see Father, right back here, ready to get his wife and daughter and head for home.

"Since we're all here, we need to discuss how we're going to manage caring for Virginia Belle." Melissa had a lot of the Yateses' take-charge skills that Vince saw in his father and himself.

"Tina, Jonas offered your services."

"That's when I said you worked at the diner and the saloon." Vince smiled at Tina, enjoying her stormy expression.

"I *picket* the saloon," Tina said, then glared at him with her pretty blue eyes. "I'm trying to get the place closed. That's a far sight from working there. And I'd be glad to help care for Mrs. Yates."

That the stubborn little thing offered without a moment's hesitation warmed Vince's heart, and that was good because his heart was currently ice-cold.

"Thank you. And I apologize for my earlier comment. Vince and I will certainly have to help." Melissa said it almost like she expected him to say he wasn't going to.

She probably really did suspect Vince was like Father. And it was a good bet Father never once took a turn caring for his wife. Julius Yates had a lot of money, and he used it to make problems go away.

Jonas still hadn't moved his hand.

For some reason that bothered Vince, and considering all he had right now to be bothered with, that was just stupid. Still, he didn't need any more aggravation, so he moved to the side, so Jonas was on his left, and took hold of Melissa and dragged her across in front of him until she was on his right.

She gave him a startled look but didn't punch him in the nose, so Vince figured she was fine.

Dare said, "Here's what we're gonna do."

Since Dare was a doctor, Vince decided to let him talk.

"We'll do some work on Asa's place."

"You mean the Yateses' house?" Vince couldn't keep the sarcasm out of his voice.

Ignoring him, Dare went on, "Asa doesn't even have a lock on the front door. We need to get one on the front and back. Those are the only doors I know of. Vince, I want you to go over the place carefully. Is there a cellar? If so, is there a way out of it?"

Vince was nodding. He usually took charge, but it was nice having someone else do it for a change. He was too upset at the moment to do much hard thinking.

"That's not good enough." Melissa was the expert, after all. "She'll still find a way to—"

"Let me finish," Dare cut her off. "You're thinking of that big mansion in Chicago. A house with so many doors and rooms and ways in and out, it was impossible to keep track of her without having your eyes right on her. Asa's place isn't like that. We need to do some work on the windows so your ma doesn't slip out that way. Asa doesn't have shutters. We can add them so your ma can't break a locked window and get out. But once we do that, your ma oughta be reasonably safe."

"It sounds like you're building a prison." Vince's stomach twisted as he thought of the time he'd spent locked up.

"It's for her own safety, Vince." Jonas slapped Vince on the back. "Any resemblance to Andersonville will be in your own head."

Dread twisted his stomach at the mention of Andersonville.

"The way I see it, your ma is going to have a lot more freedom and privacy than she had in Chicago. She can have free rein inside the house. Sleep alone at night. We'll lock the door to her bedroom at night and have someone sleeping on either side of her, but during the day we're not going to stand guard over her, not inside. We'll make sure she can only get outside when one of us is with her." Dare tipped his head, looking at Melissa.

Melissa gave a weak smile. "Maybe she can learn the house and not feel so disoriented."

"This isn't your job, though, Dare." Vince looked at Dare Riker, possibly his best friend in the world. And right there beside him, Jonas Cahill, the man Vince respected more than any other. Both men willing to give up any sort of normal life to help him out. "I can't let you do this."

Dare snorted. "I seem to recall you standing outside my house, keeping watch in the cold for weeks because someone was trying to kill me."

"Well, yeah, but—"

"And I remember," Glynna interjected, "you running into an avalanche to save me and Dare." Glynna reached out a hand and clasped Dare's.

Vince saw a look so full of love pass between them that he was glad all the way to his soul that he'd helped them find a life together.

"And you're providing me with a home," Melissa said, giving him a sad sort of smile.

"I don't mind doing that, little sister." Vince was finding that discovering he had a sister wasn't bothering him all that much, after all. Jonas seemed to be taking to it, too.

"I remember you taking a bullet to the head for Luke when Greer stole his ranch," Dare added.

"Don't anyone say anything about this to Luke," Vince said quickly. "He doesn't need to start riding all the way into town to take a shift."

"And in Andersonville," Jonas said, "I remember you stepping between me and a thrown fist too many times. You made a joke out of it. Said a man who wanted to be a preacher hadn't oughta get into fights."

Tina made a small sound, and Vince turned to her, wondering what she was going to say that made it right for her to spend so many hours looking after his mother. He'd never done much besides torment her, and she'd deserved every bit of it.

She rolled her eyes at him and gave him a smirk. "I'm sure if I'd been around longer, you'd've ended up doing something special for me eventually."

Vince was sorely tempted to do something special for her right then, like drag her into his arms and see how her smile tasted.

"Spending time in a comfortable house with your sweet, if slightly addled, ma isn't even close to paying you back." Dare pulled Vince's thoughts away from recklessness.

Jonas spoke in his strong, wise voice. "When I say 'there is a friend who is closer than a brother,' I mean that about all the Regulators. But none more than you, Vince."

"Regulators? What're they?" Melissa asked.

"We met in Andersonville, a Confederate prison camp." Vince found that after the time they'd spent here in Broken Wheel, it was easier to talk about those days. "We fought for the Yankees and were all prisoners of war. It was the meanest, cruelest, darkest place on earth. And we, along with others, got the job of bringing law and order to thousands of starving men, who'd been reduced to near animals from all the deprivation. There were bad men there who didn't want anyone bringing peace. And there were good men there who thought when we punished the bad, we were taking sides with the Reb guards. Those good men considered us traitors to the Union."

"I had a man drive a knife into my back once and claim he was serving God by ridding the world of a pack of living, breathing Benedict Arnolds. Treasonous turncoats." Dare squeezed Glynna's hand harder. "Vince dragged that man off of me before he could strike again, knocked him

144

cold, then pulled the knife out of my back and staunched the bleeding."

"That kind of anger focused on us from so many directions created a bond closer than brothers." Jonas leaned forward to talk to Melissa across Vince's body. "That's what I'm talking about. We learned to depend completely on each other, and that trust has served us well even now, long after the last shot was fired in the war."

Jonas looked at Melissa a bit too long, then turned to Vince. "So, I'd say I can sit with your ma for a few hours a day and not feel put upon."

Vince wanted to protest. He didn't mind helping others, but it wasn't right when they helped him back. He had money. He'd been privileged all his life. They had families and serious responsibilities, like being a parson and doctoring the folks hereabouts. He did more or less nothing. Which reminded him he oughta check in on Lana Bullard here pretty soon.

Jonas patted him on the shoulder. "One or two of us will always be around. We'll figure it out."

Vince nodded silently. He was a little choked up from his friends offering so much help. It had been a while since he'd seen Mother, but right now if he went in there and she didn't recognize him, or worse, called him Julius, he wasn't sure he could bear it.

He took the coward's way out. "I'll see if Tug Andrews has a couple of locks for the doors, and if he doesn't, I'll see if Sledge Murphy can rig something. A blacksmith oughta be able to come up with a latch of some kind. If he can't figure it out, I'll order 'em." Vince wanted to get a few steps away from his friends until he could get ahold of himself.

Jonas stepped away almost as if he knew Vince needed some time and space. Jonas was wise like that. Then it appeared Jonas reconsidered because a warm hand rested on Vince's shoulder. He looked down, surprised to see it wasn't Jonas. It was Tina. She wasn't so wise. But he looked in her eyes and saw nothing but kindness.

"We'll stay with your ma until you're ready to move her," she offered.

Vince broke the eye contact before he did something stupid. "I'll be quick," he said, then hurried away. Honestly, he as good as ran.

By the time he got to the general store, he had ahold of himself. Tug Andrews wasn't a lot of help. His suggestions amounted to either chaining the door shut or clapping a ball and chain around Mother's leg. What it amounted to was Tug had some chain to sell and thought he saw a buyer.

Sledge was more help. He agreed to rig a hook for the windows first thing tomorrow—a big job, as there were a lot of windows. He said he'd do that and afterward start building wooden shutters. At Sledge's suggestion, Vince found two men in town who had locks on the doors of their houses, who agreed to swap their doorknobs with those without locks. That took care of the front and back doors of the Yates house.

CHAPTER 12

Between working on his new house and keeping an eye on Lana Bullard, his prisoner, Vince managed to stay away from his mother the whole next day—and he knew without a doubt he wasn't hurrying to see her. The plain truth was he was hiding, delaying the moment he had to take over the care of his mother.

Dare came in to help with the house, but Vince ran him off.

Porter pestered him about letting Lana out, and Vince took some pleasure in thwarting the man.

Glynna came over to the boardinghouse bearing his dinner. It was tasty, but Vince didn't insult her by asking who had cooked it. They both knew it didn't even need to be said that it wasn't her.

Jonas stopped by a couple of times to try to get to the bottom of what was eating Vince. Or at least to try and cheer him up.

Melissa showed up at the house to unpack and get the room ready for Mother. She at least was nice enough, or uncomfortable enough, to ignore him.

Vince just worked harder.

As he carefully adjusted the last of the hooks, which

Sledge had made in a clever way so they weren't easily un-done, Vince knew he was dragging his heels about fetching Mother. He berated himself for his cowardice even as he tinkered with the window latch in the room that would be Mother's. He was stirred up inside. Furious at Father. Hurt by Mother. Startled by his brand-spankin'-new sister. Honored by his friends' generosity. Confused and enticed by Tina. A creaking floorboard told him someone was here. Probably Jonas trying one more time to get Vince to bare his soul, share his pain, open all his festering wounds.

Vince wasn't gonna let that happen.

Bracing himself to politely send Jonas away, Vince turned around to face . . . trouble.

"Do you need anything, Vince?" Tina stepped into the room. That same kindness on her face that had been there earlier. He couldn't keep away from her when she was picking at him. How was he supposed to resist when she was being so sweet? He closed the distance between them and faced her with only inches separating them.

"I can think of just one thing I need from you," Vince snapped, wishing she'd run. Protect herself from what he had in mind. Wishing he wasn't so stirred up that he couldn't stop himself from doing something stupid.

Instead she rested one hand on his upper arm. "What is it? You know I'll do whatever it takes to make this work."

"This? Make *this* work? There's a word that could mean anything."

From Tina's furrowed brow, Vince knew sure as certain she didn't mean it the way he wanted her to.

Her touch set off a shudder of longing that shook loose the last of his self-control. His thoughts ran wild to that first moment he'd seen her. One good look and he'd walked faster, intending to drag her right out of Jonas's grip. Then he'd tripped over the steps, which had slowed him down.

By the time he was standing again, moving forward again, she'd burst into tears. That had blown those wild thoughts out of Vince's head with the force of a Texas cyclone.

Vince had gotten himself and his unruly thoughts under control. A couple of times since then, he'd almost lost his grip on sanity. But each time he'd gotten a handle on the turmoil inside him. Each time it'd been harder, but he'd won.

This time he lost.

He grabbed Tina around the waist, hoping she'd slap him and run. Hoping she'd be smart enough for the both of them.

Instead she blinked those pretty blue-bonnet eyes at him, and a little gasp shaped her lips into a perfect little pucker—almost like she did mean it the way he wanted her to.

He wanted someone to hold, someone who was truly his. No, not just someone—*her*. And he was through pretending he didn't. He did what he'd wanted to do ever since he'd seen the prettiest woman on earth held in his good friend Jonas's arms. He lowered his head while he lifted the little pest to her tiptoes and took a good long taste of that sassy mouth.

Holding her, kissing her was like finding a resting place. A resting place in the center of a cyclone. The swirling madness of his worries was pushed aside.

⁂

Tina's knees buckled as she wrapped her arms around Vince's neck to keep from melting into a puddle on the floor. She might've been able to resist him if she hadn't seen the hurt when his ma didn't know his name.

And his vulnerable pleasure when she did.

It'd touched a raw place in Tina's heart, for she who had no memories of a mother or father. Only starchy, critical, cold Aunt Iphigenia.

Vince, always so confident, so take-charge, seemed wounded . . . just like Tina. Even knowing it was a dreadful idea, she'd wanted him to kiss her for a long time. Before, when they'd come close, there were good reasons why they'd stopped. But right now, she couldn't think of a single one of them.

Vince eased back, and Tina made a quiet sound of protest. His hands came up to her shoulders, and he held her away from him—not far away, just enough that he could look her in the eyes. That look held. It stretched between them like a lasso dropping expertly and tying her. To him. His look reached her heart and bound it tight.

Then, like ripping flesh, he tore his eyes away.

It hurt more than Tina could believe.

"I'm going to say this once, then never again." Vince, who was bold, quick to smile in the teeth of danger, always in charge and always on guard, couldn't meet her eyes. "You saw my mother."

"What does your ma have to do with anything?"

Vince finally looked up. She saw longing in his eyes. Except there was a place in her so lonely to be held, so desperate to be loved, that she wondered if she was imagining it.

When Jonas had hugged her, when she'd first come to Broken Wheel, it had been almost painful. Jonas lifting her up and whirling her around, smiling, welcoming her

150

had been a rain shower in the parched, cracked, isolated desert of Tina's life.

That love and touch from her brother had filled an empty well in Tina's heart. But Vince was different. She'd never known anything of romantic love. She'd given it little thought.

Now she knew what it was like to be held and kissed. It was wonderful. She wanted more of it so badly that she couldn't trust herself to speak, afraid she might start to beg.

"My mother's a madwoman, and the daughter of a madman. And my father's a tyrant. Whichever one of them I am, no woman should tie herself to me. I'm never going to inflict myself on a woman and most certainly not on a child."

That made her want to strangle Vince Yates, but she was afraid if she got close enough, instead of wrapping her hands around his throat, she might wrap her arms around his neck instead and pull his head down to kiss her again.

"Fine." Her voice was low and breathy. She cleared her throat. "We'll pretend that didn't happen then."

Shaking her head, she tried to remember why in the world she'd come over here. "Dare said we need to . . . to . . . that is, she's . . ." Tina steadied herself and went on. "He thinks it's time to move your mother here." Tina rubbed the back of her neck. "I'll go back to Dare's and walk Virginia Belle over."

"Tina, we need to . . ." Vince made some motion with his hand as if he meant to reach for her. Tina wasn't sure which was worse: that he reached or that he checked the motion.

"I'll be right back with your mother." Tina spun around and ran down the stairs. She knew that whatever he was going to say would amount to an apology.

Sorry I kissed you. Sorry I held you. Sorry I had a weak moment and wanted to be near you.

To be kissed, to be held, to be wanted were things Tina had never known in her life, until recently with Jonas. For Vince to apologize for offered affection, then snatch it back made her feel worthless.

She knew she'd had a strange upbringing with her chilly, taciturn aunt and a home that didn't welcome friends. But she discovered in herself as she hurried along that it was easy to believe the reason no one had loved her all those years growing up was because she was unlovable. She hadn't given it much thought before. She'd thrown herself into the cause of shutting down the saloon, proud of the fact that she was disliked. She called it persecution and embraced it. But now this hollow place inside her seemed to cry out that no one would ever love her, that no one could.

As she rushed across the cold dirt that stretched between Vince's and Dare's, she heard the door behind her open and close. Vince was coming, but he wasn't rushing to catch up. In fact, he was moving slow, making sure to keep plenty of space between them.

That was wise of him. She promised herself she'd be just as wise.

She'd enjoy caring for her brother, whom she'd as good as forced herself on—and he was too kind to throw her out. She'd pursue justice for Lana Bullard. She'd battle demon rum.

And she'd do it all with her heart tucked safely away.

❧

Vince didn't know if he was going to get his mother or chase after Tina. Both were probably a bad idea.

Tina got inside Dare's house ahead of him and shut the door rather sharply. Sharp enough to stab a man, in fact.

Vince came in a few seconds later and came face-to-face with Mother, dressed, her hand on Melissa's arm, her coat on, obviously ready to head for home.

Mother smiled. "Julius, darlin', I declare I've never seen you get home before the sun sets."

The little foxhound stood at Mother's heel, its tail wagging, watching his mistress's every move.

Vince forced a smile, even while he thought that his father wouldn't have smiled, so Mother wouldn't expect it. "I came to walk you to . . . to . . ." Vince was stumped. He couldn't help taking a quick look at Tina, who met his eyes and then quickly looked away.

Not that he blamed her.

Dare broke up Vince's irritation when he came up and said, "Your mother's ready to go, Vince. She's going to be fine." He turned to his patient and spoke sternly, "You must not go outside alone. It's dangerous." In a kinder but still bossy tone, he added, "Now you mind me, Virginia Belle. I'm your doctor and you must do as I say."

Mother gave Dare such serious attention that Vince hoped somehow Dare had gotten through to her and she'd remember what he told her and behave as he asked.

A man could dream. "Are you ready to go?" Vince asked.

His mother, the woman he'd loved so desperately, the woman who'd taught him to do almost anything to stave off her tears, smiled her bright, beautiful, confused smile, and nodded.

"Let's go, then." He began moving toward the door.

Melissa gently helped Mother forward.

Vince decided to let Melissa lead Mother out ahead of him, the dog at their heels. He glanced back at Dare and said, "Thank you."

Dare nodded. "Good luck. Come get me if you need help in the night."

"Or me," Glynna offered. "I'd be glad to sit with her."

Vince took a quick peek at Tina.

"Jonas and I will be glad to help, too." She said it, but somehow her words sounded like a warning. She might as well have said, Don't you dare come near me, you big kiss-stealing oaf.

And that was exactly how Vince wanted it. He nodded and left to follow Mother home.

Vince let Melissa and Mother go upstairs together. He waited downstairs until Melissa opened the door and looked down over the railing.

"You can come up now." Melissa went back in.

Vince climbed the stairs and went to Mother's room and knocked on the door.

"Come in," Melissa said.

Vince went in to find Mother in her nightgown, her hair down and braided. Melissa might pass as a lady's maid, but to Vince it seemed like someone putting a child to bed.

"I've come to say good-night, Mother."

Mother looked nervously around the room. "Aren't we leaving, Julius? Why would we sleep in this place?"

Vince just didn't know how to handle this. Was he to

154

pretend to be his father? Did he have to spend the rest of his life being taken for Julius Yates? That was Vince's own idea of hell. He didn't know what was best for Mother, so he just tried to be honest.

"It's me, Mother. It's Vince. Your son Vince. This is my house. You're staying with me now, and this is your new home." Bought and paid for by Father. And Vince had found such a generous amount of gold coins that Judas Iscariot would have been green with envy.

Mother's delicate brows lowered. "Vince? My son Vince?" She wrung her hands together in agitation. Her voice rose. "Julius, what do you mean by that?"

Vince exchanged a glance with Melissa, who stood quietly beside Mother. Melissa turned to her charge. "It's time to get to bed now, Virginia Belle. It's been a very long day. You must be exhausted."

"Well, bless your heart, Missy." Mother spoke to Melissa as if she'd never been worried by Vince, as if he weren't in fact still in the room. "You are such a sweet thing. Yes, I am so tired. I believe I will turn in."

"Good night." Vince stifled the urge to add *Mother*. He needed to give this time. He'd find his way through this mess somehow. He'd bought a lot of books. He'd read them all to find out how to get Mother to come to her senses.

Melissa had been dealing with this for a while. He needed to talk to her, see what advice she had.

"Good night, Julius dear." Mother reclined.

"I'll just sit with you awhile." Melissa drew the covers up and tucked Mother in as gently as she would a child. Melissa looked at Vince and whispered, "I'll stay until she's asleep, and make sure the door is secure when I leave."

Nodding, Vince stepped back out and pulled the door shut, wondering how he was going to manage. Wondering why it felt so wrong to lock Mother in a room overnight.

He'd been assigned the room to the west of Mother's. Melissa was on the east. They had her surrounded. He went in and got ready for bed.

Then he lay awake, so mixed up he was afraid his thoughts would churn all night. But his exhaustion caught up with him and he was asleep in minutes.

And dreaming of becoming his father.

Of being hunted by a pack of slavering hounds.

Of kissing a blue-eyed picketer.

Two of those dreams were nightmares. The last one was bliss. And that might be the biggest nightmare of all.

Chapter 13

Vince was in the middle of the sweetest dream of his life when the pounding started. He jerked awake.

"Vince, get out here!"

Vince was on his feet, his pants on, dragging his shirt on before Luke's fist hit the door for the fifth time, and his friend was pounding hard, so that was saying something.

"What? Is Mother missing?" That was all Vince could think of. Well, that and Tina Cahill, but unless it was Jonas, come to shoot Vince for kissing his sister, there was no reason for door pounding.

Luke stood, chest heaving, furious. "Get dressed and get out here. This is business for the town sheriff."

Vince had forgotten he had that job. "I'm coming."

The door next to Vince's rattled. "Julius, why is this door locked?"

Mother's sweet Southern voice sounded frightened. Melissa came out wrapped in a dressing gown. She took one look at Luke, squeaked, and darted back into her room.

"I'll mind your mother, Vince," Melissa called from her room. "Can you and your friend please leave? I'm not decent and I need to see to her. I dare not wait until I get dressed."

Mother shook the door. "Someone help me!" Her voice broke, and through tears she cried, "Someone get me out of here."

Vince would rather take a beating than listen to his mother cry. Nope, Melissa didn't dare wait. "Yes, we're going."

"Sorry, miss," Luke said. "I'll wait outside." He sped down the stairs.

Feeling like a coward, Vince darted into his room. He grabbed his boots and gun and coat and anything else he thought he might need, while Mother wept and Melissa fumbled with the key to Mother's door.

Vince was right behind Luke. He stopped at the front door to pull on his boots, then hollered up to Melissa, "The house will be empty now. Do you need help? I could send Dare over."

"No, just go. I'll be fine on my own."

"Glynna's going to send breakfast over, so you don't need to go out." With that, Vince stepped outside and faced his furious friend. Vince did a quick search of his brain and knew that, though Luke had a sister, she lived far away in Colorado and was married, and Vince hadn't done a thing to offend her.

"Dare's waiting at his house."

Vince stopped short. "I've got to see to Lana. Stoke the fire, get her some breakfast."

"Dare already did both of those. He filled me in on your ma and your move to Asa's. Dare's got coffee brewing at his place." Luke strode away, not waiting for Vince to say yes, no, or maybe.

"What's going on?" Vince buttoned up his shirt while he walked and hooked on his gun belt. He didn't bother pulling on his coat, even though the morning air was sharp. They'd be inside again about the time he got it on. He'd lace up his boots once he could quit jogging to keep up with Luke.

"I'm only telling this one time." Luke picked up the pace and jerked Dare's door open without knocking. Glynna wasn't there, nor were her children. No Tina.

They were all busy running the diner. No one to help Melissa with Mother.

"Did you bring your wife along?" Ruthy didn't like being left behind.

"She's in the diner. I hope she's not helping cook. We didn't get much sleep the last two nights, and I don't like seeing her get worn out in her condition."

"Glynna convinced Ruthy to go abovestairs at the diner." Dare gestured them in, then went into his kitchen. "Come on back. I've got coffee ready."

Jonas was already there.

Dare shoved a cup into Luke's hands. "Ruthy hasn't come back down. Glynna checked on her and she's asleep. Ruthy must've been plumb tuckered out."

"Thanks." Luke settled into a chair. "Glad to hear Ruthy's resting. Doubt it'll last long."

Dare poured coffee, then handed a tin cup to Vince. "I got Lana's breakfast, too."

"Thanks, Dare." Vince took a long sip of the coffee, hoping it would get his brain started.

"Tell us what happened, Luke." Vince set his cup aside and crouched to tie his boots.

Dare paced. Jonas sat down and held his cup in two hands, drawing the heat from it.

Luke tipped his chair onto its back legs. "Someone took a shot at me two nights ago."

Vince finished with his boots, rose from his crouch, retrieved his coffee, and took up a position by the door. Mostly there wasn't a thing to watch for. Broken Wheel had gotten purely peaceable lately, not counting mothers who were tetched in the head and runaway fathers and unexpected full-grown sisters and pretty little spitfire neighbors.

But there hadn't been much shootin' trouble for quite a while. Until now. Vince looked at Luke. The man looked as grim as the Reaper.

Not purely peaceable anymore.

"Who was it?" Dare quit pacing to pay attention, though he never stood still for long.

"One of my hired men said he saw an Indian," Luke began.

The coffee steamed in Vince's cup, but he felt so cold that none of the warmth reached his insides. He knew Luke considered some of the Kiowa people as personal friends, and he'd never had much trouble with them. No one wanted that to change.

"He might be tellin' the truth," Luke continued, "but he has reason to lie, too. Whoever did it, those gunshots could've hit Ruthy. They came within inches of hitting me and Dodger. I've got to get to the bottom of it and quick. I spent yesterday tracking, figured I could get to the truth myself, but now I'm asking for help."

"We'll help." As he said it, Vince thought of Mother.

How could he help Luke when his life was chock-full of problems already?

Luke had probably barely heard that Vince's life had gotten so complicated, and he wasn't paying much attention right now. Luke surged to his feet, strode out of the room, and returned with a burlap bag. The bag made a sharp clinking sound.

"After my cowhand told me he saw an Indian, I went tracking. I found what might be a boot track in one spot. It's rocky, and not much sign is left of a man passing through on foot, even less if that man was wearing moccasins. I just can't be sure of what I saw. There was definitely someone out there, but then I knew that from the bullets. What trail I could pick up led me to a small canyon where I found this." Luke upended the bag, dumped its contents onto the floor. Whiskey bottles tumbled out. Too many to count at a glance.

Jonas set his coffee cup down on the table and leaned forward to take a look.

Frowning, Vince stared at the bottles. "Some are caked with old dirt. Whoever dropped them out there has been drinking for a while."

"Yep, and if it's one of my men, he's been drinking steady while he's working my cattle and riding my horses. He's going around armed doing dangerous chores, and he's supposed to be ready for trouble."

"No man who's a steady drinker can say he's thinking right." Dare stopped pacing and crouched down beside the bottles. He picked them up and studied them.

"Which might explain a gun going off accidentally, or a man taking a shot at a house without considering why that was a mighty bad idea." Luke sat back down and took a long swallow of his coffee.

It occurred to Vince that a lawman ought to be studying the evidence, so he left his position by the door and came up to look at the bottles.

Vince knew his friend Luke real well. He took a deep breath, thinking to learn all he could from a man who could read sign like the written word.

At that moment the door swung open in the other room, and Janny, Dare's eight-year-old stepdaughter, came running in. She skidded to a stop in the kitchen doorway. "I took breakfast over to Missy and Vince's ma. There's trouble. Not serious, but Missy asked if someone could come lend a hand."

Vince wheeled to head out.

"Wait." Jonas's voice stopped Vince in his tracks.

Vince turned impatiently and saw those bottles again. He needed to go to his mother. He needed to help his friend.

"I'll go." Jonas rose from the table and went for the back door, so Vince didn't even have to get out of the way. "Luke's trouble is a job for a lawman. I can be of more help with your ma, Vince. I'll come a-runnin' if it's something I can't handle."

The door opened and closed so fast that Vince didn't have time to stop Jonas. Caring for Mother was Vince's responsibility. But for now, Vince turned back to Luke.

"Dare said your ma came to Texas, Vince, and that she's not well. I'm sorry to bother you right now while she's visiting. I don't think this can wait, but I'll understand if you don't—"

"Waiting won't help. Mother's not here for a visit; she's

162

here to stay. I'll help unless Jonas comes for me. But he oughta be able to do whatever Melissa needs."

"Who's Melissa?" Luke paused from scowling at the bottles.

"She's my sister."

"You have a sister?"

"She's an adult woman, and the first I ever heard of her was two days ago. My father had a child he kept hidden, but he brought her along on his trip to see me."

"Your pa's here, too?"

"Nope, he's long gone now. He dropped Mother and Melissa off, waited until we weren't looking and took off." Vince decided maybe Luke didn't want to think about his own problems, so he was questioning Vince about his. He explained quickly what had happened.

Luke immediately jumped in to offer his help. "Ruthy and I can come in and see to your ma if you need us. All you've gotta do is ask. I won't soon forget you took a bullet for me fighting to get my ranch back."

"All I remember about that fight is I let myself get bushwhacked and wasn't there to help you in the final fight."

Luke gave a humorless laugh. "Not surprised you'd see getting shot as a failure to your friends. You ask a lot of yourself, Vince. Just remember I'd be proud to help out, and you know Ruthy. She'll probably be in here organizing things. I doubt I can stop her." Luke smiled, but the smile didn't last. "She might be safer in town until I get to the bottom of who's behind this shooting out at my place."

That turned Vince's attention back to why Luke had

come. Vince could be his usual calm-in-the-face-of-trouble self when it was someone else with the problem.

"It's unlikely that whiskey came from somewhere other than here in Broken Wheel." Vince's head cleared from his family woes as he thought about how to track down whoever had fired the shots at Luke's place.

"Duffy sells it," Luke said. "That's the only place in town you can get a drink."

"It's gotta have come from his saloon." Vince straightened and set his empty coffee cup down on Dare's kitchen table with a sharp click. "Let's go talk to Duffy. We'll get a list of every man who buys whiskey by the bottle. Then we'll have a long talk with each of them."

"Shouldn't take long," Dare said. "It might not even be a list. Not too many hombres around here who buy this much whiskey. They're a lot more likely to have a drink or two in the saloon and have done with it."

Vince gave a nod at the empty bottles. "Bag 'em up and bring 'em along."

Glass clinked as Luke put the bottles back in the sack.

"Duffy stays at the diner as long as possible," Vince said, leading the way out of Dare's house, "but he oughta be done with breakfast by now and be alone. Not much business at the saloon in the morning hours. I'd as soon not have this talk in front of a crowd, especially if someone there's got something to hide."

The three of them trooped out of the house and went around the row of buildings. That row on the east side of Main Street had the diner at the far south end, an empty shop, the general store, and Duffy's Tavern. There was a matching row of buildings straight across on the west side that had five small buildings with shared walls, except for a thin alley midway down the row. An empty building anchored the north side. Then came the jailhouse, two more empty buildings separated by an alley, then Vince's law office. There was a small bedroom upstairs, which had been his home in the months since he'd come to town to back Luke in his fight.

Now he had possession of the law office and the former boardinghouse. If you added in that he was the sheriff with the only set of keys to the jail, Vince figured he was the biggest landholder in town. Not sayin' much.

Those buildings were about all Broken Wheel amounted to. The blacksmith had a big barn on the north end of town, set at an angle. The burned remnants of Dare's old house sat straight across from the smithy.

There were scattered buildings behind the row of businesses on the east side, including the church, Jonas's house, Dare's, the house Duffy and Griss shared, and about a dozen others. The men who lived in them were trappers and hunters mostly, those who'd found a reason to live way out in the middle of nowhere.

Broken Wheel was in Indian Territory. There was almost no law here. Vince being sheriff for no pay and against his will was proof of that. And the folks who came and stayed were a scruffy, disreputable lot—barely civilized, most of them. Vince liked to think that his Regulator friends were the exception, but it sounded like Luke's father was an old curmudgeon who fit in pretty well in this wild land. And because his pa had liked it here, Luke ended up out here, and that had brought Vince and his friends.

Indian Territory . . . had one of Luke's hands really seen one of the native folks running from the shooting?

True or not, Luke had himself a problem, and there was no choice but that Vince would try to help him. Except Vince had so much trouble already that he honestly wondered if he could fit another crisis into his life.

CHAPTER 14

Tina was doing her best to feed her morning herd and keep up with all that was going on in town at the same time. And considering her only view was out the back window of the diner, she was doing pretty well.

She'd been the one to send Janny off to deliver breakfast to Mrs. Yates. She'd seen Janny come running, empty-handed, from the boardinghouse and head straight for Dare's. She'd sprinted past the window in Glynna's kitchen, gone into the home where she now lived with her new pa, Dare, then come right back out and returned to the diner. Glynna's little daughter reported that Melissa had asked for help and Jonas had volunteered.

Tina saw Jonas striding toward the house the Yates family had just moved into. She wondered if her brother was taking a shift watching Mrs. Yates, or was something else going on? Janny didn't have any answers.

Tina was too busy to think about it during the breakfast rush, but she had a good view of the stretch between Dare's house and Vince's. She never saw Jonas return and she began to worry something had happened that required a parson's care.

It wasn't much later that Vince, Dare, and Luke came out of Dare's place and moved away from Vince's house. They seemed to be heading for the north side of town. Maybe they were coming over for coffee and cobbler. Tina glanced at the pan left over from breakfast and was glad she had it to offer. She was also glad she'd been at this cooking business for a few months so she didn't have to pay much attention to it. She could spend her time instead puzzling over what was going on.

It was far more interesting than cooking.

Vince swung open the batwing doors of the saloon. Stepping in, he was hit by the stench. Old whiskey, heavy tobacco, no interest in scrubbing. Those were all reason enough not to visit this saloon, though it was his not being a drinker that always kept him away.

Duffy Schuster stood behind the bar, leaning on his elbows, talking with his brother. Those two were a big part of the smell. It wasn't just the floors that didn't get scrubbed in this place. In fact, there were still smudges of mud on Duffy's neck left from Tina's picketing mud fight. Duffy needed to be careful or something might grow in all that dirt.

Duffy straightened. Griss turned, leaning on one elbow as he watched Vince come in with Dare and Luke a step behind. None of them were customers, so Duffy knew there was another reason for the visit.

The familiar *whap-whap* of swinging doors told Vince his friends were now inside.

"Coffee on the stove, men. Pour yourself a cup if you've

a mind. No charge." Duffy was none too bright. Vince had always figured the man was doing good to keep his saloon in operation. But it took cunning to find an Indian tribe and then contract with them without getting into trouble. For many an Indian brave would fight to prevent the encroachment of firewater into his tribe. So maybe Vince had underestimated Duffy.

The man's dull look and heavy Texas twang might be covering a sharp mind. Or maybe Duffy wasn't selling liquor illegally, and someone had staged the trouble at Luke's the other night to point at the native folks.

Vince glanced back at Luke, who carried the gunnysack of empty bottles. "We'd like to know if these came from your saloon." Luke upended the bag, this time with a lot less care than he'd shown at Dare's house, and a few of the bottles shattered when they fell to the floor. "And if this whiskey came from here, I want to know who bought it from you."

Duffy looked from the mess on his floor to the anger in Luke's eyes and got very quiet. He came around and bent down beside the bottles. Plenty of them were still unbroken, so the man could see they were the same brand of whiskey that stood in bottles behind the bar.

Shaking his head, Duffy said, "Hardly no one takes a full bottle out of here, let alone this many." Duffy rose to face Luke head-on.

"Only someone did, Duffy," Luke said, defiant. "I found these on my land, and I had a hail of bullets fired at my house the other day that barely missed me and my wife. I followed a trail to the bottles, all of 'em empty, and no one around here deals in this devil's brew but you."

Duffy's eyes seemed to look past Luke, as if he were straining his brain to remember. "Looky here, Stone. I'm telling you, I don't do that big a business in here. You can check with the mule skinner who brought in the last load of supplies. He'll tell you he unloaded a case of bottles, nine in all. I've still got four of 'em under my bar. And that was going on two weeks ago, before New Year's Eve night, and I served a heap of that case of whiskey then. One drink at a time."

Luke scowled at Duffy, who took a nervous step back. Luke was whipcord lean, with the muscles of a Texas rancher who spent all day wrangling cattle that outweighed him by a thousand pounds. And he was as hard as the land he fought to wrest out a living. It spoke well of Duffy's common sense that he was scared.

Dare strode over to the bar, and the sudden movement made Griss straighten. As Dare went around back, Vince noted that neither man wore a gun, though it was well known that Duffy kept a shotgun on a couple of hooks under the bar.

Reaching down, Dare pulled up four still-corked bottles, holding them by the necks, two in each hand. He set them on the bar with a loud *clunk*, then brought up a fifth bottle that was half full.

"And I've got the empties for the other four bottles on the lower shelf," Duffy said. He acted like Dare was producing proof positive of his innocence by finding those bottles. "You see—all my order is accounted for."

"The empties are down here, sure enough," Dare said. "But just because these bottles are here doesn't mean you

170

didn't buy more and sell 'em to someone. The word of a saloonkeeper isn't worth much."

"There's no reason to go and talk that way about us," Griss cut in. "We've always done an honest business here in Broken Wheel, and no one can say we don't sell good liquor for a fair price."

"How are we supposed to question a mule skinner who's been gone for two weeks?" Vince asked, drawing Duffy's attention away from Luke.

Duffy's eyes were moving between Luke and Vince and Dare. He looked nervous enough to make a run for it.

No new orders came in, and as Tina did preparation for dinner and cleanup from breakfast, she wondered what the men were up to. Tina, who'd spent her life cooking for two while living with Aunt Iphigenia, was finding a talent for feeding a crowd.

With soft splashes she dropped the last of the peeled and cubed potatoes into the water. She'd started a huge rack of venison roasting for the noon meal before she'd cracked the first egg for breakfast. She lifted the heavy potato pot and set it on the hot stove. The potatoes would be tender and ready to mash shortly before the men came storming in for dinner. An apple brown Betty was ready to pop in the oven when the venison came out. Tina liked serving the dessert warm.

Glynna picked that moment to come into the kitchen, and Tina braced herself to do more cooking. It wasn't unusual for a straggler to ask for a late breakfast, and Glynna always got a few coffee drinkers midmorning.

Instead of asking for more eggs and hashbrowns, Glynna blew at blond hair wisps hanging in her eyes. She toted a tray loaded with dirty plates and utensils and coffee cups. She looked worn out.

"This is the last of it. I locked the door." Glynna smiled at Tina. "I'm not letting anyone in for morning coffee today. I'm hoping Ruthy will wake up and we all can get a chance to visit, though I won't wake her. She must be exhausted. I've never seen her sit still, let alone nap."

"Coffee and a visit sound wonderful, but would you mind terribly if I ran over to the boardinghouse first?" Tina rolled down the sleeves of her blue gingham dress.

"Do you need to see Vince for something?" There was a strange tone in Glynna's voice that made Tina look at her sharply.

Glynna couldn't know anything. Surely the fact that a man kissed a woman wasn't apparent on that woman's face.

"I saw Jonas go over quite a while back." Tina buttoned her cuffs, focusing overly on the chore so she wouldn't have to look Glynna in the eye. "I'm a bit worried after Missy asked Janny to go for help. I don't know where the rest of the men are. I saw them leave your house with Luke. Since they all left Mrs. Yates alone with Missy, and Jonas went over and didn't come back, I just want to make sure there's no trouble."

"You go check on your brother." Glynna set the tray down beside the sink. "Give Missy a break if she needs one, too. We'll finish the cleanup just fine on our own. We're all going to have to work a bit harder until we figure out all that Mrs. Yates is going to need."

Tina untied her apron and hung it on a nail by the back

door, then pulled on her coat. "I'll see if Missy can come here for coffee, otherwise maybe we could go there and include Mrs. Yates in our visit."

Glynna's face brightened. "That's a good idea. Either one has to beat serving food to a horde of starving men."

Smiling, Tina hurried over to Vince's. She reached the front door and decided to just slip inside quietly. It seemed more like a boardinghouse than a private home, and anyway, what if Mrs. Yates was resting?

She heard muted voices coming from the back of the house. So she headed back there, walking down a hallway that sided the stairway, thinking to invite everyone to the diner. It was mostly a female gathering, but Jonas could come or he could go find his friends. Luke Stone had been upset about something this morning, though Tina hadn't heard what. A door stood ajar near the back of the building, and she swung it wide to see . . .

Jonas jumping away from Missy as if she were a hot potato. But he was still too slow. Tina had seen exactly what was going on.

Vince moved closer, pinning Duffy to the spot with his cold eyes.

Sounding falsely belligerent, Duffy said, "I'm telling you that's all the drink I've got, and no one ordered more. You've got my word, and that's all the proof you're going to get."

"You got a bill of sale?" Luke shoved on Duffy's shoulder to earn the man's full attention.

Scowling, Duffy said, "I don't hold with all that fuss. I can't read anyhow, so what good is a pile of paper going to do me? The mule skinner brings me the same order every time, and he takes away the same amount of money to pay for it. A man's word is his bond out here in Texas, and my word is good. You can't find a single man in this town to say different."

Luke cocked his head sideways and seemed to burn a hole right through Duffy. "I'll tell you how I see it, Schuster. Someone's buying a lot of drink in this town, and you're the only man who has it to sell. It's been long enough that freight wagon should be through Broken Wheel again any day, and you can believe I'll be askin' him some questions. And if I don't get answers I like, I'll be back."

Luke pressed closer to Duffy and towered over him. "If my wife had been so much as scratched, you wouldn't still be standing when I left this place. So if you're lying, you'd better tell whoever's buying from you that you're out of the bottle-at-a-time business."

Duffy cowered like a scared rodent, but he didn't change his story. "I can't stop doing what I ain't doing to begin with, Stone."

Vince wanted to try a little rough justice on Duffy, see if they could pound some answers out of him. But Vince was the law in Broken Wheel, and that wasn't the way a lawman conducted himself. He'd learned that from reading his volumes of Blackstone's *Commentaries*.

After Sheriff Porter's disregard for the law, it didn't sit right with Vince to follow the man in his corruption.

"We'll talk to the freighter." Vince came up beside Luke just in case his friend needed to be restrained. "And if we don't like what we hear, we'll be back."

Vince waited until Luke quit trying to burn the truth

out of Duffy with his blazing eyes and stormed out. Dare came out from behind the bar and followed Luke. Vince was right behind them. The three of them strode down the steps and into the deserted street.

"He's lying." Luke turned to go back to the tavern, ready to get answers with his fists.

Vince grabbed Luke's arm and stopped him cold. "We don't know that, Luke."

Turning on Vince, Luke said, "I'm not leaving town without some answers."

"You're not going to find them in there. Duffy is either telling the truth or he's covered his tracks. We have to wait for the supply wagon to come back."

Luke looked frustrated enough to swing a fist at anyone who thwarted him. "Those bullets came too close to Ruthy. I won't let anyone hurt her, for sure not a low-down polecat like Duffy Schuster." Luke took a step forward until he was nose to nose with Vince. They were close in height, yet Luke probably outweighed Vince by twenty pounds, all of it iron-hard muscle.

Vince was tough, but he didn't figure he could win a fight with the kid. "Luke, I'd let you pound on him, except I got a bad feeling in there."

"What do you mean, 'bad'?" Dare asked.

"Duffy was sure enough afraid, no doubt about it. But I listened to a lot of men tell stories both true and false while I was spying during the war and policing at Andersonville, and to me, Duffy sounded like he was telling the whole truth."

Luke turned to face the saloon. "Then it's Griss. Maybe he orders bottles on the side."

"Griss sounded like he was telling it square, too." Vince stood side by side with Luke. Dare was to the far side of the kid, and he faced the tavern, too. The three of them in a row, frustrated. Angry. Vince admitted he was also worried. Flying lead wasn't a good fit for a lady with a baby on the way. Come to that, it wasn't a good fit for anyone.

"Then if it isn't them, who is it?" Luke asked. But they all knew there was no answer, not here and not now.

"We'll get to the bottom of this, and we'll do it fast. Let's start by going back to where you found those bottles and look harder for tracks." Vince added, "How sure are you that the Indians weren't the ones who left those bottles?"

"It ain't them. I know it in my gut. But I've got no proof." Shaking his head as if to escape his bleak thoughts, Luke turned toward the diner. "I want to go see my wife. I can hardly bear to let her out of my sight."

Dare said, "I've got a book for her to read about having a baby, Luke. Come on back to my place and I'll get it for you, then we'll go sit with the womenfolk for a while."

"I'll go get my mother and Missy and Jonas and bring them over, too," Vince said. "Jonas and Missy are probably long past ready for some help."

CHAPTER 15

"Tina?" Jonas ran one hand over his red curls. But it was no use. Missy's fingers had clearly left a trail.

Missy blushed to the roots of her dark hair and clutched her hands together in front of her. She would have put those hands to better use covering her lips, swollen from kissing Jonas.

Tina's brother kissing Vince's sister.

They'd only just met.

"I . . . I didn't mean to . . . to . . ." Tina was speechless. And that certainly never happened. "I'll just . . . that is . . . Mrs. Yates should—"

Tina spun away and almost ran out of the room, her head full of confused images. Her brother had been holding a woman close whom he barely knew.

And where had Mrs. Yates gone to? As she rushed away, Tina's temper began to build. Jonas shouldn't be kissing a stranger. Why, Tina had known Vince for months now, and when they'd kissed she'd been astounded by it, not ready for it at all. And anyway, these two were supposed to be watching Mrs. Yates. Where was she?

"Tina, wait!" Jonas came running after her and caught

her just as she was ready to go check Mrs. Yates's room. "What you saw back there was . . . was . . ."

The front door opened, and Vince stepped in. He looked right into Tina's eyes and there was a flash of memory between them. Then Vince's brow furrowed, and Tina wondered what in the world she must look like. Vince looked past Tina. His eyes locked on something. Tina looked back to see Jonas, lapsed into silence.

"What's going on here?" Vince asked, sounding like the crack of doom.

Missy peeked out of the doorway but stayed back. Vince's sharp eyes went past Jonas to his sister, then back to Tina. He arched a brow at her.

Which helped her to regain her speech.

"It was what, Jonas?" Tina thought she sounded rather steady. Calm, in fact. Cool and unruffled. "You were about to say what I saw was . . . ?" Tina let the word hang.

"It was Missy agreeing to . . ." Jonas's always ruddy skin turned a vivid red. He swallowed hard, looked at Vince, then squared his shoulders as if someone had ordered him to stand at attention. "Missy was agreeing that I could court her."

"She what?" Vince exploded.

It was such an unexpected answer, Tina's knees sagged, and even though she was gripping the banister, she sat down hard on the second step. If that step hadn't been there, right under her backside, she'd have slumped all the way to the floor.

Vince seemed like the type to catch a collapsing woman, but he didn't even notice.

"You just met her!" Tina hadn't meant to shriek exactly, but that was how it came out.

And one completely selfish stab of jealousy told Tina she was no longer going to be as important to her brother. In fact, if Jonas and Missy married, Tina was most likely going to be asked to move out. And if they were too kind to ask her to leave, she'd still know they would look on her as unwelcome. A feeling she'd had most of her life.

Jonas shrugged and scrubbed both hands through his hair, then turned and reached one hand out for Missy. She came forward with a shy but steady smile and took his hand.

"You're courting?" Vince sounded somewhat like a screeching bird. He had the nickname Invincible Vince, but he must've had too many things happen too fast, because this situation had gotten the better of him.

"I know this seems sudden." Jonas pulled Missy close.

Tina studied Missy. They really knew nothing about her. There could be little doubt she was Julius Yates's daughter, but how had she really lived these last few years? Was she an honest woman? Maybe she was looking for a home and grabbed the most gullible man she could find. Maybe Jonas meant nothing to her. Maybe she'd been overly generous with her favors, allowing a man to kiss her. Tina caught herself on that when memories of being in Vince's arms subdued her growing moral outrage.

"It doesn't *seem* sudden. It *is* sudden." Tina really didn't know what to say. And that never happened. Tina always knew exactly what to say.

"Where's my mother?" Vince sounded cold as the grave. "You were supposed to be watching her, but it looks to me like you got distracted."

Melissa gasped, gave Jonas a worried glance, then

whipped around him and threaded between Tina and Vince to run upstairs.

When she was gone, Tina exchanged a long look with her beloved brother. Vince stood silent.

"I know it's come from out of the blue," Jonas said, "but from the moment I saw her, I felt like God was opening a door in my heart I never even knew was closed. I've never been more certain of anything in my life. If it were up to me, we'd be getting married this very day."

"Today?" Vince croaked, and for a second Tina thought he was going to join her sitting on the steps. He looked none too steady.

A movement at the top of the stairs drew Tina's attention, yet that wasn't a surprise. She was eager to look away from the besotted expression in Jonas's eyes. Melissa came out of the room with Mrs. Yates on her arm.

"I believe Missy is the woman God prepared for me," Jonas went on. "I feel like I've found my other half." He watched Melissa descend the stairs as if she were walking down an aisle with a bouquet of posies instead of an addled woman. Tina and Vince and Mrs. Yates might as well have melted into the floor, because Jonas and Melissa only had eyes for each other.

Finally, Melissa was near enough that Tina had to move or block the stairway for the two ladies. Tina struggled to her feet. Her knees wobbled. Vince caught her under the arm and kept her upright.

"I want you to trust me, Tina." Jonas reached for her, but Tina stepped back, pressing against Vince, out of her brother's reach. "I know the voice of God, and He's telling me I've found my wife."

Jonas wanted her to approve. He wanted her blessing. But right now that was too much to ask.

"I came over here to invite you all to the diner for coffee." Her voice was frigid.

"Tina, I—"

Slashing a hand at her brother to shut him up, she pulled herself free of Vince's grip. "We've locked up until it's time to serve dinner. Ruthy is in town with Luke, and we wanted a chance to visit uninterrupted. I'll head on back now. Come if you want."

Tina dodged around Vince and left the house at a near run.

"Wait!" Jonas called out. "Tina, come back!"

Tina only moved faster. She needed someone, a witness, a buffer. She looked back and saw Vince's broad shoulders blocking the doorway. Apparently he wanted a word with his friend.

As she rushed away, Tina wondered where she was even going. Back to the diner, where Jonas and Melissa would no doubt soon arrive?

Back to Jonas's parsonage where, judging from Jonas's determined look, Tina would soon be living on sufferance. Except the way she'd foisted herself on Jonas uninvited, that was all it'd been all along.

If she stayed, it would be as an unwanted intrusion. Only the fact that Jonas pitied her would keep her from being cast out . . . again. She was a fool to let that break her heart. After her parents left her. After years of Aunt Iphigenia's coldness. After the awful new uncle who wanted Tina in a way that turned her stomach. She should have expected this.

Why had she come here?

Why had she let herself believe that Jonas would make a home for her?

Why hadn't she just gotten on with her life, gotten a job somewhere and taken care of herself, instead of being a little fool who wanted home and family and love?

After all those years of hearing Aunt Iphigenia say a woman needed to know how to take care of herself, Tina had ignored that sound advice, tracked down her brother, and forced from him something he hadn't wanted to give.

She rushed through the back door of the diner and was sorry she'd come. Now Jonas would catch her here and say all the painfully polite words about her always having a home with him. Jonas was kind, but he'd gone out West after the war without stopping in to see her. And she'd chased him practically to the ends of the earth and made it impossible for him to send her away.

Not like Melissa. Jonas had known her for only hours before asking to court her.

And meanwhile Tina had kissed Vince. It was hard to imagine that kiss was less passionate, less powerful than the one shared by Jonas and Melissa. And there'd been no request from Vince to court her—quite the opposite. He'd apologized, said it never should have happened.

Whatever word God had whispered to Jonas, He had withheld from Vince. Which meant Vince didn't want her, either.

❧

"You're carrying on with my sister? My sister you just met?" Vince realized that the last day had worn him right down to the nub. Punching someone would suit him, and to his way of thinking, Jonas had just volunteered.

"I'm not carrying on." Jonas tried to follow Tina, but Vince blocked the parson from leaving.

"Let me past. I need to talk to Tina. She's upset."

Vince's fist tightened. In a flash he remembered he was Invincible Vince Yates. His Regulator friends had given him that name when he'd found a knack for solving problems in Andersonville. If they needed supplies, Vince found them. If bad men were planning trouble, Vince got wind of it and gathered the Regulators together in time to head things off. If the Confederate guards were in one of their sadistic moods, Vince had a talent for dodging them or calming them down or turning them against each other.

Nothing much got the better of him.

So his father turning up, his mother being abandoned, a sister materializing, a new house being landed on his head, a feisty little lady coaxing a kiss out of him, and now *this*. It had all seemed to be more than Invincible Vince could handle.

In a distant way, Vince realized this was nothing compared to cannonballs and starvation and a prison with thirty thousand men, about half of whom thought sticking a knife in his back was the will of God. But it was still beyond him.

And punching the latest bearer of bad news would make him feel a whole lot better.

"Now, Vince," Melissa said calmly, "there's no call to—"

"Get out," Vince snapped.

"Vince," Melissa said, her lips forming a tight line, "I do not answer to you."

"Take Mother over to the diner for coffee and let me have a little talk with Jonas."

"Go on." Jonas ran a hand up Melissa's back, and that stopped her from whatever she'd been planning to say. "Take Virginia Belle with you. I need to talk to your brother alone."

Melissa's eyes, a perfect match for Vince's, flickered between Jonas, Vince, and Vince's fist. "I'll go." She glared at Vince. "But you have no say in this."

The snap of her voice was even like Vince's. He'd met a female version of himself and wondered, for all her quiet ways, if Melissa might not be invincible, too. If she was, Jonas was going to have his hands full.

"Come along, Virginia Belle. We're going to have our morning tea." Melissa walked straight for Vince, who got out of her way, not so sure he wouldn't have gotten run over.

"Good morning, Julius." Mother rested one of her gentle hands on his arm. "Will you be joining us?"

"I'll be right along." Speaking civilly to Mother had a calming effect on Vince. It was hard to be so careful with her while contemplating slugging somebody.

Vince watched the ladies leave. The door clicked shut, and the minute it closed, Vince whirled back to face Jonas, only to see him sinking onto the stair step. Right where Tina had been when Vince had come in. This whole thing seemed to be having an ill effect on the ability of everyone to stand upright.

"I'm out of my mind." Jonas buried his face in his hands. He didn't seem to be having one second of worry that Vince might throw a fist.

"If you're this confused, why in the world are you talking about getting married?" Vince felt a tug of sympathy, maybe even pity, for his friend. Leaning back against the door with his arms crossed, he stood guard like always. He was waiting for Jonas to make sense.

Jonas scrubbed his face with both hands, then ran his fingers deep into his hair, making the red curls run riot. Finally, dragging his hands down, Jonas's eyes emerged from between his fingers and his whole face appeared. He shook his head and looked Vince square in the eye. Jonas wasn't one to shirk from taking responsibility for his decisions.

"I don't even know what happened. We've talked a bit the last couple days. From the first word, from my first look at her, I was so drawn to her." Jonas gripped the banister like he was going to stand, and then he just gave up and stayed on the step. "This morning I think all Missy needed was someone to stay with your ma while she ran to the privy. I came in, Missy thanked me and stepped out while I visited with your ma. Then Missy came back, and Virginia Belle said she was tired and she lay back down. Missy was worrying about how things were going to work out here, and we started talking. I was being a parson. I was trying to encourage her and cheer her up and help her see God's hand in all of this."

"Even though none of us have a single idea what God has in mind?"

Jonas jerked one shoulder in a shrug. "It was the most wonderful talk. She's so sweet and . . ." Jonas shrugged again. "We just ended up in each other's arms. It was the simplest, truest thing that's ever happened to me. Like she belonged there. Like I've been waiting for her all my life."

Jonas looked up. "I promise you, Vince, there's been no disrespectful treatment of your sister. I'm just sure she's the woman God has set apart for me, and we're supposed to be together. I know it's unwise to rush into marriage, but right now I would gladly marry her. I'll help her with your ma and support Melissa in whatever she needs to do. The reasonable side of me tells me we're being rash. But everything in me who feels led by the voice of God tells me I've found my future, and I need to join my life with Missy's without delay. I'm completely sure of it, and I don't intend to refuse this gift the Lord is offering me."

Jonas stood, his wobbly knees apparently restored now. Still, Jonas didn't seem much interested in how upset Vince was. He was too focused on his own future. "I'm going after her. I don't even like being separated from her for these few minutes."

Heading for the door, Vince slapped a hand on Jonas's shoulder to stop him.

Jonas frowned. "You're not going to pretend like you have some say in Missy's life, are you? I've known her every bit as long as you have, so don't start acting like a protective big brother."

"You're right in saying that, but I think I'm more worried about you than Melissa. This isn't like you to go off half-cocked, Jonas. You know nothing about her background. It sounds like her mother was no better than she ought to be, considering a lifelong affair with a married man—my father. Now Melissa found her way into the Yates family. It's true, she treats my mother with kindness, but that's also been her way to a comfortable home and money coming in."

"Don't you say a word against her." Now Jonas's fists were clenched.

186

Vince raised both hands, palms flat, like he was surrendering. "I'm not saying I know a thing against her. But the point is, I don't know her and neither do you. And what's more, that's such a simple truth that you can't possibly deny it."

Jonas frowned, glaring at Vince. But no fight broke out. Finally, with a short, hard jerk of his chin, Jonas said, "I know you're right. That is the simple truth."

"So you'll slow down and give this some more thought?"

Jonas drew in a breath so slow and deep his chest visibly rose and fell. At last he said, "Sure, but I won't wait too long." Jonas then stepped around Vince and pulled the door open, knocking Vince forward a few steps. He took off running, on his way to catch up with Melissa.

Vince stood at the door. Of his own house. A big house. A house with a mother living in it. A sister. Which raised the question: was Jonas going to live here, with Vince? He almost had to, because Vince couldn't manage Mother without Melissa.

And if Jonas lived here, what about Tina?

Lifting his eyes to the top of the stairs, Vince looked at the row of four bedrooms. Melissa on the far left, with Jonas soon in residence, unless Melissa planned to abandon Vince to care for his mother alone.

Mother's room was next, then Vince's. He looked at that fourth door. Was Tina going to be moving into that bedroom?

Vince couldn't let that happen, and yet, if Jonas moved in, then Tina would have to.

And if Vince wasn't careful, before he knew it, there'd be another wedding, because Vince was mighty sure he couldn't live next door to Tina Cahill and not end up doing something as crazy as marry her.

And speaking of crazy . . . if he married her, he'd end up with children, because those things just followed like summer followed spring. And then there would be little ones who might be cursed with a madman for a father—if Vince took after his mother's family.

And that was the kind of fate Vince could never bestow on a wife, to have a husband to care for year after year with only the burden of it.

Vince couldn't do that to a wife or a child. Surely God would consider such a thing as the worst kind of selfishness.

Or maybe they'd have a tyrant for a father—if Vince took after his father. If that happened, then he was destined to ruin his children's lives and have them leave him as soon as they were able.

And yet Vince's eyes went to that fourth door. He saw no escape from Tina and the almost unavoidable result of being so near to her.

It was all Vince could do not to run for the hills like his father had done. So which one of his parents was he most like? His cruel, hot-tempered, arrogant bully father who'd raised a son to always be on guard, or the madwoman he had for a mother?

Both were a cruel fate to anyone foolish enough to join her life with his. And Vince wasn't selfish enough to let that happen.

CHAPTER 16

"Is Missy bringing . . . ?" Smiling, Glynna came into the kitchen—warm and savory with the aroma of roasting venison—but the smile vanished when she saw Tina. "What happened? Did Mrs. Yates run into trouble again?"

Tina shook her head and wondered what her expression must be for Glynna to sound so urgent. A notion came to Tina that was better than nothing. "I'm a good cook, aren't I, Glynna?"

"Yes, you're a wonderful help in the kitchen." Glynna's concern changed to flat-out worry. "Are you quitting? Are you getting tired of cooking for the whole—"

"I'm staying," Tina said, cutting her off. "Don't worry about that."

Heaven knew this was no time to quit her job. Tina made decent money, and she could be a cook anywhere, too. It was just a big old shame that she hadn't hopped on that carriage and left when Mr. Yates had snuck out of town. She could be a cook in Chicago. Of course, yesterday she hadn't known she would become permanent unwanted baggage for her brother to tote around. "But I was wondering if I could move into the rooms upstairs."

Glynna looked surprised. "You don't want to live with Jonas anymore?"

"I want a place to call my own. I want to earn money and take care of myself and stop depending on the sufferance of others."

"Sufferance?" Glynna blinked just as the door opened and Melissa stepped in with Mrs. Yates on her arm.

Tina saw that the women were alone, which meant Vince had collared Jonas.

"Hi, Missy, Mrs. Yates." Glynna took a second to be polite, then went right back to quizzing Tina. "What do you mean by 'sufferance'? Jonas likes having you live with him. You didn't start another mud-wrestling match on Main Street when I wasn't watching, did you?"

"Mud-wrestling match?" Melissa said, looking nervously at Tina.

"Why, whatever do you mean by that?" Mrs. Yates touched the collar of her dress with her fingertips.

"Never mind. It's in the past." Tina stepped sideways so Melissa and Mrs. Yates could join their circle. She arched a brow at Melissa. "There are far more interesting things happening around here than my picketing the tavern."

Melissa shook her head. "Let's all just sit down and discuss this. Tina, nothing is decided yet. And when it is, you're still going to live with us."

"No, I'm not." Tina was determined. And *you're still going to live with us* sounded very much like things were decided.

"Us?" Glynna's voice rose.

"Melissa and Jonas are . . . are . . ." Tina's voice trailed off, and she noticed her hands had formed fists, but not so

190

she could punch someone. It was to hold on tight to her nerves. "They're courting, and if they end up married, it's only proper to give the newlyweds their privacy."

"Bless your heart," Mrs. Yates said, and patted Tina's arm. "You're the most thoughtful girl." She leaned closer to Tina. "Have we met?"

Glynna quit listening to Tina's request for a roof over her head and turned to Melissa. "You only just met."

Tina had that very same thought. So had Vince. So would anyone with a working brain.

"I know. But we're not rushing into anything." Melissa threw her arms wide and almost knocked Vince's ma over.

Glynna dashed to Virginia Belle's side and steadied her, the only one in the room able to think clearly enough to catch the sweet lady.

Tina had heard the excitement in Jonas's voice when he'd nearly said wedding vows while watching Melissa descend the stairs. And she'd seen the way Melissa looked at him, affection in her eyes. She suspected there was some rushing coming.

"I don't know how it happened. But Jonas is so wonderful."

Tina had thought her brother was wonderful too, though she was less thrilled with him now than she had been an hour ago.

With a wild glance at Mrs. Yates, Glynna turned to Tina. "And you're moving in here?"

Virginia Belle said, "I appreciate your kind offer, but I don't want to move. I am quite fond of the plantation."

Glynna gave her head a tiny, violent shake. Then, with her arm around Mrs. Yates's waist, she said, "Let's get you a cup of coffee, ma'am. Come in and sit down."

Without waiting for much cooperation, Glynna guided Mrs. Yates from the kitchen.

As she left, Tina called after her, "So can I move in here?"

"Get the coffeepot." Glynna snapped out the order just like she was the boss of this diner, which was highly questionable. "Then get in here and sit down. We're going to talk this out right now."

Missy followed Glynna, and the swinging door to the dining room slapped shut. Tina felt rejected for about the tenth time today, and it wasn't noon yet.

Her shoulders slumped. She snagged four tin cups, slipping a finger through each handle. Then she hoisted the half-full pot, left from that morning, and followed Glynna out of the room.

Missy had abandoned her duty as caretaker to Mrs. Yates. She was sitting at the nearest long table with her head in her hands.

Glynna took care to get Vince's mother comfortable on the bench seat. Tina poured the coffee. Glynna and Virginia Belle sat with their backs to the kitchen. Tina and Missy were side by side across the table—not overly close to each other—Tina's choice, for Missy seemed beyond moving.

When they were all settled, Glynna said, "So, Missy, what happened?"

"I'm out of my ever-loving mind." Missy spoke to the table, or maybe herself.

"And now you want to move out, Tina?"

Missy lifted her head at that. "Good heavens, Tina. I have no intention of throwing you out of your home."

"You're not throwing me out." Tina sounded strong, steady. She was getting the hang of pretending to be completely happy that her life had just been blown to bits. "I just need to get my own life in order. I need to stop depending on others." And expecting them to love her. "I am a self-supporting woman. Glynna lived here as a single woman before she married Dare, and I see no reason why I shouldn't live here."

A woman needs to know how to take care of herself. Aunt Iphigenia had been absolutely right, the old bat.

"It's not proper for you to live alone, Tina," Glynna said. "I was a widow with two children. Completely different situation."

◦◦◦◦◦

Vince gathered his wits enough to rush after Jonas. There had to be a way to head off Tina Cahill's moving in. Being stuck with her could turn into a trap Vince never escaped. A trap for Tina too, if she had the sense to realize it.

But keeping Tina out probably meant keeping Jonas out, and that meant kicking Melissa out, which left Vince to care for his mother, at least through the night. And with the personal needs of a woman, Vince wasn't sure if that was even legal.

He needed to read over his volumes of Blackstone a little more closely.

Maybe he was the one who needed to get out. Leave them all alone in his place. He could move back to his tiny room over his law office and just help with Mother during the daytime.

Of course, she was his mother, so he probably needed to take responsibility for her by staying in the same house. Vince rounded the back corner of the diner in time to see

Jonas slam the door. The man was in a hurry to get on with his courting, the idiot.

Pausing at the door, Vince considered banging his head against it for a while before he went inside, but then decided he'd better not take the time. He needed to get in there before his whole life got rearranged without his consent.

He barged through the kitchen to see that Luke was coming down the stairs with Ruthy. Dare was pacing near the front door, looking at Jonas as if he'd lost his mind.

Vince was just in time to hear Jonas say, "You'll always have a home with me, Tina. We'll need to live in the boardinghouse to care for Mrs. Yates, but there's plenty of room there for you, too."

"No there's not!" Vince said, panic in his voice.

"I'm not living there!" Tina spoke right on top of Vince, saying pretty much the same thing.

Everyone fell silent. Vince's eyes locked on Tina. She was fuming. What was worse, she looked hurt. Jonas had hurt her. Vince had too. Blast the little pest, she was making him feel like the worst kind of lout for wanting to kick her out before she'd even moved in.

And he didn't want to hurt her. He just didn't want her anywhere near him. Which wasn't hurtful; it was common sense.

"Well, we'll figure all that out later." Jonas broke into the deadly silence with all the sensitivity of a starving dung beetle. "For now, since we're all here, I want everyone to know my intentions toward Melissa are completely honorable."

"Can anyone tear themselves away to help me track down whoever shot at me and Ruthy?" Luke seated Ruthy as if the tough little Irish redhead were made of spun glass. He yanked his gloves out from where he'd tucked them behind his belt buckle and appeared to be strangling them. "Vince, you're the law in this town."

Leaving town right now seemed like a top-notch idea. "Can someone watch my mother while I go do some sheriffing?"

Vince wondered if that question had ever before been asked in the history of the world.

"Mrs. Yates, how do you feel about pouring coffee?" Glynna asked. The woman had put everyone else in town to work for her, why not Mother?

Virginia Belle Yates, Southern princess and rich Chicago socialite turned waitress. Vince had never imagined such a day.

"Why, I dearly love pouring tea." Mother acted like she'd be presiding over a refined ladies' gathering. The woman was in for a surprise.

"I'll see to her, Vince," Glynna offered.

A hard rap on the front door showed a couple of men coming for the noon meal. Tug Andrews, who always looked like the image of a rough mountain man, pointed at the doorknob, scowling through his shaggy beard. He seemed to think they might have locked up accidentally.

A line was forming behind him.

Ruthy said, "I'd be glad to help get the meal on. You men can all go to—"

A door in the back of the diner slammed, and only then did Vince notice Jonas and Missy had left. Neither of them were going to be much help for a while.

Tina glared after the happy couple, her arms crossed, her

toe tapping in annoyance. "I'll go mash the potatoes." She stormed out of the room.

Glynna rested a guiding hand on Mother's arm. "Come to the kitchen and I'll show you how to make coffee."

"Make coffee? Well, I declare," Mother said, fluttering her eyes, "that would be lovely."

Vince saw Sledge Murphy in line behind Tug Andrews. Sledge shoved Tug aside and banged on the door with the side of his fist. Tug shoved back. Words were exchanged that made Vince want to cover his ears.

Lovely wasn't the word that came to mind.

Mother and Glynna left. Vince looked from Luke to Dare. "Let's saddle up."

The three of them headed for their horses, unlocking the diner door for the noon rush on their way out. It was all Vince could do not to hop on his horse and ride all the way to Mexico.

CHAPTER 17

Tina's life might have hit a rough patch, but the mealtime ran as smooth as silk. The men all treated Mrs. Yates with an unexpected amount of kindness, as if they knew she was fragile. Or maybe she just made even the biggest lugs in town miss their mothers.

Mrs. Yates surprised Tina by working hard, too. The genteel woman, though somewhat confused, was a sturdy woman beneath her fluttering lashes and flirtatious smiles. She behaved as though this were a fancy party and the ramshackle crowd of unwashed men were her guests. Tin cups and gallon coffeepots didn't stop her from being a gracious hostess.

Enough of the men in town had heard of the way Mrs. Yates had run off yesterday and that she was a bit addled. On more than one occasion, when the Southern belle tried to leave the diner, the men would abandon their venison steaks and redirect her, usually by asking for more coffee. Add to that Ruthy and her inability to stop working, and the absence of Vince and his Regulator friends, including Jonas—who was absent for his own reasons—and it was the easiest dinner since Tina had somehow gotten stuck with this job.

Which didn't mean her life wasn't collapsing on her head.

Finally the men finished and cleared out. Tina made up plates of steak and potatoes for the work crew. Paul and Janny took their plates to Dare's house, along with one to deliver to Lana in jail, and a meaty bone for Livvy. Glynna called after them, reminding them of their schoolwork.

Tina, with Ruthy's help, carried in four plates. Tina's feet hurt enough that as soon as she'd helped Mrs. Yates to the table, Tina sank onto the bench seat across from her. She chose a seat with her back to the front door, thinking she could better block an escape attempt from Virginia Belle. Tina was distracted from her feelings of rejection when Ruthy sat next to Virginia Belle and ran a hand over her rounding belly.

Glynna sat down next to Tina, across from Ruthy. Tina waited until all three ladies had food in their mouths, the better to avoid hearing their opinions, and announced, "I'll be sleeping here tonight, Glynna."

Mrs. Yates was apparently too refined to ever have a really large bite of food in her mouth, so she was able to respond immediately. "You can't stay here alone, dear child. No, that would be improper, even scandalous for a single lady to live alone."

Vince's mother said it as if it were a pronouncement from on high and she'd settled everything. She took another tiny bite of her steak.

Glynna said, "Are you enjoying your meal, Mrs. Yates?"

"It's lovely." It was a testament to how hungry Virginia Belle was that she was diverted by the mention of food. Tina thought maybe Vince's mother should work hard every day. It might keep the woman at the meal table and prevent her from waking at night. They could use another waitress in this place. It'd give the youngsters a bit more time at their studies.

"Now then, it's a simple thing to sleep here and come down to work in the morning." Tina said a brief but sincere prayer to be forgiven for her extremely bad attitude toward her brother's happiness.

"I saw two bedrooms upstairs," Ruthy said. "Luke and I can stay here with you. Luke said he doesn't want me going home until we find out who shot at us."

"Land sakes!" Mrs. Yates's hand went to her throat. "Someone shot at you?"

Ruthy flinched, and Tina was pretty sure Glynna had just kicked her in the ankle. "Mrs. Yates, that is such a pretty dress."

And it was. Mrs. Yates made the rest of them look like the very first frontierswomen. Tina's dresses had taken a beating since she'd come West. And putting on hoops and petticoats was just more trouble than it was worth.

Virginia Belle had on dark blue silk with a matching bonnet and reticule. The woman had a lace fan and any number of petticoats, most likely a corset and any number of other unmentionables. Getting the woman dressed in the morning wasn't a job for amateurs.

"Someone," Glynna said ominously, "will have to be at the boardinghouse in the evening to make sure"—she gave Vince's ma a significant glance—"that all personal and intimate needs are dealt with. And that includes through the night when help might be required. The current boardinghouse owner can't be expected to deal with such things."

"Well, if Jonas and Melissa marry, they'll have to stay at Asa's, and I can't stay there." Not even to spare her own life would Tina change her mind about that. "A single woman and single man under one roof would be far more improper than staying here."

Glynna shook her head.

"Tina . . ." Ruthy's eyes narrowed as she studied Tina's face. Tina was afraid a blush was creeping up her cheeks. "Your brother living there is enough to make it proper. Surely you and Vince can—"

The front door behind Tina swung open, which distracted Ruthy, thank heavens.

"She's gone!" Paul rushed into the room with Janny just a step behind him.

Janny yelled, "Mrs. Bullard broke jail!"

The little brown-and-white foxhound came racing in with the children, yapping for all she was worth.

"She could be after Dare again." Glynna jumped up and spun around so fast she nearly fell headfirst over the bench. She steadied herself and cried out, "We have to warn him!"

"Dare's an hour's ride away and we have no idea how long Lana's been gone." Tina knew the prisoner had been fed breakfast very early. But with the confusion of the morning, no one had been in the jailhouse since.

"Go get Jonas." Tina had an un-admirable feeling of glee to give that order.

"Get Tug Andrews instead," Ruthy cut in. "Jonas and Melissa have gone for a walk somewhere, and there's no point in anyone traipsing out into the wilderness after them. Tug can close the general store for a couple of hours and ride out to our place. Lana may have run off, but if she's still close by, I'd prefer to have one of Luke's friends stay near."

The dog rushed to Mrs. Yates's side and barked at her as if they'd been separated for ages. Oblivious to the unfolding crisis, Vince's mother fed the hound a chunk of venison and patted its head.

"I'll go with you." Glynna skirted the table. "I don't want you children running around town alone. Paul, let's get your gun first."

"No, Ma," Paul said with a loud voice. Glynna, who was on her way to the back door, stopped and turned around. The boy had worn a pistol on his hip for a spell, mad at the world and determined to protect his ma. He'd calmed down since Glynna and Dare had married and had taken to leaving the gun and holster hanging from a hook at home. "I don't think we should go home to get it. If Lana's up to causing trouble like she did last time, Pa's house might be where we'll find her."

Tina hadn't been in Broken Wheel when Lana burned Dare's house down, but she'd seen the pile of blackened timbers. And she'd arrived in time to staunch the blood when Dare had been stabbed. Then Tina had stood guard over Glynna's children until Lana was caught and locked up. Since she'd been arrested, Lana hadn't acted crazy at all. Yet Tina knew a thread of madness flowed through Lana Bullard, and no one could be sure when it would surface next.

Glynna hesitated, then said, "Tug is right next door. We'll go straight there."

Though her desire to pester Jonas was uncharitable, Tina wondered if her brother was safe. They really did need to warn him. "Go on. I'll stand at the door and watch. Janny, you stay here with us. Ruthy and I need to keep an eye on Virginia Belle."

Glynna looked between her daughter and son with such worry that Tina felt the weight of it.

With a jerk of her chin, Glynna said to Paul, "Let's go."

They were gone, with the door slammed behind them, before anyone could think of more to worry about.

Tina rushed to the front door to watch them dart safely into Tug's store.

Turning back to the room, Tina noticed Ruthy standing by the door to the kitchen, guarding against an escape attempt by Virginia Belle. It was a good idea for them both to keep Mrs. Yates's safety in the forefront of their minds. Having her wander off, and possibly run into Lana outside of town, could turn a jailbreak into a tragedy.

They were near the entrance to the canyon, on the trail where Luke had found the whiskey bottles. The plan was to look for tracks, which was something Luke excelled at.

Vince figured if Luke couldn't tell more about who'd left behind those bottles, none of them could.

Luke raised a hand, signaling the group to stop. "Red Wolf should be close," he said.

Red Wolf, Luke's Kiowa friend who'd taught Luke to read sign, would be a better hand at tracking than Luke. Vince's hopes rose.

A harsh sound that might be some kind of birdcall came from behind a tumble of flat red rocks, all stacked this way and that, some the size of wagon wheels, and others big enough to serve as a foundation for a one-room cabin.

Luke responded with a similar bird cry. Soon Red Wolf stepped out from behind the boulders. Luke rode forward and swung off his horse to shake his friend's hand, both of them grabbing each other by the elbow. Luke said something in Kiowa that Vince couldn't understand.

It could be "Hello," or it could be "Is one of your people trying to kill me?"

Vince had learned a few words when he'd helped care for Red Wolf's Kiowa village during a measles outbreak. But unless Luke or Red Wolf said, "Swallow this medicine," Vince wasn't going to be of much use.

Red Wolf started heading for the canyon. Luke ground-hitched his horse and followed him. Vince had a well-trained horse, so he did the same as Luke, yet he waited for Dare, who was busy tying his cantankerous mare to a mesquite tree. They were a few steps behind and got into the canyon in time to see Luke and Red Wolf crouch down by a patch of dirt.

"Come in careful," Luke said, pivoting on his boots. "We don't wanna stir up any tracks."

Vince and Dare both slowed. They exchanged a glance and then began scouring the ground around their feet before every step.

There wasn't much to see, and Vince considered himself to be a fair hand at following a trail. The ground was rocky, and plenty of sand scudded along in the buffeting winter wind, erasing any tracks that had been left.

Luke and Red Wolf moved farther apart, eyes fixed on the ground.

Vince had about decided it was a pure waste of time when a scrub juniper blew sideways and something glinted right near its roots. The roots grew next to a big round slab of shale or sandstone about two feet high and six feet in diameter.

"Luke, get over here," Vince called. "And mind where you walk." Kneeling well back of the shiny, mostly buried object, he tried to make it out without disturbing the ground around it. A glance up told him that Red Wolf wore some bright beads, and Vince remembered others in his tribe liked to adorn their clothing.

But this didn't quite fit. Luke and Red Wolf came close, searching for tracks so thoroughly that it took a long time. Glancing sideways, Vince saw Dare hanging back. He knew better than to get too close, but he was paying attention.

"What is it?" Luke was near enough to see what looked like the glint of metal, though maybe it was a shiny streak in the rock. Not being sure, Vince wasn't ready to start digging.

Using English, Red Wolf said, "I had a young warrior come in stumbling, acting the fool because he'd had the devil's brew you white men sell."

The devil's brew, that had been on Tina's placard. Or was it demon rum? Kinda the same thing, and she'd had several signs over the past few months. Vince had to squelch a smile as he thought of her and her feisty battle against Duffy and his saloon.

She was so pretty that the men mostly *liked* her standing outside the tavern. They considered her a slightly pesky greeter at the door and weren't averse to hearing a few words from her, looking at her soft blond curls that made a man think she wore a halo, and getting a close-up view of her bright blue eyes that glowed like the blue at the heart of a clean-burning lantern. Yep, they liked that moment of her time even if it meant they got a finger wagged under their noses and a sermon on the evils of demon rum. And that accusing finger . . . she had the prettiest, most delicate little hands, and even when scolding someone, her voice rang like the song of church bells. She even—

"Vince!"

Jerking his thoughts back to the present, Vince looked at Luke's annoyed eyes. "What?"

"I asked you if you could, real gentle-like, brush the dirt aside from whatever that is. I don't want to get any closer." Luke's black brows lowered to a serious straight line. "What's so interesting that you're not payin' attention to the best clue we've found yet? Aren't you supposed to be the sheriff around here?"

Luke edged nearer, not taking another step until he'd checked carefully for tracks. Red Wolf stayed back; he must have eyes like an eagle or really not want to disturb the ground. Dare had moved halfway to the canyon mouth, looking farther afield for any sign of who'd been in here.

Ignoring Luke's question because the answer had no business coming out of his mouth, Vince reached for the little bright object and brushed the dirt aside. "I think it's just a bit of brass. That's what glittered. It doesn't look like anything I've seen on a bottle at Duffy's. What are the chances he buys two different kinds of whiskey, one to sell to . . ." Vince swallowed the next words because he'd been going to say *sell to the Indians*.

Once Red Wolf had told about his brave coming in

drunk, Vince realized he'd decided that shot had been fired at Luke and Ruthy by someone from the tribe.

Clearing his throat, Vince finished, "One to sell by the bottleful to someone."

Red Wolf met Vince's eyes, and it was clear the man knew what Vince had been going to say. Opening his mouth to apologize, and no doubt make everything worse, a cocking gun cracked behind them. Vince spun to face a glowering cowhand with a Colt six-shooter aimed right at Red Wolf's heart.

"I reckon I found the man who shot at the boss. Don't move a muscle."

Luke was crouching on the far side of the red rock slab, so he was barely visible. Vince was right there, but apparently this cowpoke was riveted on Red Wolf. Dare was out of his line of sight.

"You're coming with me to the house, and I'll pull this trigger if you so much as look at me wrong."

"Wilcox!" Luke surged to his feet.

With a shout of surprise the cowhand jumped and his gun went off.

Red Wolf launched himself sideways.

A roar of fury erupted from Luke's throat. Dare sprinted toward the Kiowa brave. Vince charged right into the path of the cowhand's gun. The man was shaking his head, his eyes wide with shock, and the gun fell to the ground.

Vince got to Wilcox, scooped the gun up, then shoved the man hard enough to land him on his backside.

Tearing his eyes away from Wilcox, Vince saw Dare drop to his knees beside the warrior. Blood bloomed on Red Wolf's chest.

Luke was one step behind Dare. He knelt so fast his hat went flying and his overlong black hair drooped into his eyes.

"How bad is it?" Luke's voice was awful to hear. So much fury and fear and grief. The sound of it made Vince turn back to Wilcox, who saw Vince's expression and scrambled away, still on the ground.

Leaning down, Vince grabbed the man by his shirt front and jerked him to his feet. And that was when the waves of alcohol on the man's breath hit.

"You're drunk." Vince plowed a fist into the man's face. It wasn't enough.

"Vince!" Dare's voice cut through the haze of Vince's rage. "You can beat him up later. I need my bag off my horse. Get back here fast."

Sparing one hard look at Red Wolf, Vince saw the Kiowa warrior's shirt was soaked in blood. When he let Wilcox go, the staggering fool sprawled on his back, his nose and lip bleeding. Leaving him there, Vince sprinted for Dare's horse.

Tug Andrews rode out of town at a full gallop. Tina watched him go and sent a prayer winging after him that he wouldn't meet a madwoman. Then she turned to her little group of warriors.

Paul had a gun. Rather than risk going home, he'd bought it from Tug. Armed now, he and Glynna had hurried back to the diner, where they holed up. The men would be at least two hours returning, and that was if Tug found them right away.

Tina could feel Lana lurking behind every door, every building. A knife in hand, or a torch. If she'd gotten into Glynna and Dare's house, she might have a gun. It was as if a dark, heavy fog hung over the whole town of Broken Wheel.

"She probably ran." Tina, along with Glynna and her children, and Ruthy and Mrs. Yates were huddled in the diner. "She broke jail. She probably ran far and fast. Stole a horse maybe. We need to check and see if anyone's missing a horse."

"We need to stay here," Ruthy said. "There's safety in numbers. We'll simply wait here until the menfolk come back."

"No." Tina felt her spine stiffen much like it did when she was preparing to picket the saloon. "I am tired to the bone of Lana Bullard and her nonsense. I have no wish to cower here. My aunt Iphigenia always said, 'A woman should know how to take—'"

"Care of herself," Glynna and Ruthy said together.

"We know," Glynna said.

"From stories you've told about all the chores you did," Ruthy said, "it sounds to me like your aunt mostly made you take care of *her.*"

Glynna shrugged and said sheepishly, "Iphigenia really does seem like a nasty old—"

"I think," Tina said, cutting Glynna off before she could finish in some unfortunate way, "it's time to have done with this nonsense. 'A coward dies a thousand deaths, a brave man but once.'"

"Is that your auntie, too?" Ruthy asked.

"I think it might've been Shakespeare."

208

"Do you often get your aunt mixed up with Shakespeare?" Glynna went and stood in the kitchen doorway.

"Almost never. Although she might've been quoting Shakespeare, so I may have given her credit for a lot of things she didn't deserve. Did Shakespeare ever say a woman should know how to take care of herself?"

"I don't know, but he did say, 'Fools rush in where angels fear to tread.'" Ruthy went to the front door. Glynna and Ruthy were guarding against Lana, but they were also blocking an escape attempt by Mrs. Yates.

"Would anyone like tea cake with their afternoon coffee?" Mrs. Yates asked.

Paul was pacing, an unfortunate tendency he was learning from having Dare for a stepfather. "I'm going to get Jonas."

"No, Paul," Glynna said. "I saw them walking to the east of town. You'd have to go hunting them, and Lana might be out there."

"We'll signal him to come back to town with some gunfire. Then I'll tell Sledge to shut down the forge and help us search the town." Paul checked the load on his pistol. "Once we're sure Lana's on the run, we'll pick up her tracks, form a posse, and get set to head out after her. Pa and his friends oughta be back by then."

He looked at his mother and sister. "Stay here. I'll bring you a gun as soon as I can." He dodged around Ruthy and went out the front door. He might want to take charge, but Tina noticed he didn't try to get past his mother.

"Paul!" Glynna called. But her boy was gone, maybe for good. Maybe there was only a man left.

"Let him go, Glynna," Tina said. Since they couldn't

stop him anyway. "Lana has never focused her anger on him." Much. Tina did seem to recall one scuffle.

"Once he rousts Sledge, maybe they can go together to find Jonas," Ruthy said. "Then we'll probably have Missy in here, too." She added dryly, "I imagine she's eager for our company."

Three shots split the air. Paul was right, that'd bring Jonas running.

"Missy is coming back?" Mrs. Yates smiled. "I do hope she brings my blue silk shawl with her. This is unseasonably cold weather for Georgia."

Red Wolf's eyes flickered open and blazed with pain.

Vince was back with the battered black leather doctor's bag before Dare got Red Wolf's buckskin shirt slit open.

Luke translated Dare's question into Red Wolf's guttural Kiowa language.

"It's not terribly bad." Dare heaved a sigh of relief as he removed a bundle of rags from his doctor's bag. "The bullet sliced the skin along his ribs, and he's losing a lot of blood, but I don't think it even broke a rib." He glanced up at Luke. "He'll be okay. He needs stitches, and there's the danger of infection, and he'll be weak from blood loss for a while, but in time he'll mend."

Exhaling until Vince thought he might deflate, Luke passed the news on to Red Wolf.

"Hunt for my sutures and the silk threads and the carbolic acid." Dare shoved the bag into Vince's stomach as he pressed a rag against the freely bleeding wound. "Hand them to me when I ask."

Dare snapped orders as he treated the fast-flowing wound and stitched it up. He soaked a bandage in his beloved carbolic acid and pressed it to the sewn-up bullet furrow.

"You'll need to change this bandage daily, and I'll send a bottle of . . ."

While Dare explained wound care to Red Wolf, Vince finally looked around to see where the drunken varmint was who'd done this. "Wilcox is gone!"

"I saw him stagger off a while ago," Luke said. "Don't worry about it. *I'll get him later.*"

It was a promise given with such quiet menace that Vince felt a chill run up his spine.

"What good is it to get him?" Red Wolf asked. "Do you think your law will arrest a man for shooting an Indian? Better chance he would be given honors for the deed."

Since Vince was the law, that stung a little. At the same time he knew it was true. Vince could arrest Wilcox and force the stumbling fool to face a judge, but the chance of his going to jail was somewhere between little and none. "He's almost for sure who shot at you, Luke. We can charge him for that, too."

"A drunkard with a gun." Luke's dark eyes flashed with rage. "It ain't a fit combination anywhere."

"So he's the one drinking in this canyon?" Dare finished bandaging Red Wolf and eased back on his heels. "But Duffy denies selling it to him. And whoever sold it to him likely sold it to Red Wolf's brave, too. We need to figure out if it's Duffy, or if maybe your man Wilcox got it somehow and he's the one who sold it to the Kiowa. That's against the law. And join that with shooting at Luke and shooting you, Red Wolf, and he'll be spendin' some time in a jail cell."

Luke nodded, staring at the canyon mouth. "It's gonna be my pleasure to put some hard questions to Wilcox."

"Best go about arresting him mighty careful." Dare gathered up his bottle of medicine and a few other doctoring supplies. "He's been drinkin' and he'll find himself another gun, and you know he didn't even mean to pull that trigger. He jumped and it went off, so you can't hope to reason with the yellowbelly coyote when you catch up with him." Reaching down, he offered Red Wolf a hand.

Red Wolf slapped Dare's hand aside and stood. Then his knees gave out. Luke grabbed Red Wolf around the waist, supporting his friend's wounded left side. A groan escaped Red Wolf's tight lips.

Dare put the supplies he held back into the bag, then caught Red Wolf from the other side. Luke let Dare bear Red Wolf's weight to ease the strain on the bullet wound.

"I reckon when I catch up with Wilcox, I'll handle him without much trouble." Luke was a tough man for a fact. Vince forgot that sometimes when Luke was busy being a husband, all chipper about a coming child.

"Let's get Red Wolf into the house." Dare gently helped the Kiowa chief along. "You need to rest for a few hours."

"While you're regaining your strength, I'm going on a manhunt," Luke said. He lifted his hat, smoothed his hair back, and clamped the hat back down to hold it out of his eyes. He needed to see everything that moved for the next several hours.

The approach of thundering hooves stopped them all

cold. Vince had his gun out before he'd made a conscious decision to draw.

Luke's foreman, Dodger, led that old mountain man Tug Andrews into the canyon.

As soon as he saw them, Tug shouted, "Lana Bullard broke jail. All the womenfolk are holed up in town. Lana's going on another killing rampage."

CHAPTER 18

Jonas stormed into the diner. He had one six-shooter holstered on his hip, another in his left hand, and a Winchester Yellow Boy rifle in his right. Tina hadn't realized just how scared she was until her brother walked in and made her feel safe.

He looked disheveled, but the anger in his eyes drove out her annoyance at his courtship. She remembered Jonas had ridden the outlaw trail for years before he'd found God in the middle of a Civil War battlefield.

Melissa was right behind him, her shining brown curls loose around her shoulders. It had been neatly twisted into a bun when she'd left.

Paul brought up the rear with his gun drawn.

Tina realized she'd started thinking of her as Missy until she'd caught the woman kissing her brother. It had been *Melissa* ever since.

Tina was going to have to get over that.

"Paul said Sledge Murphy will be here any minute." Jonas took charge and began rapping out orders like a general. "I'm going to roust Porter and make him help us. He's been in visiting Lana more than anyone. If she has anywhere she'd run, Porter has a better chance of knowing about it than anyone. I'll go get him." Jonas turned to Paul. "I want your help."

Tina saw Paul stand up straighter and nod.

"Ruthy, I'm putting you in charge. I know you can fire a gun." Jonas handed her the pistol he had in his hand. "This is Paul's. I got it out of Dare's house."

"Did you search the house for any sign that Lana might be hiding there?" Tina thought of the houses scattered around town. Lana could be lying in wait in one of them.

"Sure. I was careful, and I know what I'm doing. And Dare has good locks on his house now. Lana couldn't get in with a skeleton key like she did before." There was a sudden softening in Jonas's tone as he turned to Melissa. "I've got a lot to live for, so I'm going to be very careful."

He slid one arm around Melissa's waist and gave her a quick kiss. Then he got back to business. He rested his rifle on its butt, tilted against the table, then drew his Colt and checked the load. He holstered it and then made sure the Yellow Boy was loaded.

Looking up, Jonas said, "You women stay inside. Paul, let's go." He charged out just as suddenly as he'd come in. Paul slammed the kitchen door as he followed Jonas on the search for Lana.

A silence hung over the room for a moment. Then Melissa, her hands clenched together in front of her rather nervously, said, "He seems awfully comfortable with firearms for a man of the cloth."

Tina squashed the urge to tell Melissa a few hair-raising stories. "Make sure the back door is locked, Glynna."

Ruthy was already set by the front door, clearly up to

the challenge of this fight. Tina considered herself a strong woman, but perhaps not in the Western sense of the word. Letting Ruthy guard the door was just good sense. Ruthy was getting round with a baby, though. Tina found a chair so her friend could sit while she stood guard—sat guard? Tina wasn't sure what to call it.

Ruthy took the chair without complaint. "Thank you. I seem to wear out mighty fast these days." She'd taken a long morning nap, but Tina thought she looked like she could use another.

The tension in the room was thick.

"Janny, why don't you show Mrs. Yates your studies?" Glynna suggested, giving Janny a wink and nodding her head toward the stairs. Getting Mrs. Yates upstairs and out of the way seemed like a good idea.

Janny took Mrs. Yates by the hand. "Tell me about one of your tea parties, ma'am."

After they left, Tina said, "I'm going to put something on for supper." She saw Missy following after her toward the kitchen and braced herself to have a talk with the girl. But Missy got busy mixing up biscuits, and the only talk concerned where to find flour and bowls and such. Tina cut up the venison that wasn't fit for steaks, seared the meat in a big Dutch oven, then covered it with water.

"Don't you think you should fry that longer?" Glynna asked from where she stood guard by the back door.

"Don't be giving me cooking advice, Glynna." Tina smiled at her to take the sting out of the words.

Glynna shrugged. "I just hate raw food. It can make you sick, you know."

"I'll be careful, I promise." Tina set the meat to simmering to get tender for stew. She threw in onions and potatoes and left it toward the back of the stove, where it would gently steam the afternoon away without boiling dry.

"How are the biscuits?" Tina asked Missy.

"They're coming along fine. I'm a dab-hand at most baking. My ma and I had to do for ourselves. I didn't grow up in the Yateses' household, you know."

"Thank you for helping." Tina tried to be gracious. She wasn't sure how well she covered her resentment, but she knew it wasn't fair, so she suppressed it to the best of her ability and hoped Melissa wasn't the sensitive type.

The biscuits were mixed up in no time, and then without asking, Melissa set to making a batch of bread. Tina was impressed and wondered if she could lure the unsuspecting woman into helping at the diner full-time. An extra pair of hands would give Tina more time to picket the saloon.

Maybe Mrs. Yates could sign on as a waitress too, make herself useful. There wasn't much she could mess up about serving meals, short of pouring boiling hot coffee on the men's laps.

Finally, as the afternoon stretched toward evening, Jonas and Paul came back. Ruthy jumped out of her chair by the front door or she might've gotten smacked.

"Porter's gone and his horse, too. I'm sure those are his tracks along with Lana's leading out of the back of the jailhouse. He probably helped with the escape. They've been planning it, I reckon, waiting for a chance when everyone was distracted."

"How can you tell it was planned?" Tina asked.

"We found where another horse was tied outside of town. Looked like it had been there a long time. I only followed them a short while, but they were heading straight west at a gallop. We can't be sure they won't circle back, but I think for now we can hope they're making a run for it."

"Aren't we going to chase after them?" Glynna looked fierce for such a delicate woman.

"No, at least not until we get more men. We'll wait for everyone to get back from Luke's." Jonas gave Glynna a rather weak smile. "Would it be so bad to just let them get away?"

Gasping, Glynna said, "She tried to kill Dare three times."

"I know," Jonas said, sounding a little sheepish, "but she seems to have calmed down lately. And we haven't had much luck figuring out what to do with her. I think we should just let her go. She's already out of Vince's jurisdiction. He doesn't have a badge that lets him do much sheriffing that far outside of town. We can sure go after them, but we might be gone for days, maybe weeks."

Jonas gave Melissa a look of longing, clearly not interested in being away from her, not even for one day. "We could get the Texas Rangers after them, yet by the time we rustle up a Ranger, Porter and Lana will be out of Texas. After that it's the U.S. marshals' job, and I don't know how to go about finding a marshal. Ride to Fort Worth, I 'spect, or maybe send a wire to someone—not sure who."

Tina felt a whisper of relief to think Lana and her madness might be someone else's problem. "Maybe, since her lunacy was mostly aimed at Dare, she might not be too much trouble once she gets away from him." Tina looked at Glynna. "What do you think?"

"I don't know." Glynna flung her arms wide. "I don't

want Dare on her trail for days, either. But what if she comes back? I'd have to be convinced she left the area."

"I could track her," Ruthy said, looking fierce. "I can out-track anyone in these parts, and that includes my husband. I wouldn't even hesitate except my belly's slowing me down some."

"As it is," Jonas said, "we have no choice but to wait. When Vince and the others get back, we can decide then what to do next. I could go after Porter and Lana myself, but I don't like leaving you all here unguarded."

"Well, if they really are running for the hills, it gives them more time to get clean away." Tina wasn't sure if that was a good or bad thing. "I've got to finish supper. We can all eat together here at the diner."

She headed back for the kitchen, wondering if being turned loose in the Texas wilderness with that low-down Mitch Porter might be the perfect punishment for Lana's crimes.

Just as Tina stepped up to the stove to thicken the broth around the meat, hooves pounded outside. She leaned to peek out the kitchen window, afraid Lana had come back. It was Vince—leading a line of horses into the clearing at the edge of town.

CHAPTER 19

Vince had been riding in a flat-out panic the whole way home. His long-legged thoroughbred was game. They'd made the trip from Luke's in record time. Dare and Luke were right on his tail, but he'd gotten a jump on them while they gave orders to care for Red Wolf.

The sun had dipped below the horizon as he neared town. In the winter dusk he listened for bullets, imagining his mother being gunned down. His new sister dying in a hail of flying lead. Tina lying dead, all the fire and sass gone.

As they'd neared Broken Wheel, Vince heard no gunfire. Was it over? Was everyone dead?

He raced for the diner and pulled his well-trained gelding to a halt so hard it reared up. Vince's feet hit the ground before his horse's did.

With his gun drawn he sprinted for the diner door, wondering if he needed to go in low. Wondering if the women were being held hostage. Would he meet armed resistance? The diner door swung open just as he was reaching for it. Ruthy smiled, sitting in a chair, holding the doorknob in one hand and a gun in the other.

Vince skidded to a stop before he plowed over Luke's

pregnant wife. "What's going on? I thought Lana was on a rampage. Tug said she was loose." Vince heard his friends thundering up behind him and moved farther into the clearly unthreatened diner.

"We're fine." Ruthy shrugged, then looked past Vince and her face lit up with a smile she only used with Luke.

"Lana Bullard broke jail." Jonas rose from where he sat playing checkers with Paul. Melissa, Tina, then a step later, Glynna came in from the kitchen. It was about the most peaceful scene Vince had ever encountered.

"Porter helped her. The two of them hightailed it straight west. Paul and I tracked them for a while, but they'd probably been gone for hours. We think they made the break right after you rode out of town, and we didn't miss them until after the noon rush was over. They had enough of a jump on me I never caught a glimpse of them. I broke off the chase because I didn't want to leave the women alone."

Vince had his hands full not collapsing into a heap on the floor as the tension seeped out of every muscle in his body. He'd never been this scared in his life, and he'd fought in the Civil War.

Dare pushed past Vince and headed straight for Glynna. "She didn't try anything?"

Glynna's eyes filled with tears as she shook her head. "No, we never even saw her. We found out she was gone when Paul and Janny went over with dinner. I just let them go right in there. She could have been waiting. She could have hurt them . . . and I s-sent them." Her voice broke, and Dare quickly wrapped her in his arms and held her as she sobbed.

Dare looked at Vince from where he stood holding his

wife. "I'm taking Glynna home. We can't start after Lana tonight. Tomorrow is soon enough."

Jonas said, "We checked your house thoroughly and there's no one there."

"Thanks," Dare replied. "Paul, get Janny and come with us now."

Paul ran up the stairs and soon returned with Janny and Mrs. Yates. Dare steered his family toward the back door.

"Wait!" Tina rushed to the kitchen. "Let me send you with a meal. I made enough for everyone. There's no sense letting it go to waste."

Dare gave her a grateful smile as she ladled a smaller pan full of the stew. No one knew better than Dare this was the best chance he had of eating well tonight. Tina filled a plate with biscuits and covered them with a red-and-white-checkered cloth.

Paul had the pot of stew. Janny took the biscuits. Dare drew his gun. The family left, and Tina locked up after them. When she returned to the dining room, Jonas and Melissa were gone, and Ruthy had fallen asleep with her head resting on the table.

"Where'd Jonas go?"

Vince gave Tina a dry look that told her she didn't want to know.

"I'm taking Ruthy upstairs for the night." Luke eased Ruthy into his arms and together they left the room. They could hear his heavy boots clomping on the steps.

"Would anyone like to play a hand of whist?" Mrs. Yates looked around the room. "Now where did I leave those cards?"

Tina quickly set a plate of steaming stew in front of Mrs.

Yates, and she must have been hungry because she forgot about cards and dove into the meal. Tina fed Vince and then threw a meaty bone to Livvy before sitting down to her own meal.

She set out plates for Jonas and Melissa and Luke, assuming they'd be back to eat.

By the time Tina was done eating, Mrs. Yates was nearly asleep where she sat on the bench. "Can you walk us over to the boardinghouse, Vince? You stand guard while I get your mother to bed."

A deep snore sounded from overhead; there was no chance it was Ruthy. So Luke wasn't coming back. "I'll set the stew back on the stove so it won't burn, and if Luke and Ruthy get hungry in the night, they can come down and eat something. Maybe Jonas and Melissa are over at Asa's." Tina realized then she was talking quite fast and not giving Vince much chance to arrange the evening. But all she could think about was getting Mrs. Yates settled, which meant shutting the woman in a room with Tina on the inside of the door and Vince on the outside.

Vince came around the table to where Virginia Belle sat next to Tina, and with a strong hand he helped his ma to her feet. "Let's get you to bed now, Mother," he said.

They walked to the boardinghouse, and Vince saw Tina and his ma all the way to the bedroom door.

"Tina, I think we should talk about—"

"Not now, Vince," Tina interrupted. "Your ma is exhausted." She then shut the door before he could say anything more.

◦◦◦◦◦

Tina took her time getting Vince's ma ready for bed — not that hard to take time at it because the woman was wearing all the underpinnings of a fine lady. A corset and chemise, petticoats and hoops, drawers and stockings and other things that Tina barely recognized, let alone figured out how to remove. Half of this wasn't going back on the woman tomorrow, not if Tina was the one who had to get her dressed.

While she worked, she listened for Jonas's voice, but it never came.

Tina finally admitted that her brother was so caught up in Melissa he'd forgotten he had a sister, a sister now left in a seriously improper situation.

If he did give it any mind, Jonas probably thought Ruthy and Luke were staying here.

Dare had herded his family home, wanting to get inside with the doors locked while Lana was on the run, not even thinking that within minutes Jonas and Melissa would abandon the diner to resume their courtship.

Then Ruthy had fallen asleep at the table, so tired she couldn't keep her eyes open. The question was left open as to who would be chaperoning Tina and Vince. And Luke had probably never heard of the word *chaperone*.

Now here was Tina, wondering when Melissa would come back so she could take over the care of Mrs. Yates, and Tina could leave here and go to Jonas's house. Until then, there was only one other person besides Mrs. Yates left to stay in this house with Tina, and that was Vince.

Which left Tina pretty much on her own with the most attractive man she'd ever known. A man whose intentions toward her were the exact opposite of honorable.

Tina's excuses for staying closed in this room ran out

when Virginia Belle quietly began to snore. Livvy lay on the floor near Virginia Belle's feet. For a moment Tina considered sleeping right there with Livvy. Why not bed down beside the dog? But she had no nightgown, the floor was hard and cold, and there were no blankets to make up even a simple pallet.

Melissa had to come back sometime. *She had to.*

Tina knew Jonas to be an honorable man, so she'd come. Yet Tina could picture the two of them, sitting in front of the fireplace at the parsonage, talking and getting to know each other. Courting.

Tina couldn't interrupt them.

I'll just duck out of this room and wait downstairs. Vince may have already gone to bed. We won't even see each other.

That was a sound plan.

Quietly she stepped out of Virginia Belle's room.

Vince stood at the top of the stairs, leaning against the wall, arms crossed. Standing guard.

"Uh . . . go on to bed, Vince. I'll wait downstairs for my brother."

Get away before he speaks. Before you find yourself kissing him!

Tina turned toward the stairs.

"Stop." His voice was deep and smooth. It touched a chord in her that rang like music.

Like a brainless ninny, Tina turned back to face him. To face the big dumb charming varmint.

"I'll come with you, Tina. We need to talk."

Oh, there was no doubt about it. She was a complete half-wit where Vince Yates was concerned, because she headed for the stairs without a word of protest.

She had to slip past him, and when she did, her skirts brushed against his legs. Her arm touched his. She felt those brief touches all the way to her bones.

Lifting her skirts to keep from tumbling, she took a firm grip on the banister and hurried down before her knees grew as weak as her will—both tended to happen in Vince's presence.

She went into the front room. Cantankerous old Asa hadn't been one to open his home for social gatherings, which explained why everything in this room was shabby and coated with dust. Vince must have lit the two lanterns that burned here, then gone upstairs to lie in wait for her like a hungry cougar . . . only better looking.

Tina had no idea how long Asa had owned the boardinghouse, but she got the feeling the furniture had been here before him. There was a threadbare sofa that might have been green once upon a time. An overstuffed brown chair with what looked like horsehair poking out in spots. Two small tables stood on either side of the sofa, each with a lantern. All of it was centered around a fireplace that looked as if it'd never been lit. It was stone cold, but it hardly mattered. Tina wasn't planning to sit in here long enough to need a fire. She sank into the overstuffed chair that was at a right angle to the sofa and faced the door to the hallway.

Vince followed her into the room. She tried not to look at him, instead straightening the skirts of her blue dress as if her life depended on tidiness. He took a seat on the old sofa, as far away from her as he could. A second later, he stood back up and moved to the hearth and leaned against it. The man was as restless as Dare Riker. Next he went to the door that led to the hallway. He opened the door wide and stood so he could see upstairs yet still keep an eye on Tina.

"Well? What is it, Vince?" Tina felt what little composure she possessed slipping away. "I'm tired. Unless it's really important, let's have this talk in the morning." *Or never.*

Vince crossed his arms, then uncrossed them. He ran both hands through his hair and made a mess of it. Tina had to fight back the impulse to go smooth his hair back into place.

"How's Mother?" he asked.

Tina knew beyond a shadow of a doubt that Vince hadn't brought her down here to discuss his mother. Still, it was a safer topic than any that were on Tina's mind. "She seems fine. She asked for Missy a couple of times."

Shaking his head, Vince said, "Looks like your brother will be marrying my sister. 'Course I just learned a little while ago I had a sister."

"Love at first sight. Jonas believes he's found his perfect mate, the one God chose for him."

Vince shrugged. "So Mother wasn't upset that Missy was gone?"

"Not really. She thinks I'm a housemaid. I told her my name, but she called me Clara a couple times today."

"I don't remember a Clara from our home in Chicago. Maybe it's someone she knew when she was a child." Vince sighed so heavily that Tina had to let go of some of her anger out of sympathy for him.

"Don't worry, Vince, we'll figure out a way to take care of your mother. Once Jonas and Melissa are married, Jonas can move in here with you and that will be one more helping hand. But it's not proper for me to be here with you. I think I should go stay in your mother's room until Jonas brings Melissa—"

"About that kiss . . ." Vince began, cutting her off.

She'd really hoped she could avoid this conversation for tonight. Honestly she'd hoped to avoid it forever, but one night at a time. "It was a mistake, that's all." Tina talked fast. "You were tired. I was upset. Let's forget it ever happened."

Vince jerked his head up, and his eyes blazed. "I'm having a little trouble forgetting."

"You'll have to apply yourself."

"How about you? Have you forgotten?"

Silence stretched between them. At last Tina said quietly, "I'll have to apply myself, too."

"Which means no."

Tina closed her eyes. There was silence again. This was the moment when a man with honorable intentions would propose. Vince seemed decent enough . . . except in his dealings with her.

"I'll tell you simply, Vince. Seeing Jonas and Melissa meet and fall in love and instantly begin talking of marriage . . . well, that's not how I think a couple should behave."

"I agree with you there."

"Jonas probably calls it love, and I'm hoping it grows into that, but the truth is, what they feel"—Tina dug deep and found the courage to look Vince straight in the eye— "is what we feel. That draw. That tug of attraction that's almost too strong to deny. Yet my brother wants to put the word *love* on it. You, on the other hand, want to ignore what passed between us, or deny it, or possibly just tell the truth about it—that we're attracted to each other but it's not the same as love. So we need to behave in a more circumspect way. There will be no more kissing. And despite the attraction, you're not the man for me any more than I'm the woman for you. We'd spend our entire married life at each other's throats."

"Oh, I think there would be some good moments." Which sounded like Vince had considered joining their lives together. Considered it, and then rejected it. "But I'm never going to marry, Tina. I should never have kissed you, no matter how much I want to."

"You want to?"

"Oh yeah, I do." Their eyes locked. "But there's something that stops me every time I think of spending my future with you."

Tina waited to hear that she was a nag. She was too willing to fight for her causes. She was too stiff, too fussy, too unlovable. It was all true. She accepted that, and yet here was Vince in a seemingly honest mood. No doubt he would share all her shortcomings and why he refused to contend with them. She could hardly blame him. Some days she wouldn't stay around herself if she could get away.

"Which one of my parents do you think I'm like?"

Startled out of her lowering thoughts, Tina said, "Which are you like? I don't really know either of them that well. I was around your father for a total of maybe two hours, and your mother isn't herself."

"I think it's almost a law that a child is raised in the way he will go. I believe that's in the Bible, in fact. I'm either like my tyrant of a father, and believe me, I feel that inside me."

"Really? You don't seem all that tyrannical. Bossy maybe."

"Or I'm like my mother. And that could well mean I'll lose my mind as I age. Which one of those two people would you wish on someone, Tina? And my mother's madness is passed down from her father, so I carry the seeds of it. I will most likely pass it on to a child. Do you wish that for yourself? Do you wish for a life spent, in your own declining years, caring for an addled husband who doesn't know his own wife?"

Vince's voice rose with every word. "Do you wish to watch your children go mad? Or would you prefer to live with a tyrant who can be so frightening he'd raise up a son who doesn't know how to ever let down his guard? Which of those people do you want to marry?"

"Don't pretend this is about you." Tina rose and stormed right for him. "I know I'm not a lovable woman." She got right up under his nose, furious. This was the unpleasant part of herself, the snippy, nagging part no one could warm up to. Well, he might as well know the truth of who she was. "I know my aunt was rigid, but even rigid people love children most of the time, and she couldn't find anything about me to love. She loved her new husband easily enough, but not me. And I know Jonas is only letting me stay here out of pity."

Jabbing a finger at his chest, she went on, "I know if a man really cared about a woman, he would be willing to do anything to have her in his life. I'm going upstairs now, and I don't want you to touch me again or make excuses for why you want to kiss me one minute and shove me away the next."

"You're not going anywhere until we settle this." Vince

brushed her jabbing hand aside. "We're stuck together caring for my mother, and we need to clear the air."

"This is what happened before. We argued. We got too close. You grabbed me and I let you. Well, that's not going to happen again. I'm going up to your mother's room and I'm locking the door. I will remain in there until my brother comes to deliver your sister and return me to my home. You go to your room and stay there." Tina whirled and started for the steps.

She felt Vince grab for her, his hands just barely missing as she moved. He wanted to force her to stay and listen to his excuses. Just as he probably wanted to kiss her again.

She rushed upstairs. When she reached the top, she realized there were no thundering footsteps chasing her. She looked over her shoulder to see Vince standing where he'd been, watching her, his eyes burning with temper and something more.

He hadn't even cared enough to chase after her, not even in the heat of the moment.

In the heat of the moment Vince wanted to grab her and kiss her and probably make a bunch of promises he had no business making and no intention of keeping.

Their eyes held for a long while, and only fierce self-discipline kept him from running up those stairs. Then he realized that what he was seeing in her eyes was not anger, but hurt. It broke his control just as she spun and disappeared into Mother's room. From way downstairs he heard the harsh *click* of the key turning in the lock.

Smart lady.

Jonas had no business leaving the two of them alone, even though Jonas almost certainly wasn't thinking they were alone. With every Regulator right here in town, how in the world had Vince ended up alone with beautiful Tina? Well, alone except for his mother.

His gelding would've made a better chaperone than Mother. And Vince was sorely tempted to go sleep with his horse, except that would leave Mother and Tina alone in the house, completely unprotected with Lana Bullard on the loose.

With that in mind, Vince turned to check the lock on the front door. He'd gone all around the house twice while Tina had spent an interminable hour tucking Mother in. The house was secure. Lana couldn't get to them, and she probably wouldn't think to come here even if she did return to town.

Every time he thought of Tug racing toward him and the panic that had spurred Vince back to Broken Wheel, his heart lurched—even now after he'd assured himself they were all safe.

"*Killing rampage,*" Tug Andrews had said. Vince's mother, his sister, his friend Jonas, his . . . He thought of Tina but she certainly wasn't *his*. And yet she'd been far too much in the front of his thoughts as he'd spurred his horse toward town.

How had he gotten to be the man with so much family to protect? Sure, Luke and Dare had wives in danger. Dare had two kids. Luke had one on the way. But Vince figured he had more on the line than the both of them.

Vince hoped Lana and Porter pushed hard all the way to California. That might be wrongheaded for the town sheriff to hope his prisoner got clean away, but keeping

Lana locked up had been a pure nuisance. The choice of places she might end up was brutal. Everyone was tired of feeding her. And good riddance to that no-account Mitch Porter. Vince was glad to see the back of him. If Vince could depend on the couple staying away, he wouldn't even consider chasing them down.

When Tina had entered Mother's room, Vince had heard her turn the key. He'd double-checked the closed latches on the windows in Mother's room earlier, so Mother couldn't do any nighttime wandering.

That left Vince with a long night and no hope of sleeping.

He went to the north window in the front room that looked down the length of Main Street. A second window on the east gave him a nice angle on Dare's house.

That was who needed watching.

Vince leaned against the window frame, settling in to stand guard through the night. Without even asking, Vince knew Luke would watch later, and that was why he'd gone to sleep early. No doubt Dare was up and alert, too. Vince knew his friends well, his faith in them absolute. The only one Vince wasn't counting on was Jonas. And even at that he'd have been on guard, except he knew Vince, Luke, and Dare were all in town.

It was getting late enough that soon Jonas would come and take Tina away. Maybe then Vince would get himself a couple of hours' sleep in a chair stationed at this window. If he didn't, he'd somehow get through the day without it. Vince had learned at an early age never to relax. Keeping watch was the only way he'd ever found to truly feel safe.

A lesson learned from a father who would kill a harmless little pony and think he was doing it for his son's own good.

It was a way of life that had served Vince well, and he wasn't going to abandon it now . . . especially since he wasn't going to sleep anyway. Not with Tina so close he could practically hear her breathing.

Standing watch, though, wasn't keeping his unruly mind under control.

He thought of that first moment when he'd seen Tina. When she'd gone flying into Jonas's arms. Jonas had lifted her off her feet, whirled her around, and Vince had looked right into her eyes. More had passed between them in that first glance than he'd ever shared with a woman in his life. He'd seen all the way to her heart.

Clenching his hands, he could still feel the weight of her when he'd lifted the bedraggled little pest out of that mudhole. He'd wanted her in his arms. Carrying her to the diner, no matter how annoying she was, had been a pleasure.

When he'd foisted the job of sheriff on her, she'd been horrified but too stubborn to admit the job was beyond her. Vince had known Dare and Jonas were around to help out, so he'd gone right ahead and handed over his badge.

Then he'd come riding into town from New Orleans, filthy, exhausted, starving. And she'd come charging out of the jail to greet him, smiling that smile that made a man feel like the sun had come out from behind a cloud. Oh, she'd said it was because she was tired of being sheriff. But it had been purely nice to have her welcome him.

And then he'd kissed her. He could still taste her lips. Even if he spent a lifetime avoiding her—which he fully intended to do—he'd never forget how sweet she was.

Nope, he wasn't going to sleep so long as she was in this house, and that was that.

He had an addled mother.

A little sister who was supposed to help but who had instead, at least for now, abandoned Mother to anyone else's care.

His friend Red Wolf had been shot by a drunk, who'd made a clean getaway.

He had someone selling whiskey to the Kiowa tribe.

And he had a runaway prisoner who he oughta round up first thing in the morning—even though it might mean he'd be gone for days when he shouldn't abandon his mother for more than a few minutes.

All that should give a man plenty to occupy his mind. But all he could think about was pretty, feisty Tina Cahill. And the fact that the two of them were stuck together minding Mother.

He shifted his stance to get a better look at Dare's house and did his level best to think of something else.

And failed miserably.

CHAPTER 20

Tina finally got out of Vince's house for the night, but she was right back in the morning because Melissa had asked for help when she'd arrived home. Melissa would need a few moments to run to the privy and such. Most likely before Mrs. Yates was up and dressed for the day. Vince watching her would never do.

She woke to an unusual rainy morning, for it was a dry land here in Texas. She wasn't prepared for the sand to stick to her shoes as it had, and she'd only been in the house long enough to pull off her muddy shoes when she heard the crash. All she knew was that if Mrs. Yates was breaking things, it was bad. Barefoot, she rushed for Virginia Belle's room. A cry of alarm from behind the locked door nearly made her drop the key they'd left in the lock.

Livvy yelped from inside, then broke into a whine.

Tina fumbled the key for a second but held on and got it turned. She wrenched the door open.

Mrs. Yates held a lit match in her hands.

She stood amidst shards of glass from a broken lantern, looking around as if she wasn't sure what the match was for. The front of her long white nightgown was soaked in kerosene. If she dropped that match, she'd light herself on fire as well as the whole room, and with the fuel soaking the floor the whole boardinghouse could go up in flames.

The poor little foxhound stood outside the circle of glass, focused on her mistress but unable to get to her. Livvy had probably stepped on the glass.

Tina took one step toward Virginia Belle and stopped. Her feet would be cut to shreds, but the match in Virginia Belle's hand was burning down. Tina couldn't let the match drop, even if it meant walking on broken glass with bare feet.

Before she took the next step, Vince thundered up the stairs.

She looked back, and their eyes met for a moment. She could have cried, she was so relieved to see him.

He pushed past her, crunched over the glass. He was wearing his shoes . . . and wearing the same clothes . . . and he'd come from downstairs.

He'd kept watch all night. But he must have slept or he'd have come out to torment her when she arrived.

Vince crossed the room to his ma, plucked the burning match from her fingers and blew it out, then swept his barefoot mother up in his arms.

"Missy made this mess, Julius." His mother looked stern.

"We'll clean it up, don't worry." Despite his soothing voice, Vince's expression of worry put lines in his face. How could they keep her safe?

It had never occurred to Tina to take the lantern and matches from the room, but now it seemed so obvious. What other things were they forgetting? Mrs. Yates looked like a befuddled child.

238

"Stay back, Tina. I don't want you to get cut." The concern in his voice almost drove out the memory of how he'd rejected her last night. "Get your shoes on, then come back and gather some clothes for Mother. I'll take her to my room. We'll need to wash the kerosene off her. You can do that and get her dressed while I clean up this mess." Vince looked toward the dog. "Livvy, come."

Slowly the dog followed him out of the room. At first glance Tina didn't see any wounds, but the dog's yelping had sounded like pain. She'd check Livvy's paws as soon as she could.

Tina dashed down the stairs and yanked on her sodden half boots. She heard Vince's orders as if they still echoed in the house. He was a man who knew how to lead. Tina didn't think that was a bad thing, but she suspected Vince only saw his natural take-charge reactions as a regrettable resemblance to his father.

Soon Tina was back in Virginia Belle's room. Mindful of the shattered glass, she stepped carefully as she gathered up a fresh bundle of garments for Mrs. Yates.

Tina went into Vince's room and saw his mother sitting on the bed. Vince knelt at her feet, head bowed as if he were before royalty. He spoke softly to her as he lifted one foot and examined it carefully for cuts.

"You didn't cut yourself." Vince sounded so loving as he cared for his mother.

My mother is a madwoman, and my father is a tyrant. Whichever one of them I am, no woman should tie herself to me. I am never going to inflict myself on a woman and most certainly not on a child.

That was what he'd said when he rejected her. And yet

here he knelt, a picture of decency and love. Not like either of his parents.

"I think Livvy cut her paw." Vince said it so quietly, it took Tina a second to realize he'd aimed the statement at her rather than his mother.

Before he had to give more orders, Tina went to Livvy. The dog was standing there resting her chin on the bed. Tina stooped down by the dog, which put her shoulder to shoulder with Vince. When Tina lifted the injured paw, she noticed a few drops of blood on the floor. Nothing serious, but the dog would be hurting for a while.

After checking, Tina said, "There's no glass stuck in her paw, and it has stopped bleeding already."

"Good, because we need this dog."

"Livvy is hurt?" Mrs. Yates reached down and patted the foxhound's head. "This is Missy's fault." Mrs. Yates turned to Vince. "Julius, I insist you dismiss her at once."

For all the things she was forgetting, what if Virginia Belle remembered Missy breaking the lantern and refused to be around her? That would take an important pair of hands away from the job of caring for Vince's mother.

"I have to ride out and hunt for Lana and Porter, and we need to track down the man who shot Red Wolf. If we don't settle things to the Kiowa's satisfaction, well, we don't want the tribe to start feeling hostile."

Focusing on the dog's paw, Tina knew what would come next. The job of caring for Mrs. Yates was going to fall even more heavily to her. And that still left her job at the diner.

She looked out and saw the sun was pushing back the night. Tina barely had time to get Mrs. Yates cleaned up and dressed before she'd need to get to the diner and start her morning's baking of bread.

Well, Mrs. Yates was just going to have to pour coffee today, because Tina couldn't watch her over here and cook over there. And giving the lady a big pot of boiling hot coffee no doubt qualified as one of those potentially dangerous things they should make sure she be kept away from.

Of course Glynna could care for Mrs. Yates. She could be spared far more easily at the diner. A sad but true fact, though the menfolk in town thought getting a private moment to speak to Glynna was an important part of their meal.

None of them had much to say to Tina—what with her scolding them for their drinking habits. But that was just fine, as she was too busy scooping up food for the polecats. And maybe they'd start liking her more soon, because with cooking and sheriffing and now tending Mrs. Yates, Tina hadn't found time to picket for quite a while.

"You know, I saw protesting Duffy's Tavern as a mission field." Tina gave Vince a disgruntled look.

Vince didn't answer as he examined his mother's other foot, but Tina thought she heard a quiet moan come from him.

"And my mission is even more badly needed in light of the drunken cowpoke at Luke's and the shooting of Red Wolf."

"Not sure you waving around a placard would've changed all that. Besides, Duffy denied selling any bottles of whiskey."

"Well, he would, wouldn't he?" Tina decided kneeling beside Vince was too friendly. It made her feel as if they were kneeling at the altar. She'd heard of couples doing such during a wedding ceremony and she had no wish to emulate that, however slight the comparison.

She rose from the floor, scooped Livvy into her arms, and sat beside Mrs. Yates, who reeked of kerosene. "Livvy and I are going to get more water. I believe Mrs. Yates is going to need a bath."

"I have a fair supply of water already heating," Vince said.

"When did you do that?"

"I had plenty of time because I didn't get any sleep last night." Vince looked up at Tina, and she saw the dark circles under his eyes.

"I'm sorry if you're tired, Julius." Tina said the name with relish, and Vince's expression promised retaliation. Good luck to him. "It's just that I don't have much time for sympathy, what with having two jobs and being on the verge of being evicted from my home when the day comes that Jonas casts me aside for a wife."

"He won't cast you aside." Vince looked at her hard, and the heat in his gaze reminded Tina of every time he'd touched her.

Tina felt her resentment grow. She liked being angry better than feeling hurt. "I've got less than an hour before I need to start breakfast. I'll be back with a tub and the water."

Stalking toward the door, thinking of how heavy it was all going to be while a big strong man was right here and not offering to help, she was in the hall when Vince said, "Tina, wait."

His commanding voice had her stopping without really

choosing to, which annoyed her. But she turned back. Maybe he was going to offer to do the heavy lifting at least.

"It'll be a lot easier for you if you leave the dog here." Vince smiled a cranky smile that let her know he was tormenting her deliberately.

"Fine." She let Livvy down, and even the dog she'd been tending abandoned her to worship at Virginia Belle's feet.

As she tromped down the stairs, Tina thought back to the day she'd come to town and moved into Jonas's house. A single woman caring for her bachelor brother in a quiet little Texas town hadn't seemed like it was that big of a job. But honestly there weren't enough hours in the day.

CHAPTER 21

There just weren't enough hours in the day for all Vince had laid out in front of him.

Vince had seen a lantern come on in the diner, and after nearly wrestling the bucket of water away from Tina and carrying it, he'd left Mother in Tina's care. He wanted to help any way he could, but he had no role in getting Mother bathed and dressed. So he'd come over to the diner to find Dare and Luke already there, while Ruthy made coffee and put bread on to bake.

"We have to go search for Quince Wilcox." Luke sat at the table, his eyes so cold that Vince felt the chill as if he'd never stepped indoors. "Red Wolf's people aren't that happy with me, anyway. Dodger said he'd get Red Wolf home last night, and Red Wolf will stay friendly, but if the Kiowa are upset enough, he may not be able to control every warrior in his band. We need to lock Wilcox up and make sure the Kiowa know we aren't going to stand for him shooting their chief."

"No." Dare slashed a hand to silence Luke. "We can round up Wilcox later. We have to go after Lana. She's more dangerous than the Kiowa."

245

Luke slapped the table. "Lana Bullard is *not* more dangerous than a tribe of restless Indians."

"Well, she tried to kill me, Glynna, Paul, and you, Vince. The Kiowa haven't done that."

"Not yet."

"We need to do both," Dare said. He began pacing so fast it was making Vince's neck hurt to follow the man.

"Jonas thinks she's running," Luke said. "If that's so, then there's little chance she'll come back, and we'll never catch her with this much of a head start. I'm not about to follow her trail all the way to California."

"But she could circle back." Dare's back-and-forth path started curving, as if *he* were circling back. "I need to make sure she isn't going to attack Glynna. That's got to come first."

Dare and Luke glowered at each other, then together they turned to Vince.

Invincible Vince. He knew—even though it was never spoken of—that he was their leader. It had always been that way. And now he had to say what was on his mind.

"Mother came within seconds of burning the boardinghouse down this morning. Even if we could've gotten the fire out, she'd have been badly hurt because she broke a lantern and spilled kerosene on herself while she stood there holding a lit match. I don't dare run off right now chasing after an escaped prisoner."

"So you're saying," Luke growled, "that our choices for today are between heading off a tribe of Indians, tracking down Lana, or tending to your ma?"

Vince had never felt less invincible in his life. "I wouldn't put it exactly like that."

246

"We can't let Wilcox get away." Luke shoved himself to his feet so hard the bench under his backside tipped over. "There could be trouble that might spread through the Indian Territory. The whole tribe could turn on folks in the area. Lives could be lost—"

"All right!" Vince said. "I get it. We'll go after Wilcox."

Dare shook his head. "You're gonna let Lana just ride off? That woman held a knife to Glynna's throat. She almost killed—"

"Dare!" Vince cut him off. "You know I never asked for the job of sheriff, and no one pays me a cent."

"You took an oath." Luke stood, pulling on his gloves. "We go after Wilcox first. We're wastin' time—let's ride out to the S Bar S."

"No, we ride after Lana first," Dare countered. "She's the one who broke jail. She's the prisoner Vince was supposed to be in charge of."

"She's on the run and you know it," Luke snapped.

"We don't know any such thing." Dare actually stood still, though the anger in his eyes as he faced Luke was an active kind of anger. "Yes, they ran when they first broke out, but who's to say she didn't lay down a false trail?"

The diner door swung open. Luke and Dare fell silent. Tina came in guiding Mother. The woman grinned at Vince as if the sun shone from his eyes. "Julius, good morning. It's so nice of you to come home from work and join us for tea."

The dog was moving pretty well, not limping at all.

Tina brought Mrs. Yates over to Vince. "I need to start cooking," she told him. Mother was fresh and clean now, but Tina was a disheveled mess and she smelled a bit like kerosene.

Vince rested a hand on his mother's back and smiled, even as he chafed at being called Julius again. Then all his common sense and leadership skills snapped into place. "Dare."

Dare stood to attention, then caught himself and relaxed, glaring at Vince. "What?"

"We let Lana go."

"We can't—"

"You said I'm sheriff, and that's the sheriff's decision. We trust Jonas when he said she was quitting the country. You can ride out and check the trail if you're worried, but Jonas knows how to track."

"Yep, he's a tracker for sure, but he can't be trusted."

"What do you mean he can't be trusted? He's a man of the cloth, for heaven's sake."

"Chasing Lana interrupted his courtship. He was looking for an excuse to come home."

Vince had to concede the point, but Dare didn't renew his demand that Vince chase down the escaped prisoner. Instead, Dare sped up his pacing—not happy but not swinging a fist, either.

"Luke," Vince started.

"Don't say we let Wilcox go. I refuse to let that—"

"Shut up for a minute!"

Luke didn't even pretend to come to attention, but he did stop his talking.

"Wilcox is an idiot."

"True enough, but that doesn't mean—"

"Let me finish."

Luke scowled.

"Go ahead and find him. You don't need me. Go back

248

to your ranch and see if he's there. A drunkard like him might have just gone back to the ranch and to bed. We didn't have time to say much to Dodger. Tell Dodger to set your men to searching. Red Wolf's mighty upset, and arresting that fool hasn't got a chance of calming him down. He's right—no court is gonna convict Wilcox of shooting an Indian. It ain't right, but it's a fact all the same. And Red Wolf knowing it's true is what's got him and his people in a lather."

"I want to catch him and charge him and bring him to trial. It's the right thing to do."

"And we will do it, but we don't have to do it today. It won't appease the Kiowa one speck. In fact, go talk to them. Tell the Kiowa to go after Wilcox. If they want to start a war, tell 'em to aim it where it belongs."

"Which means," Dare said grimly, "you've decided that taking care of your ma is what you're going to spend the day doing."

Vince looked down at his mother, who was looking around the diner in a vague way, like maybe she was realizing she wasn't home in her Chicago mansion and waiting for lady friends to come over for tea. "That, and maybe I'll take ten seconds to resign as sheriff. I never wanted the job, anyway. You be sheriff, Dare. You decide which crime you want to solve next."

The front door to the diner swung open, and Sledge Murphy came clomping in. "Breakfast ready?"

Glynna emerged from the kitchen with a coffeepot, smiled and said, "Virginia Belle, would you like to serve tea?"

Mother brightened and headed straight for the hot, heavy

tin pot. Sledge hurried forward and got the pot and took the cup Glynna had in her hand. "Let me pour it, Mrs. Yates, ma'am. It's mighty heavy for you."

Mother smiled and produced a fan that Vince hadn't noticed before. She fluttered it in front of her eyes. "Why, bless your heart, you are a fine Southern gentleman."

Luke and Dare both made about the rudest sound Vince had ever heard. And he'd spent nearly two years in Andersonville Prison, so that was saying something.

Sledge poured the coffee. "Actually, ma'am, I'm from Wisconsin. I killed me a passel of Rebs during the war. But you sure do remind me of my ma, except she smoked a pipe, and last I knew she didn't have much left for teeth. Still, you put me in mind of her. Can I pour you a cup?"

"Yes, I'd love some tea, thank you." Mother smiled and fanned and sat at the table, and suddenly Sledge was a waitress. He poured just as if the job were his own dream come true, then sat down beside Mother and asked after her health.

"I'm riding out to the ranch." Luke stalked into the kitchen, no doubt to report his every move to his wife before he made it.

Dare shook his head again. "You're a poor excuse for a lawman, Yates. I'm going to go check Lana's trail. That lovesick parson probably had his head in the clouds and didn't even look at the ground."

"There's no denying that sheriffing isn't my finest gift, Doc." Vince gave Dare a sloppy salute. "And I see no sign of getting better at it anytime soon. Can I get you a cup of coffee before you go?"

Dare growled and followed Luke into the kitchen to report his every move.

⌒∞⌒

Vince had finally figured out how to be the sheriff of a town as small as Broken Wheel that paid him nothing. He quit. Or at least he ignored the job and looked after his ma instead.

Vince doubted Solomon would have approved the decision, but he made peace with it and refused to be shaken. Several had tried.

Not Tina, though. Tina seemed mighty grateful he'd stayed around town to help. Much of the care of Mother had fallen on her, and by the end of the day she'd started calling her Mother.

Jonas and Missy were off courting again. Vince wondered how long they could keep this up before they got married. Vince didn't figure it'd be long.

Mother had been moved into the last remaining bedroom of the Yates house, which seemed like a place suited for a horror story. Tina had stripped the room of all breakables, while Vince had hung and locked the shutters Sledge had built.

Vince had left Tina to prepare Mother for bed and taken up sentry duty at the top of the stairway. He saw the door to Mother's bedroom swing open and watched while Tina patted loyal Livvy on the head.

She took a hard look at him and said, "You've got to get some sleep tonight."

Which Vince took to mean he didn't look all that good. "I'm fine." Vince rubbed his heavy eyes in direct denial of his words.

"If you don't want to sleep, don't sleep." She locked Mother's door and pocketed the key. "I'm going down to wait for Jonas." She headed for the stairs.

Mother was now sleeping in the room on the south end. Vince's was next. The empty room that still smelled of kerosene was between Vince and Melissa, who slept on the far north end.

When Tina walked past Vince, he caught her arm. "Can we talk again tonight?" Vince hadn't meant for that to come out sounding quite so friendly.

"I don't really want to talk. We both had an early morning and a long, hard day. I'm sorry Luke and Dare pecked at you today."

"Luke wasn't so bad. At least he went home early on. He and his ranch hands are better suited to hunting Wilcox than I am."

Luke and Ruthy had gone home shortly after breakfast, and that had ended the nagging from them.

"Dare made it a long day, though," Tina said.

"I reckon I don't blame him for wanting me to chase after Lana. He didn't want to leave Glynna and the children alone in town, so if someone was going to go after my escaped prisoner, it stood to reason it oughta be me."

"But when you told him no, that didn't mean it was all right for him to keep pestering until he near to drove you crazy."

"Let's don't use the word *crazy* if we can avoid it," Vince said.

"I'm fine with having a talk. I think we should go over some ideas I have for keeping Mother safe." Tina gave

Mother's bedroom door a longing look as if wishing she'd stayed in there.

"Don't call her 'Mother.'"

Tina rolled her eyes. "I don't have a lot of choice."

"Why does she think she's your mother but not mine?" Sighing, Vince turned and plodded down the stairs. He didn't even check to see if she was following. If she wanted to hide, he'd just let her.

Then he heard her footsteps behind him and was a little surprised at the smile that quirked his lips. He had his back to her so she didn't know.

When they got downstairs, Vince leaned so he could see the front door, the stairway, and Tina just like he'd done the night before. Tina took the chair. Two nights and they already had a routine down . . . like an old married couple.

He let himself look at her beautiful blond hair and had one wild moment where he pictured himself pulling out her pins, one at a time, then sinking his hands into falling-down curls and getting another taste of those pretty pink lips.

Snapping his head around to face sideways before she could catch him staring, he thought with a grim unhappiness that they were most certainly not like an old married couple in several really important ways.

"We need to think ahead about how to make Mother safe."

"I said *don't call her that*," Vince shouted, then reined in his temper and raised both hands as if surrendering before Tina fired a shot. "I'm sorry, Tina. You've helped so much. It's just that . . . that . . ."

"That it hurts to have her think I'm her daughter and not think you're her son. I understand." The gentle way she'd said those words helped a little. She did understand, to the extent anyone could.

"We need to think of her as a child," Tina went on. "What would we do if we had a child sleeping upstairs?"

A child. Their child . . .

Vince needed to get his unruly thoughts under control even if he had to ram his skull into the brick fireplace to do it. "We'd make sure there are no breakables she could get her hands on."

"With a child you can move sharp objects up high and lock doors with simple latches."

"But Mother is tall enough, and knowing enough, despite her troubles, that those things won't stop her."

"The sturdy latches you and Sledge put on the windows took care of that." Tina pulled a folded-up paper from her pocket. "I'm starting a list of other things we need to do."

"No," Vince said. He strode across the room to face her. "You're trying to figure out how to keep her safe?"

Her brows arched in confusion. "Well, yes. Of course I'm trying to keep her safe."

"I don't want her safe!" It then hit him how backward that sounded. "I mean, of course I want her safe, but that's not what we need to talk about."

Looking wary, Tina said, "It's not?"

The way she said it made him think of kissing her. From her expression he suspected that was exactly what she was thinking, too. "No, we need to talk about curing her."

"You . . . you think there's a cure? Isn't it just old age? Nothing can cure that."

"She's not that old. If she were in her dotage, I'd agree that we just need to accept things as they are. But Mother isn't sixty yet, and most folks don't become addled at her age. Her father too had something wrong with him—wrong in the head. I was never sure what, though. But it's not simple old age, so there might be a cure for it." Vince swooped his arms wide in frustration. "Did you really think I rode all the way to New Orleans to find a way to treat Lana Bullard?"

"Actually, yes, I did think that. I know you were thinking of your ma also, but mostly it was because of your prisoner." Tina's blue eyes were wide, and she gave a little shrug, as if she were the tiniest bit afraid of him and didn't want to do anything to set him off. Which was how people often treated lunatics. "So you didn't go there for Lana at all?"

"No!" Vince paused, then let out a big sigh. "I went to New Orleans because I've been tryin' to find a treatment to help cure my mother."

Dead silence settled thick over the room, to the point that Vince could barely breathe.

After a minute or two, Tina said quietly, "I know this has come on her at a young age, Vince, but . . . well, I'm sorry, but I don't think she can get well from what's ailing her." Tina's words were nothing but kind, and her eyes were full of compassion.

He wished she'd have slapped him instead. It would have hurt less.

"She's been like this for years, getting worse all the time. I have to do *something*. I can't just give up on her. I can't stand . . ." He didn't know what else to say. Words suddenly seemed stupid, useless.

"You can't stand knowing that most likely she's never going to call you Vince again."

255

"She did after she fell. For that little while, she knew me."

"And she may again on occasion, just not very often."

"Which means that for the rest of my life, my mother's going to confuse me with a cruel tyrant."

Tina shook her head. "You're angry with your father, but surely he wasn't so bad you hate the idea of being called by his name. Maybe you can learn to accept it."

"My father started trying to groom me to take over his company when I was only four years old."

"Four? What can a four-year-old do?"

"I had a tutor. I spent every afternoon studying."

"Most four-year-olds spend their afternoons napping."

Vince felt a grim smile twist his lips. "My earliest memories are of being summoned to my father's office, and that was just when I did poorly in my studies. It was the only time I saw him." With a humorless laugh he added, "Mother came to me at different times. Not every day, but if she wasn't out with friends, she'd visit and we'd have afternoon tea together. She was always kind in a distant sort of way—if I behaved myself and acted gentlemanly. I used to live for those days she'd come and see me."

"I can't imagine a life where parents *visit* their children. Aunt Iphigenia was always around. At the time I wished she'd leave me alone."

"We come from different worlds, I guess. I'd have probably studied to please my mother, but she never asked much of me. And Father criticized mistakes and rarely commented when I did things right." It might have been exhaustion, but before he knew it Vince found the story of his seventh birthday pouring out of him.

"He really had the pony killed?"

Vince nodded. "After that, I enjoyed seeing how far I could push him. But a boy who pushes a man, especially someone like my father, learns to stay on guard." Vince thought of a hundred other cruelties his father had meted out, but he didn't want to burden Tina with them.

"Makes sense," Tina said. "It was the only way you could get attention from him."

"I didn't want his attention. I just wanted him to know he couldn't control me. I managed to get expelled from every boarding school he found for me. If they didn't kick me out, I'd run away. I learned to save up my allowance and sneak off from school. I could run wild all over Chicago for days, so long as the money held out."

"And that's how a rich boy from Chicago never got himself much schooling."

Vince said, "But I learned anyway, only on my own. And reading Blackstone set me on the path to being a lawyer, even without the schooling."

"Those are the books you read that taught you how to be a lawyer?"

"Yep. Blackstone's *Commentaries on the Laws of England*. And I've studied everything I can find about insanity as it applies to the law, and now I'm going to study up on the medical treatment of my mother's condition until I can find a cure."

"Vince—"

"Don't say it." He knew she was going to say it was a hopeless dream. "I won't live out my life with *his* name on Mother's lips every time she speaks to me. I won't!"

"But I hear affection in her voice when she says 'Julius.'"

Vince grimaced at the mention of the name. "I don't

deny it. When she calls me that, she doesn't sound as if she hates my father."

"Well, that's something, isn't it?"

Shrugging one shoulder, Vince repeated, "Whatever's wrong with my mother isn't the normal confusion that comes with age. It happened too young. So we have to be able to treat her, and I'm going to find out how. I'm not quitting, not when it's something as important as my mother. I'm going to keep reading and hunting for a way to bring her back." A wave of exhaustion washed over him then, and he thought that tonight, maybe just this once he could stop standing guard enough to sleep. "Let's go to bed."

Tina jumped at his words.

Vince looked at her and realized what he'd said. "Uh . . . I mean . . ." He felt his cheeks coloring, and he never blushed. But she sure did. Her head was turning the color of a ripe cherry.

"I'm sorry . . . I'm going to bed now. Good night, Tina." This was why they needed a better chaperone than Mother. Who right now was fast asleep, snoring.

"Good night. I'll wait here for Jonas." She turned away, but not before Vince saw another bright flush spread across her face.

CHAPTER 22

Jonas walked Tina over to the boardinghouse the next morning and then ran off with Melissa. Tina got Mother dressed and over to the diner. Jonas and Melissa showed up over an hour later looking incredibly happy.

Mrs. Yates set her heavy coffeepot down with a *clang*. "Missy, you are discharged." Then Mother picked the pot up again and called Sledge Murphy a honey pie.

Tina took in Missy's befuddled expression and said quietly, "Come in the kitchen."

Missy got there just as Vince came in the back door. Vince looked at Missy and said, "Good, we need Jonas. You women need to watch out for Mother today. Luke sent a hand in and told us we need to get out to his ranch and help him hunt Quince Wilcox."

Vince went on through to the dining room.

Missy arched a brow at the high-handed orders and turned to Tina. "What happened? Why am I fired?"

"She thinks you tried to burn down the boardinghouse yesterday morning."

Quietly nodding as if this were no surprise, Missy said,

"I'll work with you in the kitchen while someone else cares for her. We'll hope she forgets she's upset with me."

Tina appreciated the help. Maybe she could get off work a little early and put in some time marching her picket line. She missed the exercise. She wondered if Mother was good at tidy lettering—and maybe she'd like to have her own sign and march with Tina out front of Duffy's place.

"Glynna is making sure she doesn't leave the diner for now. We'll worry about it after we finish up here."

Tina and Missy kept busy cooking. They worked well together. A few questions flickered through Tina's mind, but they all circled back around to some version of *How do I fit in Jonas's life if he marries you?* That seemed selfish, so she just kept working.

The kitchen door swung open, and Vince poked his head in. "Can you two come here a minute so we only have to say this once?"

There was nothing that could burn, so they rushed into the dining room in time to see Vince and his Regulator friends pulling on coats and gloves. Their horses were tied in a line to the hitching post in front of the diner.

Vince looked at her, and she remembered how he'd been last night. Her heart had come near to breaking as he talked of his childhood. Neither one of them had it easy. Maybe no one ever had it easy.

"We're riding out to the S Bar S. There's no sign that Lana has come back. You'll be safe in town while we round up Wilcox, and we hope catching him will keep the Kiowa from wanting war." Vince's brown eyes slid from his mother to his horse. Then he asked a question focused directly on Tina. "Will you be all right?"

Tina knew he was asking her to watch Mother. And she was glad to do it. For all her confusion, Mrs. Yates was very kind to Tina. Too bad she'd decided to fire Missy, but hopefully a woman as forgetful as Mother would get over her upset soon.

"Go. We'll mind Mother and the diner and the whole town. And if Lana comes back, we'll catch her and lock her back in jail and throw Porter in with her."

A smile showed a flash of Vince's white teeth. "Well, a man can't ask for more than that. Thank you." He tugged on the brim of his hat while Dare and Jonas kissed their women goodbye. Vince gave Tina a sharp look that made her feel like he'd have kissed her too given half a chance. Then the men left, and Tina got back to work.

When the morning flood of hungry men slowed to a trickle, she turned her attention to putting on a ham for dinner while Missy washed up. Minding Mother and the diner and the whole town wasn't turning out to be much different from most days. But Tina fervently hoped Lana didn't show up to test Tina on the rest of her boastful promises.

Vince rode hard for Luke's ranch. Dare was at his side, Jonas just a length behind because the trail was so narrow.

"We shouldn't have left them." Even riding at full speed didn't keep Dare from being a little overactive. He was moving about as fast as a man could; it was just his brain that wouldn't quit.

"You scouted hard, Dare. You know Lana and Porter were heading in a straight line with no sign of them circling back. She's gone."

"Somehow just listening to you be so sure is enough to make me turn and ride back to Glynna."

"You don't trust me? That ain't right, Dare. You're the one who told me it was safe to ride out."

"I know." Dare glanced back at Jonas, who tossed a really contented smile at the two of them.

"Go on back to town if you'd feel better, Dare," Jonas called out. "We can handle this."

"I've given it plenty of thought. But just because I think I'm right doesn't mean I can quit worrying. I followed Lana far enough to know she was making a beeline for the West. No one who's planning to double back rides for that many hours."

Vince grunted as he rode through the tight canyon neck near Luke's place. They found Luke already saddled up, with two of his men riding with him. "I was about to leave. I've had men out scouting all night, and we found where he rode into a dead-end canyon. But he got to high ground and took a shot at Dodger when he got too close."

"Is Dodger all right?" Dare's doctor instincts were always right near the surface.

"No one was hit. But another one of my scouts, hunting in a different area, came back and said the Kiowa are riding for that same canyon. They got word about Wilcox, too. If those Kiowa kill Wilcox, the government might decide it's an uprising and send the cavalry in to strike at the Kiowa." Luke reined his horse around and took off. Calling over his shoulder, he said, "We've got to get Wilcox before they do."

Vince swatted his horse on the rump with the flat of his hand, and the gelding leapt into a full gallop, stretching out his stride, gaining on Luke. Thundering hooves sounded behind Vince, and he knew his Regulator friends were coming fast. He caught Luke and matched him stride for stride. Dare came up on Vince's right. Jonas appeared on Luke's left. The four of them raced over the stony ground of the canyon, shoulder to shoulder, together, fighting, taking care of each other. The hooves of their horses pounded out a drumbeat that felt so right, something made Vince realize he'd always thought of Chicago as home, and Father and Mother as his family. But these men were his real family. They were brothers, closer than brothers, and home was wherever they were.

"Now we have to go in slow." Luke reined in his horse. "We want to get close but stay out of rifle range."

Luke pointed to a high canyon wall several hundred yards ahead. "I'm not sure what gun he has. I want to get as close as I can and hope we're closer than the Kiowa so I can talk to them before they charge that canyon."

At a much slower pace now, Vince realized they could take a moment to talk. "Do you all think . . . ?" He fell silent.

All three of his friends caught his uncertain tone and turned to him, waiting.

Vince swallowed hard. "Dare, do you think what's wrong with Mother can be cured?" As they proceeded at a steady walk, Vince hated what he knew his friend was going to say.

"I don't think so, Vince. I've never heard of an older person getting this kind of dementia and then getting better."

"But she's too young." Vince's stomach twisted at Dare's grim prognosis. "This happens to old people. Seventy- or eighty-year-old people. Not a woman in her fifties."

"I don't know that much about illnesses of the mind. No one does. Vince, I'm sorry, but I doubt your ma is going to get better."

"Lana Bullard did." It made Vince furious, and that was better than the despair he was feeling. "What kind of God lets a woman like Lana get better, but leaves a good-hearted woman like my mother as she is?"

And that wasn't a question for Dare; it was one for Jonas. Vince almost wished they were too close to a shootout to talk, yet they had plenty of time.

"God may know Lana needs more time. God may be hoping to bring her home to himself. Your mother, well, she might be stronger in her faith in this confused state than she was when she spent her time with teas and dress fittings. We can't understand the working of God, Vince. We can only pray and hope and accept."

Silence stretched, broken only by the clopping of horses' hooves.

Finally, Vince said, "My grandfather was mad. I never got the impression it was about old age. Now Mother. Do you think the kind of . . . of madness they have is passed on to a son and grandson?"

His heart pounded at voicing his worst fears to his friends. Vince looked sharply at Dare. The doctor. Who'd just admitted he didn't know much about these things.

It was neither the doctor nor the parson who answered.

Luke said, "A man like you, who's used to thinking of himself as invincible, would have a special horror at the thought of being as out of control as your mother is. But you can't worry about what may happen when you're fifty, Vince. That makes now a nightmare for you. It makes every day of your life something to dread, and that's a terrible way to live. You have to trust God to take care of you. And for a man who's the master at taking care of himself and everyone else, that might be the hardest thing you've ever done."

Breathing a prayer, Vince tried to do it, to turn his life and his future over to God. And as he did so, everything started to become clear. By fearing he'd become his parents, he'd allowed them to have more control over his future than God. That fear was ruling him. He begged forgiveness for not putting his trust in God. As he did so, the dark fears he'd always done his best to control lifted from his heart. He knew in that moment that he was neither of his parents. He could forge his own path, have his own future. And in that future, maybe God hadn't marked him to be alone. And if he wasn't going to be alone, he knew exactly who he wanted to be with.

But first he had to catch a drunken outlaw, stop a war party of Kiowa, protect his brothers, make sure a crazy woman wasn't going to try to kill anyone, and get back to town. Then he was going to ask Tina Cahill to marry him.

It was gonna be the longest day of his life.

Tina handed Glynna a heavy, dripping skillet. It was the last of the dishes. She heaved a sigh of relief to have the cleanup done from the noon herd of men. Missy had gone to get a different dress on, after a splash of water soaked the one she'd worn all morning and through dinner.

Paul and Janny appeared out the kitchen window where Tina stood. They must have gone out the front door of the diner and rounded the buildings in Broken Wheel to go home, avoiding the kitchen for fear of being given more chores. They'd worked in the diner all morning, and Glynna insisted that her children study every day.

Tina reached for the basin of dirty water to take it out back and toss it away, but then she dropped the basin and whirled toward the dining room. She shouted to Glynna, "If Missy is changing and the young'uns are at your house, then who's with Mrs. Yates?"

Glynna gasped, and the skillet she was drying dropped to the floor with a loud metallic *clang*. They ran for the dining room, hit the door together and stopped.

Tina shoved herself through to find . . . "She's gone."

Tina remembered how they'd found Mrs. Yates the last time. "Get the dog. She'll help us find Virginia Belle."

Except . . .

"The dog's not here?" Glynna glanced around the room, calling for the dog, but she was nowhere to be found.

"That means," Tina said, swallowing hard, "Virginia Belle took Livvy with her."

Glynna and Tina exchanged a horrified glance, and together they dashed for the front door.

Vince realized just what a winding, twisting path they'd taken as they neared the narrow-necked canyon. They'd made their way back nearly to Broken Wheel.

"Luke, how close to town is this canyon?" He was thinking of the Kiowa coming and that Wilcox was too quick to pull a trigger. Vince's family and friends were all back in town, where it was supposed to be safe. But they were bringing the trouble straight for them.

Luke glanced sideways at Vince. "It's a few miles to the
west. But the land is so broken, there's no direct route back
to town, except maybe on foot."

"And of course Wilcox would never walk anywhere."
Vince glared at Luke, which wasn't one bit fair. "And Indians are known for never getting off their horses."

Luke's eyes narrowed. "I see what you mean. This trouble could spill over to Broken Wheel mighty fast."

"Not only that," Dare said from Vince's right, "if Wilcox
is holed up in a canyon close to town, we might be riding
straight toward the place where he meets up with Duffy, or
whoever is selling him liquor. And that could mean we're
riding to face more than one man."

From what should have been a simple if touchy situation,
rounding up one worthless drunk, they'd gone to rounding
up a group of men bent on keeping their illegal business
secret. White men weren't even supposed to live in Indian
Territory, which was why Broken Wheel had always been a
quiet little town full of unsociable types. Probably some of
them were hiding from the law. Yet one of the few crimes
committed against Indians the government would enforce
was the ban on liquor sales.

Vince could see this ending up with soldiers coming in,
the Kiowa being rounded up, maybe killing involved in
that, and then whoever was left alive in the tribe would
be penned up on a reservation, while every man in and
around Broken Wheel was run out of the territory. Vince
didn't have much to lose, and Jonas could be a preacher
anywhere. Lots of folks in the West would welcome a doctor like Dare. But Luke would lose everything.

As Vince and his friends rode slowly for the varmint

Wilcox, a war party of Kiowa rounded a mesa and came charging in from the south. They were all headed for the same rugged, flat-topped canyon.

Kicking his horse, Vince surged ahead of his saddle partners, driven to stop this before it turned into something a lot bigger than a cowpoke who'd drunk himself stupid and fired off some reckless shots.

He was ahead about ten paces when, just seconds later, Luke caught up to him. "You let me talk to 'em, Vince. I know you like taking charge, but I've got a better chance of calming Red Wolf and his people down."

Knowing it to be true wasn't the same as liking it. Even so, Vince eased back just a hair as they rode closer to the armed Kiowa. One of the war party screamed and raised his rifle high. A harsh guttural command given by Red Wolf stopped the next shout from his warriors.

Then, to Vince's surprise, Red Wolf shouted, "Stop, Luke!" It was so fierce that Luke pulled up. They were close now, just twenty or so yards from the Kiowa.

"I'm here to make this right, Red Wolf." Luke's voice carried across the stony ground. "The man who shot you works for me, and I will see to his punishment."

"I don't believe in your laws, old friend. I trust you, but you can't make promises for others. The best you can do is to arrest your man for another crime. You'll punish him for that, but not for shooting at me as I stood peacefully beside you. That isn't justice—not as the Kiowa understand it."

Vince felt compelled to speak for the law in this mess. "I'm the sheriff in Broken Wheel, Red Wolf. I will arrest Wilcox for shooting you. I give you my word I won't let a judge look away from this."

Red Wolf glared at Vince, then Luke. One of his warriors roared a string of words in the Kiowa language. A rapid back and forth between Red Wolf and this man was interrupted by other warriors, all of them sounding furious.

Vince knew exactly how they felt.

"The rest of you stay back." Luke spoke low enough to not interrupt the wrangling Kiowa, then rode even closer.

Luke was talking mostly to Red Wolf with some stumbling between English and Kiowa. Red Wolf raised a hand high, and Vince saw the white of the bandage around his side, beneath his shirt. The white looked garish against the natural colors of his buckskin clothes. His hair hung down in two long braids that dangled in front of his chest.

Then one of the Kiowa warriors raised a tomahawk. Vince tightened his hands on the reins to get to Luke's side. Just then a bullet blasted out of the canyon, followed by a volley of shots.

Every man among them wheeled to face trouble. Vince soon realized, as he was sure they all did, that the shooter was out of range. The bullets were kicking up dirt nearly a hundred feet away. The best rifles around had a range of about three hundred feet, and the entrance to the canyon was four hundred or more. It had to be Wilcox, and there was a good chance he was drinking again or he'd've never pulled the trigger. And he'd've for sure quit firing after the first couple of shots fell so short.

Puffs of smoke exploded up from a jumble of rocks perched high at the mouth of a canyon.

Red Wolf roared an order, and his braves dismounted. Their horses wore no saddles and the Indians didn't tie them. The animals walked away from the noise, but they didn't hightail it out of there. Instead they went to grazing.

Luke grabbed Red Wolf by the upper arm and talked so fast in Kiowa that Vince couldn't keep the words separate, let alone hope to glean any of their meaning.

Luke slashed with his hand as he argued with Red Wolf.

No good in the verbal battle, Vince studied the range of fire and said, "Dare, I'm going to try and get behind him."

With a jerk of his chin Dare said, "Let's go."

"No!" Vince said. "I said I'd go. I wasn't inviting anyone."

"You'll need backup."

"I'll need someone shooting at him from here, as a diversion."

The Indians broke off their talk. Luke slapped Red Wolf on the arm and turned to his Regulator friends. "They're going to give us a chance. One chance to catch Wilcox and lock him up."

Vince wondered how long the Kiowa would stay out of the fight. "I've got an idea, but I'm going to be the one to try it."

"We're in this together, Vince," Jonas said.

"It's risky."

"My ranch, my risk." Luke tugged on his leather gloves. Another bullet fired from the canyon mouth, and Luke studied the location of the gunman, his eyes blazing with anger.

"What I've got planned is a one-man job. I'm going to ease up to the side of the canyon mouth and scale that bluff. I'll be in rifle range for a couple hundred feet, but I should be able to stay out of sight. The cover is only big enough for one man. Besides that, there are stretches with no cover. I'm going to need him to be busy looking somewhere else."

"So we'll string out. We'll use the cover one at a time." Dare never did like to be left out of the action.

"I need the three of you fanned out here," Luke said, "keeping his eyes away from the path I'm using. And we all know which of us is better at sneaking, because that's what I did during the war."

Vince saw the Kiowa horses grazing a ways off, but the Kiowa themselves had vanished. While Luke might be better at sneaking than his Regulator friends, he didn't have a patch on the Indians.

"I'm surrounded by married—or almost married—men." Vince thought of his mother. He wasn't married, yet he had responsibilities. He gave Jonas a hard look. "If something happens to me, Missy is the closest thing to family Mother's got left, and it ain't very close. But I want your word you'll care for Mother."

"If you're making arrangements for your death, then this is a half-wit plan." Jonas was usually serene and wise; right now he looked mighty annoyed. "I don't want to go back to town and tell Tina I let you get killed."

Vince didn't like it that Jonas had said *Tina*. Why not his sister? Why not his mother? Vince preferred to think that no one had noticed what had passed between Tina and him, but Jonas had pretty clearly noticed.

"Then make sure you keep that fool focused right on you when I'm slipping up on him." Vince jerked his head toward a man-high slab of red stone sitting in the middle of the wide stretch fronting the canyon. "I'm going to try to keep him from seeing I'm gone. Let's walk over this way."

They walked, and before long the gunman fired at them.

Once they were hidden, Vince turned to Luke. "Trade coats with me." Vince wore a long black duster. Luke wore buckskin. "Yours'll fade into the landscape better."

For once, Vince wasn't wearing the black broadcloth pants that made him feel like a lawyer. For long rides he wore brown canvas pants. The color was lucky because they'd help him to blend in with the surroundings.

Looking disgruntled, Luke handed over his coat. Vince shoved his at Luke and pulled the buckskin on.

The man shot again and again.

"What is that fool shooting at?" Dare asked. "Hasn't he figured out we're out of range?"

"Probably just wants us to be too afraid to come any closer," Luke muttered. "And that doesn't have a single chance of working, so let him waste his bullets and let's hope he runs out."

"We should've checked with Tug Andrews to see if Wilcox stocked up, or with Dodger to see how hard he dips into the bullets you keep around the bunkhouse." Vince looked around the canyon. "You all stay here for a bit. Make it so one or two of you is visible now and then. That way he'll think we're back here taking shelter."

"Don't tell us how to create a diversion." Dare crossed his arms. "It's insulting and you're wasting time."

Vince left his friends to handle their part of this lame-brain plan. Out of sight of the shooter, he angled toward another jumble of stones. Wilcox—assuming it was Wilcox—was giving his position away with every shot, the idiot. Vince would have to slip along and belly-crawl when he got closer, but for now all he needed to do was keep out of the line of sight, and the stones were scattered in a way that made that easy. Vince would be up that canyon wall and behind Wilcox, able to disarm him, without the drunken coyote even knowing anyone was coming.

That was if everything went like he'd planned. When did that ever happen in a gunfight?

CHAPTER 23

"Go get Missy and the children. We need to fan out." Tina raised her voice to call, "Livvy, here girl."

Glynna had turned to run through the diner to gather help, but then stopped abruptly and grabbed Tina's arm. "Why are you calling the dog? Call for Virginia Belle, for heaven's sake."

"Should I?" Tina was surprised by the suggestion. "What chance is there that Virginia Belle will come when she's called?"

"Well, at least try that first!" Glynna shot up the steps and into the diner, a shortcut to her house.

"Virginia Belle? Mrs. Yates? Mother?" Just to be thorough, Tina yelled, "Livvy?" At this point she just wanted someone, anyone, to respond.

There was nothing except the sounds of Glynna yelling for her children, a door slamming shut, pounding feet, and shouting for Missy.

"Mrs. Yates?" Tina had no idea which direction to go. Mother had headed south last time, so Tina dashed toward that end of town just as Paul, with Janny on his heels, came running for her. She wanted to send each searching in a different direction, but she didn't dare let the children go out there alone.

More running feet and she saw Glynna enter the saloon. A woman never went into a saloon. Even Tina, who'd stood just outside the door of Duffy's Tavern dozens of times, and even peeked inside on occasion, had never entered the place. Then Glynna was back, with Duffy and Griss right behind her. They headed for the general store. A moment later, Tina noticed them twist the knob. The door didn't open. Where was Tug Andrews? Maybe he snuck in a nap after dinner?

Duffy and Griss gave up and headed for the livery.

Missy came running toward Tina just as Glynna rushed over.

"Duffy said he'd find more men. I told them we'd split up and take the south and west sides of town. He's gonna cover the north and east sides."

Missy looked at the five of them. "Is it safe to split up? What about that prisoner who broke jail? Will she be out there?"

Tina inhaled as slowly as a panic-stricken woman could. "Dare seemed sure she was long gone, and we have no choice but to trust him because we've got to find Mrs. Yates. Glynna, you take the children and go west. Missy, you come with me to the south."

Shaking her head, Missy said, "You go with them and I'll hunt on my own. I don't think Glynna and the youngsters should be on their own."

Paul drew his gun and checked the load with quiet confidence. "She's not alone. I've got a gun and I'll protect my ma."

Looking at Paul and his calm eyes, Tina decided she had to let go of her image of him as a child. The boy was grown now, and that was that.

"You're right, Paul. Glynna's probably in better hands with you than me." Tina turned to Missy. "The two of us will team up. And we need to get going now."

The first cry of "Virginia Belle" went up from the far side of town. It was Sledge Murphy's voice. Close after was another man's voice, Duffy most likely, though he and Griss sounded a lot alike. It galled Tina that the two were being so helpful.

With a quick jerk of her chin in agreement, Missy said, "Let's go."

Missy led the way, with Tina hard on her heels. As they plunged into the rugged undergrowth and dodged the red rock slabs—many of them tall enough to hide an addled woman—Tina called for Virginia Belle, and Missy even eventually called for Livvy.

Neither of them got so much as a whisper of response.

Movement was what drew a man's eye. So Vince inched forward slowly, doing what he could to blend in to the rocky ground, the clumps of winter-dried weeds and stumpy mesquite. Vince made himself to look like just one more brown lump in a brown and lumpy landscape.

He'd advanced nearly two hundred feet and was well within rifle range now. He had cover, but nothing that would stop a bullet. He slithered along, finding dips in the rugged ground, some so small he was hiding more in Wilcox's mind than in truth. He dragged himself along on his belly with waving bunches of grama grass as his only shield, then made it behind another slab of rock. He had twenty feet of open space ahead. His only hope of getting across was if Wilcox wasn't looking this direction. Then there was a copse of young cottonwood trees and a tumble of rocks, more tall grass, and then another open space before Vince reached the bluff on top of which Wilcox was perched.

Vince kept getting closer and closer. For the next twenty feet he'd be exposed, and moving so slow that even a half-wit had a good chance of hitting what he aimed at.

Even if Wilcox missed, he'd know Vince was coming and that would put an end to Vince's hopes of scaling the cliff and getting a drop on him.

Vince eased along when he wanted to clear that stretch at a dead run. He crept like one of the desert critters, blending in, staying silent. Seconds passed between each move. The day was starting to wear down, and the shadows grew longer from the canyon walls. Vince could use those shadows when he got to them, but he had no notion of waiting for them to come all this way. He didn't think the Kiowa were that patient, and truth be told, he wasn't either.

Another inch, then a foot, then a yard. Vince thought back to the war.

He'd been a spy. His mother's Southern accent was easy for him to mimic, and he'd spent time in his childhood visiting his grandparents at their plantation. He could talk to the Southern soldiers and mix in with them.

He even had sympathy for them, because he knew they were fighting for their homes. So he'd made his way to a camp and hid in the darkness, sometimes almost right under their guns. Then he'd pick a moment and join the Southern forces.

He felt like that now. Like a sneak and a spy. A lot of people would've thought those were insults, but Vince liked knowing he could keep up his guard, pretend to be who he wasn't. He was a natural at ignoring how he really felt and adopting a manner that suited him for whatever reason. He'd learned all those skills—sneaking, spying, pretending, hiding his feelings—from a lifetime of dealing with his father.

Hard to like the idea that handling his father had trained Vince for war.

A coyote's howl jerked Vince back to the present. He realized he'd gone into his daydreams for a while. Slowly he advanced another yard, then another.

A shot blasted out of the canyon, and Vince braced himself to rush for cover. The young cottonwoods weren't much, but they were closer than the rock. But he'd be pinned down there.

Thankfully the shot wasn't aimed in his direction. Soon return shots came from Dare and Luke. Vince risked a glance backward and saw that his friends had moved in closer, to just out of rifle range.

They were diverting Wilcox's attention, all right. Vince picked up speed and got himself behind the cottonwoods. He let himself rest only a few moments, then went on—faster now as he skirted the trees and the rock pile. He scrambled with speed behind the tall grass.

He saw the shadows stretching toward him. That darkness would hide him almost as well as a real barrier. Shadows wouldn't stop a bullet, but they could keep a man from pulling the trigger to begin with.

Breathing deeply to steady his nerves, he slid into clear view of the shooter and looked up. Wilcox stood behind a boulder high up on top of the canyon wall. He was concealed from anyone straight ahead of him, but Vince was off to the side and could see the sidewinder clearly. In fact, Vince could've probably put a bullet into Wilcox from where he was hiding. But a shot upward while lying on his belly was tricky, and Vince's position would be given away.

Being careful not to draw Wilcox's attention, Vince closed the distance between him and the shadow. Once there, he had thirty more feet to the wall of the bluff, where Wilcox couldn't see him anymore, not without coming right to the edge of the canyon top and looking down.

Vince glanced up. Wilcox took a long pull on his bottle. A few more feet of progress and finally Vince belly-crawled into the shadow cast by the lowering sun. Moving steadily, he picked up speed and was soon against the rocks.

He could now see Jonas, Dare, and Luke, and they saw him. Luke tugged on the brim of his hat, and Vince nodded back. Vince saw Luke talking, and neither Dare nor Jonas even looked over. They were cautious men and too savvy to give him away by so much as a glance, just in case Wilcox hadn't drunk himself cross-eyed.

From his vantage point, Vince could see a few of the Kiowa, too. They had taken cover, and he'd have never seen them if he didn't know they were there.

Vince let himself relax for a minute, then gazed straight up the canyon wall. He needed to scale this cliff and, once he was up on Wilcox's level, end this thing. He touched his

Colt, hooked with a strap over the trigger so it wouldn't fall out of his holster while he crawled.

He hoped he could avoid shooting, but he'd do what he had to do. He took off his buckskin gloves and tucked them away, then reached for his first handhold.

⁂

"She dropped a handkerchief last time," Tina said. "Why couldn't she have done that again?"

She and Missy rushed here and there, looking behind every clump of grass and rock big enough to hide a woman. They'd been at it for at least half an hour and had left Broken Wheel far behind.

"Virginia Belle, where are you?" Missy shouted.

"Maybe since she fired you, she's not answering." Tina looked at Missy and knew her furrowed brow matched Tina's.

"Then you holler. I'll keep quiet if you think it'll help."

"Let's listen for a while instead. Surely Mother or Livvy would make some sound walking along. Livvy yips all the time." Silence prevailed as they kept walking. Tina could almost hear a clock ticking away, counting down the time Virginia Belle had been lost, maybe hurt, maybe snakebit.

Tina came up close to a steep rise of rock. It had the beautiful stripes of red running crossways that made this area different from any place Tina had ever seen. She looked at that wall of rock and knew Mother hadn't kept moving forward. If she'd come this way, this would have stopped her. To go left or right? Which way?

Tina stood in front of a swaying cluster of mesquite that seemed to grow right out of the rock. Then, because she had no idea where to go next, Tina looked closer at the clump of stunted trees. It formed almost a solid wall in front of the striped stone, but a gust of wind made the mesquite bend and dance. Tina saw something she couldn't quite make out behind the thick copse of trees. She narrowed her eyes at the rock behind the trees, or rather the lack of rock.

A sudden stomping of footsteps from their left whirled them around. Tug Andrews came out from behind a couple of scrub junipers, looking surprised to see them. "Uh . . . sorry to . . . to startle you, ladies."

Tina remembered that the general store had been locked up when Glynna was looking for help. She wondered where Tug had been, and with everyone running out of town, how had he even known they were out here?

"Mrs. Yates wandered off again," she explained.

Tug swallowed hard and tugged at his bristly beard. "I heard. How long you been lookin'?"

"We've been out here for the better part of an hour." Missy's voice broke.

"Now, don't get in a fret. I'll help you find her." Tug kept worrying the gray whiskers on his chin. The beard had never seen a trim. He yanked, and Tina noticed he had a makeshift bandage on his hand. And if she wasn't mistaken, there were several spots of fresh crimson blood dotting it, so his wound must be fresh. He had a battered buckskin coat that had the look of being made by hand. It had beadwork on the fringe that looked similar to a coat Luke owned, one made by the Kiowa. Tug wore a fur cap, and his coat was tied tight with a leather belt. He was bundled up as if he planned to be outside a long time.

"Thank you. We have no idea where to search." Missy sounded sweet and very grateful to the man for helping. And honestly, Tina was herself grateful. Everyone in town had helped. Even those whiskey-hustling Schuster brothers.

"I scouted this edge of town and thought I saw a footprint. Of course, that was after you two had come this way, and I ain't done much trackin' for a heap of years. But one of the shoes was different from the two of you. I think she went this way." Tug began searching along the front of the rock wall.

"Wait!" Tina turned back to the rocks behind the stunted trees. "I want to look closer here."

"Nuthin' back there," Tug said. "Best we head out of here. I think I see a track." He pointed and started off again.

"You go ahead," Tina said. She pushed the trees aside and leaned closer.

"I thought someone said she had her hound with her." Tug's voice was a mite too loud, and it drew Tina's attention. Tug was looking at her hard, wanting her to stop what she was doing and get along after him right now.

"She does. Livvy's missing, too." Missy stood halfway between Tug and Tina, looking back and forth, as if unsure of who to follow.

"Well, the lady could fall and get knocked cold. It already happened once since she came to Broken Wheel. But the chance of her and the dog both being hurt, knocked into silence, is real unlikely."

Tug had an excellent point. "So it's doubtful she's close by or we'd've heard one or the other of them."

Missy gave Tina an impatient look. "Let's keep hunting."

The man was almost certainly right. Still, she couldn't move on just yet. "Not until I've looked behind these trees. There's something back here. Missy, can you . . . ?"

The harsh crack of a cocking gun spun Tina around to face Tug Andrews. He had a pistol aimed straight at her heart. He moved the business end of the gun toward Missy, then back to Tina. His eyes shone a cold, ruthless blue that scared Tina right to the bone.

"You shoulda come along when you had the chance, Miss Cahill. Now you've bought into the fight just like Mrs. Yates did."

"Then y-you know w-where she is?" Missy stuttered, her eyes fixed on the gun.

"Yep, I know she's in the cave behind those trees, because I put her there myself. Her and that cur of a dog." Tug held up his hand, and Tina saw the bandage was soaked with blood. Tug's blood. The dots—from what had most likely been a dog bite—had spread.

"What did you do to them?" Tina felt her fury rise at this man harming someone as decent and innocent as Mrs. Yates. "Did you kill them?"

"Nope. I ain't no killer, ma'am, leastwise I don't make a habit of it. Tyin' up and muzzling that hound was about all I was worth. They're both fine and secure in that cave. If you'd have walked on, I woulda spared you being bound. I woulda settled my business, then untied the addled woman and let her roam in the woods until you found her. But now I gotta put you in there, too. I'll make sure your menfolk know where to find you later. But they won't be gettin' the note until I'm a fair piece away. I reckon it'll be cold and uncomfortable, but you saddled your own bronc by nosing around the wrong cave."

Tug motioned toward the stand of trees. "Let's go. Time for you to pay a visit to that loony woman and her nasty dog."

CHAPTER 24

All he had to do was climb a mountain, get up to Wilcox's level, get the drop on him and arrest him. Vince had even brought shackles along—just like a real lawman.

Maybe seeing Wilcox clapped in irons would satisfy the angry Kiowa.

Vince remembered that it wasn't just Red Wolf who'd been in danger because of this coyote. He'd also shot at Luke, with Dodger and Ruthy in the line of fire. Or maybe he hadn't shot at anyone. Maybe with his head muddled from whiskey, he'd just fired his gun wild. Then like a low-down, no-account weasel, he'd blamed the shooting on someone else.

Vince would enjoy chaining him up for that alone.

The wall was mighty sheer, but not so bad Vince couldn't handle it. He shed the buckskin coat. No need now to use the earth-toned coat to conceal himself. Wind cut through his shirt as he scaled the canyon wall.

Though the first stretch was almost straight up, there were enough handholds and toeholds to keep him moving so that he made good progress. As he climbed up the bluff, being careful not to make any sound, he saw that the rock wall sloped inward the higher he got. And there were scattered stones that Vince was wary about trusting with his weight.

Soon the rock was sloping enough that Vince could go to crawling on his belly again, dragging himself along. At last he made it to the top and now was only a few dozen feet behind Wilcox. Pulling his gun, Vince watched Wilcox wobble, holding his gun more as a cane than as a weapon. He had the rifle in his right hand, braced on the ground, and a whiskey bottle in his left.

Seeing as how Wilcox had been drinking, and knowing the fool would be a poor one to reason with, when Wilcox went to take another drink from the bottle, Vince rushed him.

Vince made contact with Wilcox's head with the butt of his gun. The man went down like a felled ox. It was a good day's work. They'd be home in time for dinner.

Vince looked out and realized the rock Wilcox hid behind concealed all that had just happened. He'd need to signal Luke and the others. He was moving to snatch up Wilcox's rifle when a gun cocked right behind him.

"Leave the rifle there and drop your own gun, Yates." It was a voice Vince recognized. Tug Andrews, and he spoke without a bit of a drunken slur.

In his awkward position, bending, facing away, Vince knew he couldn't hope to beat an already aimed pistol.

Slowly he straightened away from the rifle. The Regulators still didn't know if Vince had gotten to the top of the canyon yet.

"The pistol, Sheriff," Tug Andrews said. The man who ran the general store spoke in a hard, mocking tone that

Vince had never heard from him before. "Don't start turning around before that gun hits the ground or I'll shoot."

Vince let it go, his teeth gritted. The gun struck the stony ground with a dull thud. As he turned, it came to Vince clear as day that Tug Andrews was another man in Broken Wheel who shipped things in, a man besides Duffy.

The twisting path they'd ridden to this canyon had led them close to Broken Wheel. Vince figured he even knew which bluff this was. From town it stood high and looked to be nothing but another hill. But if Tug had found a way into the canyon from the north, the side without an obvious opening, it'd make a likely hiding place for cases of whiskey. In this broken land there was every chance to be a cave that threaded all the way into the center of the canyon, or a rugged but passable trail that wound up and down the sides. Vince had just climbed it, which proved it could be done.

"I knew someone in town had to be supplying Wilcox with liquor," Vince said. He hoped the old man would start talking and forget to keep his gun quite so level.

With a humorless laugh, Andrews said, "Duffy and Griss told me you accused them of it. I stirred 'em up good, was real offended for 'em. Good, honest, hardworkin' folks like the Schusters gettin' questioned by a lawman who works at a job that pays no money. It's a shame is what it is."

"What do you want from me?" Vince knew his Regulator friends; they were close by and on edge. Unfortunately Vince had told them to hang back and give him time. They'd be coming, but none too soon. Andrews couldn't see them, not from where he was standing. So in a few minutes, hopefully, this was going to become four men against one. Andrews would've been better off to run, but he didn't know that, and Vince wasn't about to warn him.

"If you'd've arrested Wilcox, he'd've sobered up and told you I sold him his whiskey. Then you'd've known I'm selling it to the Kiowa and Comanche, too. I'm leaving the territory, but I've got money and furs, all kinda things hidden in a cave down yonder. I'm not riding out without it." Jerking his head, Tug took a step backward and pointed with his gun. "Head on down the trail. I just need you to stay quiet long enough for me to load up a couple of packhorses and get away. I won't hurt anyone if I don't have to."

The cold way the old-timer spoke and the steady look in his eyes made Vince move mighty careful.

Picking his way down the steep trail, he heard Tug close behind him, but not too close. Before long they reached the bottom of the canyon. Vince kept an eye out for his friends, but he didn't see any sign of them.

A gaping cave mouth was right near the trail's base. "Go on inside," Tug said. "I've got a big old surprise for you in there."

A surprise? Vince wondered what he meant by that. He hoped it wasn't a bullet in the back.

The cave opening seemed to swallow him up. The wind was cut off, and yet Vince felt colder than he had outside.

"Hold up!" Tug said. If the varmint really intended to tie Vince up, load up his cached wealth and take off, Vince should probably let him do it. Luke was the best of trackers. He'd find this place soon enough and set Vince free. But Tug would have to quit the country and do it fast. The question was, did the old-timer know he couldn't move fast enough? Did he know that to leave Vince alive meant almost certain capture?

A scratching noise sounded, and light popped up behind Vince. Tug had lit a match. Vince glanced back to see him touching a match to the wick of a lantern. Tug did it all without letting go of his gun. And he was well out of grabbing range.

"Thinkin' of goin' for my gun, Yates? Like I said, I don't wanna shoot you, but I will if you don't give me a choice." Tug lifted the lantern off a peg driven into the rock wall. "Move on down the tunnel and say hello."

The sneer on Tug's face sent a chill up Vince's spine. There was definitely something more coming. He moved faster, driven now to see what lay ahead. The tunnel was lit only by the lantern, though they hadn't gone far when he saw more light ahead. The tunnel widened into a cave with its own lantern burning.

Mother, Missy, and Tina sat side by side on the cave floor, bound and gagged. They all stared right at Vince, their eyes wide with fear. He noticed that Mother's gag was soaked, drenched by tears.

Tug Andrews had made Vince's mother cry. Vince could feel his anger and frustration building by the second.

A soft whine drew Vince's eyes to Livvy. The little hound lay between Mother and a stone about the size of Vince's chest. Livvy's mouth was muzzled by a strip of leather, and a rope around her neck was tied to the base of the stone. The dog lifted her head and strained against the rope when Vince came in. The high-pitched whine grew louder as the dog lunged over and over, each time followed by a muted yelp.

His stomach twisting, Vince glanced back at his weeping mother and his frightened sister, and then he looked in Tina's eyes, hating to face her terror or her tears.

She was furious. She looked like she wanted to chew her way through that gag and start scolding Tug.

Vince rushed forward just as something slammed into the back of his head. He went down hard, to his knees, then collapsed face-first as the world faded away. The blow seemed to paralyze him. He felt his hands yanked behind his back, yet he was too dazed to fight back.

The man was good. He moved like someone who'd spent time as a cowhand. In mere seconds Tug had Vince tied up like a calf ready for branding.

Old Tug stood away from Vince, breathing hard. Even that much exertion wore him out. But who was lying here all trussed up and who was walking around free? Tug was a harder man than Vince had ever considered. He'd had enough strength to best all four of them and Livvy, too. Now here they all were, with Vince as helpless as his womenfolk. All of them were firmly in Tug's clutches. And instead of rescuing them, he, Invincible Vince, lay here bound, his vision dark, his thoughts scrambled by that hard blow.

With his boot Tug rolled Vince onto his back. Vince kept his eyes closed, hoping Tug thought he'd been knocked insensible. When Tug nudged him with the same hard boot, Vince didn't react.

The old man said, "I been tyin' knots since I was a boy shanghaied onto a ship. Then later I spent time riding the grub line and learned how to hog-tie a thousand-pound steer. None'a you will be gettin' loose, so don't waste time trying. I'll leave a note in town where someone will find it, to tell 'em you're in here."

Vince, even in his groggy state, didn't like the tone of Tug's voice. Would he really leave a note? No matter, for Vince figured Luke would track them into this hole in the ground even if Tug didn't tell anyone.

Tug laughed. "I got two packhorses stashed. I knew the minute word came in about Wilcox shootin' that Indian, it was time for me to move on. I was most of the way to packed when you women stumbled onto my cave."

An annoyed snort came from Tina. Vince wanted to break loose and beat the tar out of Andrews, but for now it suited him to lay still and let the man think he was safe. As soon as Tug left, Vince would go to work getting the knife out of his boot.

He couldn't even test the ropes to see if he was able to reach his boot, but if he couldn't, he'd roll over beside Tina and let her get it.

Tug was quiet for a long stretch, and Vince figured the varmint was staring at him, wondering if he was out cold or not. Finally, Tug stomped out of the cave.

Vince sat up and wheeled around to look at the women. Tina's gaze locked on his, and the determination in her eyes helped clear the last of the fog out of his head.

Tina made an urgent sound from behind her gag.

"Just let me get my blade out first, and then I'll cut you loose," Vince whispered. He glanced at her, and she narrowed her eyes at him and said some muffled words he couldn't understand. He figured if she could talk, she'd start in with scolding him about something.

She was going to have to wait, though it was good to see

that being imprisoned didn't break her spirit. He reached for his boot, twisting his hands tied behind his back. The knots were tight. Vince got his fingers close to his right boot, but he couldn't quite get his fingers to the knife.

A deep growl sounded from Tina, but he didn't even look up. Just another inch . . . He stretched his fingers against the bonds, trying to get just that little bit . . .

Tina landed in his lap.

Vince lifted his eyes to find she'd rolled toward him and tossed herself onto him. She then rolled away and waved her tightly bound hands so that he could see—the little woman had a knife in her hands.

"Why didn't you say something?" he said.

Tina gave him a furious look, and he flashed a smile at her, then dumped her unceremoniously onto the cave floor. He turned his back to her and took the knife.

He had his ropes slashed in seconds, made quick work of getting his feet free, and cut the ties on Tina's hands loose just as footsteps tromped toward the cave.

Vince jumped up as Tina worked on freeing herself. He knew she was right where Tug could see her when he stepped into the cave, so he dragged her back to the wall even as she got her feet untied.

Vince rushed to the cave entrance, looked around and found the exact thing he needed: a nice-sized rock. He saw Tina working on Missy's hands, and Vince hissed at her and waved for her to sit still. Tug Andrews wouldn't notice that her ankle ropes were gone, not for a few seconds, coming from the light into the dark. And since Vince had been knocked down out of the direct line of sight from the entrance, he was hoping Tug would just come right on in. Vince only needed a couple of steps.

Tug came in whistling. The old fool was a happy man. Well, Vince was about to make him mighty unhappy. Tug took two steps, looked to his left where Vince was supposed to be, which exposed the back of his head to Vince. And that was enough.

Vince brought the rock down on Tug's head, returning the favor of Tug's blow.

Tug crumpled to the ground, hitting the unforgiving rock hard. Vince disarmed Tug a lot more thoroughly than Tug had disarmed him—or Tina, come to that. It felt good to regain possession of his own pistol.

A scrape from the far tunnel brought Vince's head up. He aimed as Luke poked his head in. With a sigh of relief, Vince holstered the gun. "Tie him up, will you?"

"Sure . . . Tug Andrews?"

Vince nodded. "Yep, he boasted of selling liquor to Wilcox, the Kiowa and the Comanche." He was about to check on the women just as Tina jerked her gag free. Missy was loose, so Tina turned her attention to Mother. Missy gently helped Livvy out of the muzzle and cut the rope around her neck. The dog went wild barking as if all that noise had been backing up this whole time.

Tina helped Mother to her feet, and Vince went to assist. Tina said, "He told us he'd been using this cave to stash furs and other things he traded whiskey for."

Vince kept Mother close at his side while Luke finished securing Tug, leaving his feet unbound.

Tina went on, "Tug said that as soon as he heard what Wilcox had done to Red Wolf, he knew it was time to hit the trail. He's got two packhorses outside, all loaded and ready to go."

Seconds later, Dare stepped in with Wilcox, who was barely able to walk. Jonas brought up the rear.

Dare gave Vince an incredulous look. "Never thought of Tug being involved in all this."

"Me neither," Vince said. "I don't think I'm cut out to be a lawman."

Vince wondered how long they had before Red Wolf came in with his band of warriors. Everyone else seemed to be here, why not them? "Are the Kiowa gonna trust us to punish these coyotes?"

Dare gave a nod. "He saw us pull Wilcox down off that bluff, and it seemed to satisfy him that we put shackles on him—especially since it was mighty clear he'd been whacked on the head. I told Red Wolf we'd make sure he paid for his crimes. He wasn't real happy, but he rode off with his men."

Vince felt a weight lift off his shoulders.

Mother turned to Vince, her eyes wide and childlike. "Vincent, what are we doing out here in this cave?"

Everyone in the cave gasped . . . well, except Tug and Wilcox. Tug was unconscious or he might've gasped, too. Wilcox didn't come to town that often.

The rest of them knew Mother would probably go back to calling Vince Julius just as soon as she was feeling better, which was just the worst kind of dirty shame. But for now it was nice to hear his name on her lips.

"You're right, Mother," Vince said, offering her his arm. "This is a cold, dirty place. Let's get you back home this instant."

Mother took Vince's arm and smiled. He looked around the cave, took stock, and found Luke and Jonas hoisting Tug to his feet and unbinding his hands. Tug's arm was slung over Jonas's shoulder.

"I'm going back for the horses," Luke said. "I'll bring 'em to town tomorrow when I come in for church." He turned for the tunnel that led to the canyon.

Jonas slapped himself on the forehead. "I forgot what day it is." He gave Missy a private sort of smile. "I need to write a sermon."

"You've been distracted," Tina said.

Jonas nodded. "But I know what I'm going to preach about."

Vince thought he knew, too. "What's that?" he asked anyway.

"Trusting God with your future." Jonas smiled, then half dragged, half carried Tug out of the cave entrance that led toward Broken Wheel.

"Tomorrow's plenty soon enough for the horses. If we need one, I reckon we can use Tug's. He ain't riding anywhere anytime soon." Dare shoved Wilcox along, following after Jonas.

Missy went next, then Tina. Vince walked out with Mother on his arm. When they all got outside, he saw Missy hurrying to catch up to Jonas. Tina had lingered and, with a very smooth move—or so Vince thought—he snagged her hand. She looked sideways at him, smiled and didn't pull away.

With Mother on one side and Tina on the other, they walked toward town. Livvy trotted faithfully along at Mother's side.

"So, you carry a knife with you all the time?" Vince asked his little spitfire.

Grinning, Jonas looked over his shoulder. Then his eyes went to Vince's hand, joined with Tina's, and his grin quickly faded. He arched a brow at Vince, demanding his intentions without uttering a word. Vince had thought he was being discreet with Tina, but Jonas had said something earlier that told Vince his preacher friend knew something was going on. And now they were holding hands.

"Why, yes, of course I carry a knife." Tina started to pull her hand away, but Vince hung on tight and she didn't really fight him. "You should have known that."

"How could I have known if you didn't tell me?"

Tina quit trying to get loose and smiled that shining smile that made Vince ache to marry the woman and have her all to himself. "If I've told you once, I've told you a dozen times, a woman needs to know how to take care of herself."

That surprised a laugh out of Vince.

"Amen," Missy called over her shoulder.

Jonas laughed, then Missy joined in, and Tina added her pretty ringing laughter. Vince realized he hadn't heard Tina laugh nearly enough. He right then and there vowed to change that. And he'd tell her so, along with a few other things, just as soon as he could get her alone. It better be soon, because he intended to marry her right after he asked the question.

Mother reached across Vince and patted Tina on the hand. "You're going to make a wonderful addition to the family."

Tina, caught in mid-laugh, started choking.

CHAPTER 25

Tina sensed something different about Vince. The way he held her hand, for one, right in front of Jonas and everyone. Jonas had noticed for sure.

Mother Yates had noticed too, and she wasn't exactly famous for that.

Vince leaned down and whispered, "I need to talk to you, but I want to stay with Mother until she forgets me again."

That made Tina smile. She thought Vince was finally getting used to the idea that his ma wasn't going to be thinking straight a good chunk of the time. They needed to watch out for her and enjoy her company as she was.

While Tina completely understood and sympathized with Vince's priorities, she itched to know why he wanted to talk to her alone.

They were a while locking the prisoners away and getting Virginia Belle cleaned up. Vince ignored the jail and stayed with his mother, talking quietly with her. There was no time to be alone until they sat down to dinner.

When Tina was finally done cooking—for all of them again—she hung up her apron and walked out of the diner kitchen to join the others. Vince took Tina's hand and nodded toward the kitchen. If he wanted her to cook some more, the man was in for a big disappointment.

He led her straight out the back door.

The sun was setting and it was getting cool. But the building blocked the wind, and when Vince pulled her into his arms, Tina didn't notice the weather at all.

"You know, Tina, I said I'd never marry because of my worries about being like my father or my mother. Either would be a disaster for a wife and children."

"I remember." Oh yes, she remembered it all too well. She braced herself to be told the same thing again. Otherwise why would that be the first thing out of his mouth?

"Well, I was an idiot to say all that."

Tina's head came up, and she met his eyes. Her heart sped up and her spirits lifted as he smiled that flashing white smile. "You were?"

He definitely was, but she never thought he'd admit it.

"I've wasted a lot of time, not just with you but in other ways, because I was worried about the future. Well, no more. I'm turning my life over to God, the present *and* the future. Please forget my foolishness and forgive me for the attention I paid you without honoring you as I should have with a proposal. Can you do that? Can you forgive me?"

Tina couldn't resist reaching up to touch his lips, to stop his words. "I understand why you were worried. And your worry was all for me, that you'd be a poor husband to me and a burden. Of course I can forgive that."

"I love you, Tina Cahill," Vince said, then leaned down and kissed her.

It wasn't the kiss that touched her as much as it was the words he spoke. Tina's heart ached with the pleasure of hearing those words when she'd given up on them at last. She wanted to believe it so badly she might have told herself to refuse the words, just to keep herself safe.

She might have, if not for Vince's kiss.

It was a different kind of kiss. It wasn't the stolen kiss that came out of an attraction they were trying to fight. This was an honorable kiss, though no less passionate because of that. In fact, it was more passionate because of that.

When finally Vince lifted his lips from hers, they stood mere inches apart, his dark eyes shining, his handsome face full of kindness and love.

"Marry me, Tina. Please tell me you'll join your life with mine."

The only thing stopping her was that she had a smile so wide she hardly had control of her lips to speak. But her smile seemed to be enough to make Vince wait patiently. He kissed her again, and this time he tasted her smile so thoroughly he might well have forgotten he'd ever proposed.

Against his lips, Tina whispered, "Yes, I will marry you. I want to spend the rest of my life with you."

He kissed her forehead, then her nose. "Mother will keep us busy, I'm sure. You already know how much that's going to occupy our lives. Today, finally, I accepted that she's not getting better. I understand now that I need to accept her and care for her to the best of my ability. It's going to be hard work for the both of us."

"I love your mother, Vince. I think because I didn't know her before, I don't have any idea how she used to be. All I see is a genteel Southern belle who's slightly dotty and in need of protection. I think, after I was so unkind to Duffy, only to find him helping at every turn, and that low-down Tug Andrews was the real outlaw, I might leave off my picketing and spend my energy caring for your mother."

Vince kissed her soundly. "Well, Duffy is innocent of what happened here, but you were right about whiskey being a scourge. So, if you want to picket in your spare time, I'll help you paint up another sign. And maybe, if the weather's fair, Mother can march with you."

Laughing, Tina threw her arms around Vince's neck and kissed him back just as soundly.

"Can we tell Mother now that we're getting married?" Vince asked. "I like the idea of her knowing her son's to be married to someone as beautiful as you."

"I've got a better idea." Tina took Vince's hand, weaving her fingers between his to get a good grip. "Let's go get married right now and see if Jonas wants to make it a double wedding."

Vince flashed a smile at her and kissed her again, then pulled her back into the dining room.

Tina kept up with her fast-moving, soon-to-be husband. In fact, she might have gotten a little ahead of him.

"Dearly beloved . . ." Jonas began. Earlier, he'd put on his parson's collar and led the happy couple over to the church. He and Missy had chosen to wait a bit for their own wedding. Jonas thought it might confuse Mother to have a double wedding.

"You should really wait for Luke," Dare said, standing beside Vince to act as a witness.

"I told you why I can't." Vince tilted his head toward

his mother, who stood smiling beside Jonas, almost like a second parson. But Vince wanted her to have a good view of the goings-on, so he encouraged her to be right there front and center.

"Do you, Tina Cahill, take this man . . ."

Glynna stood beside Tina, Missy beside Jonas—the man was surrounded and yet he didn't seem to care at all.

Jonas quit talking, and Tina said, "I do."

Vince felt Tina's *I do* all the way to his heart. He looked at her and couldn't stop smiling, and she smiled right back.

"And do you, Vincent Yates, take this woman . . ."

Vince had to pay close attention because this was his part. Although, honestly, the way Jonas held Missy's hand while he talked, the man almost seemed to be speaking the vows with her in mind.

Which was fine, but Vince sort of wished Jonas would pay more attention to the wedding ceremony he was performing.

Jonas sped through the service, and that might've been because they were all afraid Mother would forget who Vince was any minute.

"I do," Vince said, more sure of this than anything he'd ever done.

"If anyone here knows any reason why these two should not be wed, let him speak now or forever hold his peace."

"Well, I think he should wait for Luke."

"Drop it, Dare." Jonas broke out of his fast reading of the vows. "That don't qualify as a reason they should not be wed. Luke woulda liked to have been here, though."

"Just get on with it," Vince growled. Tina shot him an irritated look, and Mother reached out and whacked him with her fan.

Vince was learning more about women every minute that went by. Growling during a man's wedding was definitely not appropriate, and he'd never do it again. Of course he was only getting married once in his life, so any lessons learned were pretty much useless.

"A reading from the book of First Corinthians, chapter thirteen. 'Though I speak with the tongues of men and of angels . . .'"

Vince didn't remember this part from other weddings he'd attended. Of course, Jonas had married Ruthy and Luke on a dark midnight, about two minutes after Luke proposed. And those vows had been spoken when Luke was figuring to get shot in the near future.

Things hadn't gone badly, but no one was real confident when Luke and Ruthy married.

Jonas might well have lingered over Dare and Glynna's marriage vows, except Dare had been stabbed only hours earlier and he was a little pale and none too steady on his feet. Jonas married the couple up quick so that Dare could sit down before he fell down.

Jonas was lingering over this ceremony, although reading one chapter from the Good Book didn't count as a whole lot of lingering.

"I now pronounce you man and wife. You may kiss the bride." Jonas narrowed his eyes and leaned close to Vince. "As if you haven't already kissed her, Yates."

Vince grinned, and Jonas couldn't keep up his scowl. At least it was gone by the time Vince was done kissing the living daylights out of his brand-new wife.

Jonas offered Vince his hand. They shook, and Jonas clapped him on the shoulder. Dare joined in, and Paul got in on it with a handshake too, while Glynna and Janny swarmed Tina, along with Missy and Mother.

The burst of congratulations faded as Vince turned to Mother, who beamed up at him, her eyes brimming with tears.

"What a beautiful ceremony, son." Mother dabbed her eyes with her handkerchief, and it didn't even bother him to see her cry, not over an important moment like this. "I'm so glad I got to Texas in time for the wedding, even if I did have to be abandoned by your worthless father and get kidnapped."

Vince hugged her hard. He pulled back and smiled at her. "There's no one around here who doubts there is trouble to be found in Texas, and I'd say we've more than found our share."

"Well, I'd prefer if things quieted down now," Mother said, looking right at him.

She knew him. For right this moment, Mother knew she had a son and she was pleased by that. Then Mother turned and reached out for Tina, who went into Mother's arms with all the kindness of a true daughter.

Watching his two favorite women in the world share a hug was the sweetest moment of Vince's life.

Vince was waiting for her outside Mother's room. Tina swallowed hard, but when he reached for her, she went into his arms without hesitation.

He held her close, and all her fears about the wedding night eased. She was in the keeping of a fine man. She relaxed, and Vince raised his head. "Let's go."

Nodding, he led her to his room . . . their room. When
he drew her inside, she said quietly, "I'm so glad your
mother was there for our wedding." She hesitated. "Vince,
you know . . ."

"That she will likely wake up tomorrow and not remember any of it, including me?" Vince sounded sad but
accepting.

"I'm sorry for that. I know how much—" A kiss quieted
her apology.

"I consider myself a reasonably smart man, but I've been
acting like a fool thinking I could cure Mother. Being called
Invincible Vince by my friends went to my head. I let
myself believe that if I wanted to solve a problem badly
enough, I'd find a way. But part of realizing I can't cure my
mother is accepting that I haven't been anything close to
invincible in the most important things. I've never figured
out how to make my parents love me."

"Vince, I'm sure they love you." Tina touched his lips,
wishing she could hold back those feelings even more than
the words.

Vince kissed her fingertips, gently lifted her hand away
and kept talking. "Mother does. Father, well, my choices
were to obey him and be a weakling, or defy him and be
a failure."

"That's a fight you were never going to win."

"So I quit fighting and left that life behind as soon as I
was able. What's left now is making sure Mother has as
happy a life as I can arrange."

Tina ran one hand up and down Vince's arm, thinking
to comfort him.

"I don't want to talk about my parents anymore." He lowered his head and kissed her.

When finally he broke the kiss, she asked in a rather breathless voice, "What do you want to talk about?"

"It's our wedding night. I want to talk about that." He dragged her into his arms, and there was very little talking between them for a long time.

Epilogue

Vince held his little blond daughter in his arms as he watched Sal Stone toddle unsteadily across the soft rug covering the wood floor of Luke's living room. Ruthy had made a neglected house into a home.

Baby Sal, named after Luke's pa, had his father's dark hair and eyes. The boy was a year and a half now and would be a big brother before too long.

Dare and Glynna's son, Michael, with his wispy white-blond hair, squealed and chased after his slightly older friend.

"Stay with him, Paul." Dare sounded exhausted, and in truth the whole family felt that way. The boy was getting to be as active as Dare, which was keeping his family tired to the bone. Even Dare had calmed down a bit. He had no choice. He was kept running so much to prevent the boy from toddling into disaster that Dare never passed up one of his rare chances to sit down and rest for a minute.

As for Lana Bullard, she and Porter were never seen again, which saved everyone a lot of fuss.

Jonas and Missy had a little one on the way, and Vince had never seen a couple so excited. And considering the Broken Wheel baby boom of the last year, that was saying something.

Though she was nearing her delivery time, Missy, like all of the women, was in the kitchen and cooking. Well, maybe not Glynna. They might have Glynna busy setting the table.

So, while the men looked after the little ones, Vince knew the women, including Mother, were working hard at getting the meal on. He glanced around the room, watching his friends. He loved seeing these tough Regulators become good husbands and fathers.

Vince let out a sigh. "When we were all fighting to survive in Andersonville, did you ever think we'd see the day when there was so much happiness in our lives?" He cradled his daughter's head in one big tanned hand. She gave him a toothy, drooling smile. Even though she was held high in his arms, she dove for the rampaging boys and would have thrown herself onto the floor if Vince wasn't used to her tricks.

"I carried that place around with me for years," Luke replied. "For a long time I thought it had swept away all that was decent in my life. I never hoped to find home and family again."

Michael shrieked, grabbed Sal's black curls and yanked. Dare rushed in while Sal bellowed. Paul pried his little brother's fingers loose one at a time. The ruckus was normal when the Regulators got together.

Luke lifted Sal, sobbing, and held his son against his chest. Michael was fighting Dare's restraining hands, so Dare dangled him upside down for a while until the boy was giggling. Noticing their fun, Sal began demanding his father toss him around, too.

Peace reigned—not counting the squealing—as Dare said, "And I was mighty mixed up about wanting to be a doctor and not believing I should be one with only the training I got in Andersonville." Dare shook his head, chuckled. "When I think of how fired up I was to quit caring for patients . . . Now I can't imagine doing anything else."

Dare hefted his son toward Paul, who settled on the floor with both children. He was used to being a baby wrangler.

Vince's little daughter was, of course, the cutest of them all. She was the spitting image of her mother. When Vince thought about how beautiful she was going to be, and how watchful he'd need to be with all the roughneck men running wild in Texas, he broke out into a cold sweat.

They'd named her Bella after Vince's ma, who'd taken to the child when she'd been born six months ago. Mother still couldn't be trusted on her own for even a minute, but they simply took turns staying with her and mostly things were good.

Vince's father had died a few months after Bella's birth. Vince had written and told him about a grandchild being born. Father had made no effort to see his wife or son or granddaughter.

He'd left everything to Vince, even with the estrangement between them. And he didn't bother to acknowledge Missy's existence or leave provision for his wife. Vince corrected the injustice to Missy generously and continued to care for Mother. Beyond that, he used the new wealth like all the other money he'd been handed. He did his best to make his loved ones' lives a little more comfortable and left the rest in a bank to collect interest.

Vince's lawyering business was a small concern, though it didn't matter much because he was mighty busy taking care of his wife and daughter and mother, which didn't leave him much time for practicing law. He'd had a conflict of interest in being sheriff when he arrested Tug and Wilcox, and then being the lawyer who prosecuted them. But Texas was an easygoing state about such things, and there was no trouble getting the coyotes convicted.

"And I was so sure it was right to cut myself off from my father and mother. Now I can't imagine life without Mother, especially as she's like a grandma to all the young'uns. And with all of you getting hitched, I can't believe the time I wasted trying not to end up stuck together with the only single woman left in town."

Dare laughed, then Luke and Paul joined in. Jonas was slowest, but loudest. Even Vince had to laugh. The day Vince had claimed that spitfire of a woman was the luckiest day of his life.

She hadn't changed a bit, and he wouldn't have it any other way. She didn't have much to reform these days. Duffy and Griss Schuster had finally tired of having a mission field that covered their front door, and they'd left the territory. Broken Wheel was now a dry town.

"So have you decided which of our sons you want Bella to marry, Vince?" Luke asked.

Because Vince was laughing, he inhaled when he gasped

and almost choked to death. His friends delighted in asking that blamed fool question now and then just to watch the color drain out of Vince's face. He'd almost stopped getting light-headed when he heard it, but he suspected he'd gone a bit pale because Luke, Dare, and Jonas all laughed like loons.

Tina came into the living room, and Vince thought back to the first time he'd laid eyes on her. The most beautiful woman he'd ever seen. And after nearly two years of marriage, he felt exactly the same now as then, except even better because now he looked at her with love.

"Dinner's ready." She spoke to the room, but she had eyes only for Vince and little Bella. She came over and made simple, unnecessary adjustments to the collar of their little girl's dress, then looked up into Vince's eyes and smiled in a private way she saved just for him. She hadn't come over to make sure he was taking care of their baby to suit her. She just liked being close to him.

Just as he loved being close to her.

They'd filled the empty, lonely places in each other's lives. And they were both smart enough to cherish that.

The rest of his Regulator friends headed for the dinner table, leaving Vince alone with Tina for just a moment.

He'd said it before, yet Vince didn't think he could ever say it enough. "You know when all my friends were getting married and you were the only single woman in town, even though I thought you were the most beautiful woman I'd ever seen, I was scared because I didn't want to . . . to burden a woman with all my problems. And it looked like the world was conspiring so we'd end up stuck together."

Some women might have found that a bit rude, but not

Tina. She smiled at him and kissed him lightly while she rested a hand on Bella.

"'The world was conspiring'?" Tina giggled at the idea. "I think maybe *God* was *guiding* us toward each other."

"I guess that's another way to put it." Vince drew her closer, enjoying her warmth and strength and good sense. "But there's even another way to think of being stuck together."

Wrinkling her nose, Tina said, "You make it sound like we had honey spilled over our heads."

"What I'm thinking of is my friends, and now our wives and all our children, and how we've made a home in the wilderness, a decent home where our children can grow up strong. It's because we never quit on each other. None of us. Each of us ran into trouble, and through it all, right up to today, we all stuck together."

Tina took up baby Bella and then placed her hand on Vince's arm. "And we always will, because we have a bond that is closer than a brother."

Jonas's favorite verse from the Bible. That earned her another kiss.

They heard screaming coming from the other room, the little ones squabbling again.

Tina said, "Let's go eat."

"You didn't let Glynna help with the meal, did you?"

Tina laughed and shook her head as they went to join their friends.

Mary Connealy writes romantic comedy with cowboys. She's the author of the acclaimed Kincaid Brides, Lassoed in Texas, Montana Marriages, and Sophie's Daughters series. Mary has been nominated for a Christy Award, was a finalist for a RITA Award, and is a two-time winner of the Carol Award. She lives on a ranch in eastern Nebraska with her very own romantic cowboy hero. They have four grown daughters—Joslyn, married to Matt; Wendy; Shelly, married to Aaron; and Katy—two spectacular grandchildren, Elle and Isaac, and one more on the way. Learn more about Mary and her books at:

maryconnealy.com
mconnealy.blogspot.com
seekerville.blogspot.com
petticoatsandpistols.com

Don't Miss the Rest of the TROUBLE IN TEXAS Series!

To learn more about Mary and her books, visit maryconnealy.com.

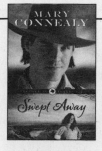

Ruthy MacNeil nearly drowned before being rescued at the last second by Luke Stone. Now, alive but disoriented, she's left with little choice but to stay with him—at least until they reach the nearest town. But is she in any less danger with this handsome cowboy than she would've been if she'd stayed on her own?

Swept Away
TROUBLE IN TEXAS #1

Dare Riker is a doctor who saves lives. But lately, someone seems determined to end his. He wants to leave the violence of his war days behind and move on—preferably with Glynna Greer at his side. But will he survive long enough to have his chance at love?

Fired Up
TROUBLE IN TEXAS #2

More Romantic Comedy with Cowboys From Mary Connealy

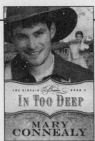

If you enjoyed *Stuck Together,* you may also like...

Brilliant but reclusive researcher Darius Thornton is not the sort of man debutante Nicole Renard could ever marry. But can she stop her heart from surging full steam ahead?

Full Steam Ahead by Karen Witemeyer
karenwitemeyer.com

Zayne Beckett and Agatha Watson have always been able to match each other in wits, but will unlikely circumstances convince them they could also be a match made in heaven?

A Match of Wits by Jen Turano
jenturano.com

When an abandoned child brings Nick Lovelace and Anne Tillerton together, is Nick prepared to risk his future plans for an unexpected chance at love?

Caught in the Middle by Regina Jennings
reginajennings.com